SWIFT & HAW
CYBERSPI

SWIFT & HAWK CYBERSPIES

LOGAN MACX

WALKER BOOKS

Copyright © 2022 by Edward Docx and Matthew Plampin

First US edition 2022

Library of Congress Catalog Card Number 2022930425
ISBN 978-1-5362-2415-3

22 23 24 25 26 27 LBM 10 9 8 7 6 5 4 3 2 1

Printed in Melrose Park, IL, USA

This book was typeset in Museo Slab.

Walker Books US
a division of
Candlewick Press
99 Dover Street
Somerville, Massachusetts 02144

www.walkerbooksus.com

MIX
Paper | Supporting
responsible forestry
FSC® C103098
FSC
www.fsc.org

FOR K, O, R, S, W–
WHO KEPT ON ASKING ABOUT IT

CONTENTS

1

EMERGENCY EXIT

Caleb Quinn had never expected to use the emergency exit plan. He went to his bedroom door, listening hard. The voices coming from downstairs belonged to his mum and a woman he did not recognize with a faintly Eastern European accent. He couldn't make out exactly what they were saying, but it was sounding less and less friendly. Something strange was happening.

He had just gotten back from school in the center of London, cycling along the Thameside path to his house in Nine Elms. It was the first week of the autumn term. After calling hello to his mum, who was working on her laptop in the kitchen, he'd run upstairs to dump his bag and grab a couple of things. His idea for the evening had been simple: have some dinner, then head outside to his high-tech computer lab, which was on a barge moored nearby at Nine Elms Pier. There he could spend a few hours working on a big content update for *Terrorform*, the sci-fi action-adventure video game that he had programmed himself.

The voices rose. Caleb decided to find out what was going on. He took out the Flex, a superpowerful computer handset that he had designed and built over the past few months; he'd been putting together devices like this since before he could talk. To a casual observer, the Flex looked like a pretty standard smartphone. But it was much more than that. Caleb had made it from an ultra-tough, flexible material that could be bent or folded into any shape. It had an operating system that was far more advanced than anything you could buy, with a unique range of special applications and functions. These were activated by coded, single-word commands. He murmured one of them now.

"Phantom. Mum's laptop."

The Phantom app sent the Flex's eyes and ears elsewhere. A view of the kitchen appeared instantly on its screen, ripped from the camera on his mum's open computer. He backed away from his door and sat down on his bed to take a look.

Harper Quinn was leaning against a counter. She was a senior CIA agent, originally from California, stationed at the American embassy just down the road from where they lived. She was dressed in a pale gray business suit, cut to conceal her sidearm, with a dark blue shirt beneath. Her red-brown hair was pulled back into a ponytail and her arms were crossed. She was wearing the no-nonsense expression that— Caleb had noticed—she used on colleagues even more often than she used on him.

Across the room from Harper was a very tall woman—at least six foot two, Caleb guessed. Her hair was an angular orange wedge, shaved at the sides, that blazed brightly in the kitchen's lights. She was dressed like a biker in a black leather jacket, jeans, and heavy boots. A silver ring glinted in her eyebrow.

Two men were also visible. One, a huge, bull-like figure, was in the passageway that led to the front door, blocking it off completely. His back was turned, his shaved head almost brushing against the ceiling. The other one, small and skinny by comparison, was standing just behind the orange-haired woman. He had a short lime-green Mohawk and squinty, weasel eyes that flicked this way and that as if seeking some sly advantage. Both were dressed in a similar style to the woman, who was clearly their boss.

Caleb studied these visitors closely. It wasn't *that* unusual for his mum to have evening meetings with colleagues and others whom she described as "contacts." But the intelligence people who came to the house were usually more . . . well, more intelligent-looking. He eased up the volume.

"So," Harper was saying skeptically, "have I got this right? You're telling me that you have important information . . . but I have to come with you to get it?"

The orange-haired woman gave her a humorless smile. "That is correct," she replied. "We have the information you requested, Agent Quinn. But more than this. Something you should see for yourself. Please, come."

Harper was shaking her head. "Our contact is based on *strict* secrecy, Ms. Szabo. You were instructed to use the designated drop in Brussels. You shouldn't be in London at all. You certainly shouldn't be at this house. I have no idea how—"

"My information concerns Xavier Torrent. And yes, you have to see for yourself."

Caleb shifted, leaning a little nearer to the Flex's screen.

Xavier Torrent. He knew that name, he was sure of it—although he couldn't say exactly where he had heard it before.

Clearly, his mother knew it too. She was impressed, excited even, but he could tell that she was trying hard not to show it. "All right," she said. "Sure. We can work something out. Meet me at exit four of Vauxhall Tube Station in thirty minutes. Then we can—"

"No." The orange-haired woman—Szabo—put a hand on her hip. "No, you must come with us now. We have an opportunity. Also—it is for your own safety." She paused. "And you must bring your son. Xavier Torrent will know that we have made contact. We act now or we lose the chance. It would be safer—for you and your son—if we all go together."

There was a long moment of silence. The weaselly man stuck a finger in his ear and started wiggling it about, as though there was something stuck inside. Caleb stared at the image of his mum. She didn't move or speak.

"You're wasting time, Agent Quinn." Szabo took a step forward, her leather jacket falling open to reveal a gun of her own, tucked away in a shoulder holster. "Go and get the boy. Then we can all leave."

"He's away tonight," Harper replied, speaking very clearly. Caleb could have sworn that she glanced over toward the laptop, as if she knew that he was listening in. "He's staying at his friend's house. Brian Beasley."

Caleb caught his breath. Brian Beasley . . . did not exist.

Whoa. He passed his hand through his hair. Brian Beasley was a code word—a secret instruction from his mum, a name that they had come up with together. *"If you ever hear me say 'Brian Beasley,'"* she had told him, her face suddenly serious, "then you get the hell away. Don't worry about me, I'm trained for this stuff. But you get away. Go back to school. Wait for me to call."

Caleb had promised that he would. Ever since his dad had died a couple of years earlier, he'd grown more and more used to his mum's secretive espionage activities. One time, not long after Christmas, the two of them had gone away to Edinburgh for a weekend. On the first evening, Harper had gotten a priority call from the agency; Caleb had to leave her at their hotel and travel alone across the unfamiliar city to the US Consulate General. But they'd never had to use this particular code word before. There had never been any trouble actually *in their house*. His earlier hunch was right: this was an emergency.

Szabo was sharper than she seemed. She had realized what had happened. In one movement, she crossed the kitchen and took Harper's gun from inside her jacket. There could no longer be any doubt—this was an abduction.

"He's here," she snapped. "Pyke, go upstairs. Get him."

Reluctantly, the Mohawked man took the finger from his ear. "But she just said—"

"Idiot! That was code! Go and get the boy!"

Caleb was already out of his chair, pulling on a black hoodie. He folded the Flex into his back pocket and grabbed a crumpled ten-pound note from the desk—all the money he had in the world. Then he crept out through his bedroom door.

The emergency exit plan involved him leaving the house via the bathroom window. The bathroom was on the other side of the wide landing, however, and he could already hear

Pyke tramping up the stairs. Damn. There was no way he'd be able to get over there in time. Making a split-second decision, he swerved into his mum's bedroom and rolled down under her bed.

But Pyke, of course, had no idea where he should be looking. To Caleb's horror, the weaselly, Mohawked man passed straight by his room and barged into his mum's, banging the door back as he did so.

Caleb bit the inside of his cheek and tried not to breathe. The slightest sound and he would be caught. The smell of stale cigarettes and beer wafted through the room. He watched a pair of battered motorcycle boots walk slowly around the bed, treading dirt into his mother's pale blue carpet.

Pyke was clearly in the habit of talking to himself. "The kid ain't gonna be in 'ere, is he? This is the mother's room. Or else my eyes deceive me—which never happens, Pykey, my friend. Oh, 'allo—what's this, then? *Very* nice picture . . ."

The thug had stopped by the side of the bed. Caleb could have reached out and undone his frayed laces. He turned his face away and tried to edge backward.

"This must be the lad we're after." Pyke snorted. "Looks like a right cheeky little scumbag. Nothing a few days with the boss wouldn't put right, eh?"

Caleb could hear his mother at the foot of the stairs. "I've told you, Szabo," she was saying firmly, "he's not here. You can search all you like."

Szabo was ignoring her, though. "Krall," she said to the huge man, "go and see what that moron is up to."

Pyke dropped what he was holding onto the floor and stood on it, cracking the glass. Caleb flinched. It was a framed photograph, taken about a year earlier: Caleb sitting proudly on the prow of his barge, his auburn hair a little shorter than it was now, grinning in the sunshine.

Krall's heavy footsteps mounted the staircase. Pyke hurried back around the bed, as if he was afraid of the man coming up.

"He's not in 'ere," he said, going out onto the landing. "This is his mum's room."

Krall grunted. The two of them seemed to be looking around, deciding where to search next. Caleb took a breath, trying not to inhale a lungful of carpet fluff. He was going to need a distraction. He slid the Flex from his pocket.

The Quinns lived in a small converted warehouse, set back a short distance from the river. When they'd moved in, the CIA had installed a top-grade internal security system, fitted as standard in the homes of high-ranking personnel. The software that controlled it was hack-proof—or so they thought.

"Spider Monkey," Caleb whispered.

This was the all-purpose hacking app that he'd programmed into the Flex. In less than ten seconds, Spider Monkey had bypassed three supposedly unbreakable passwords, giving Caleb full and invisible access to the security system. He crawled from under the bed and rose to a crouch.

Out on the landing, the two thugs had split up—Pyke heading toward Harper's office while Krall heaved into Caleb's bedroom. He had the horrible feeling that Pyke was actually the more friendly of the two agents; Krall moved and sounded like some kind of prehistoric monster. Caleb held his breath and waited until he was sure that both men were through their respective doorways. Then he sneaked as quickly as he could across the landing.

He made it to the bathroom just as a volley of swear words erupted from the office, along with the sound of several boxes falling off a shelf. Pyke must have opened the junk cupboard where his mum kept all her old case files. He was throwing stuff onto the floor, kicking at it wildly—and twisting back toward the landing as he did so. In a couple of seconds, he would be out and searching the bathroom.

It was now or never. Caleb pulled up the hacked security system and tapped the box marked LOCKDOWN: DOORS.

Immediately, reinforced steel panels slammed across every doorway, slicing out from inside the frames. An alarm started up—an earsplitting electronic shriek that tore through the entire house.

Caleb went to the bathroom window, slid up the pane, and stepped out onto the kitchen roof. The fresh air was a relief. In the dips of sound, he could just about hear Pyke and Krall, banging their fists on the panels and calling down to their orange-haired boss.

Balancing carefully, Caleb walked along the edge of the roof, pausing to peer in through the skylight. Szabo was going over to the base of the stairs, Harper's semiautomatic pistol in her hand. She began yelling up at Krall and Pyke, trying to make herself heard over the deafening racket.

Harper hadn't moved from the kitchen counter. Caleb knew that she could have easily taken this chance to disarm Szabo—to turn the tables. But she had stayed where she was. As he watched, she took out her phone, made a series of quick movements with her forefinger, then put it away again.

The alarm stopped, the steel security panels retracting as rapidly as they'd slid out. An instant later the Flex buzzed. A message from his mum.

Nicely done. Get to school. Find Professor Clay. X.

A tiny icon next to the message thread told Caleb that she'd deactivated her phone.

"False alarm," he heard Harper say through the glass of the skylight. "One of your guys must have triggered it. Can we put a stop to this, Szabo? I told you—the boy isn't here. We're wasting time. I'll come with you. Let's go."

Caleb read the message again. He realized what was happening: his mum was going to *let* them take her, to see what she could find out and give him a chance to escape. He gazed up at the sky for a few seconds. It was a clear, deep blue, tinted to the west with the first traces of dusk. He had a mission: get back to school and find Professor Clay. She would know what to do.

Caleb went to a special computing and technology school called the ARC Institute—which stood for AI, Robotics, and Cybertech, three of its main areas of study. The ARC was based in a tall, gleaming, ultramodern high-rise, just a few streets away from St. Paul's Cathedral. Getting there from Nine Elms took about twenty-five minutes on a bike—although Caleb's record was twenty-one. Professor Tilda Clay was the ARC's deputy principal. She lived in the tower and looked after the ARC's forty or so boarders from around the world. She would be in charge of the whole place now that the school day was over. Clay was a world-famous cybersecurity expert who was known to have close links with several intelligence agencies, and so it made complete sense that Caleb's mum had told him to find her. But still, he didn't exactly relish the prospect—Clay had a well-earned reputation for being the strictest teacher at the ARC. She could be severe. Caleb had already gotten a couple of detentions for things that were totally not his fault. In all honesty, he was a little bit scared of her.

Caleb climbed down a trellis into their backyard and let himself out onto the path behind, which ran alongside the river. Crouching in the shadows, he eased himself up to the corner so that he could look toward the street.

A black van was parked on the cobbles at the front of the house. Another thug was standing by its back doors, alert for any sign of the police. These were serious people. Caleb hoped his mum knew what she was doing.

He stole away from the corner as quietly as he could and set off along the path. Light from the late-afternoon sun shimmered on the surface of the water. The Thames could look so different day to day, even hour by hour: sometimes sparkling, sometimes dull and brown, as if it were alive and had moods of its own. A short distance along the bank he stopped where a gangway led up to Nine Elms Pier. He glanced around, then took out his key, unlocked the white gate, and stepped onto the pontoon. Upstream was Battersea Power Station, its four giant chimneys stark against the horizon.

At the end of the marina was an old Dutch barge, painted dark green and blue with some faded floral patterning on the side panels. The portholes were all covered by blackout blinds, and a compact, state-of-the-art satellite dish had been mounted on one corner of the roof. On the barge's prow, written on a scroll on elaborate letters, was *Queen Jane, Approximately*. It had been converted by Caleb's English father, Patrick, who'd named it after his favorite song. He'd been a pioneering computer scientist—a specialist in medical AI. The *Queen Jane* had been his laboratory before he fell ill. Now it was Caleb's HQ and the place he loved most in the world. He touched an icon on the Flex's screen that put the barge into maximum-security mode, which made it impossible to break into without drawing some major attention to yourself.

Caleb's bike was stored in a little sheltered rack next to the water. He took it out, quickly wheeled it back to the gate, then rode onto the riverside path and began pedaling downstream. That summer, he'd won a medal at the London BMX School Games. He was fast—but he seldom went at race speed in the city. This trip was different, though, and soon he was absolutely flying—around the modern tower precincts, around the MI6 building, under Lambeth Bridge, past the Houses of Parliament opposite. The way narrowed just before the London Eye and he had to swerve around a large crowd of pedestrians. A few minutes later he was spearing across Blackfriars Bridge, riding toward St. Paul's and the ARC.

Caleb's mind buzzed with questions. What was going on? Who *were* these people, with their leather jackets and luminous hairstyles? Why had they taken his mum? And what was Clay going to do about it?

11

2

BEETLEBAT

Caleb cut down a side street, bunny-hopped a low chain strung between two concrete bollards, and raced across the paved square in front of the ARC tower. The facade was a huge sheet of curved glass, reaching thirty-five storeys above the ground, reflecting the shapes and lights of the city and a broad sweep of the evening sky beyond. He rode around the side and locked up his bike.

The ARC Institute occupied the top ten floors of the tower and had a separate, smaller entrance around the back. Caleb waved up at the security camera. There was a harsh buzz as the doors slid apart. The lobby was modest compared to the main office entrance at the front, but it still had a high ceiling and a polished stone floor. A large screen showed a silver arc, the school's symbol, rotating slowly against a blue background. To the left stood the reception desk, and beyond that, the elevators were set into the far wall. It was now just after 6.30 p.m. and all the regular staff had gone home. A lone security guard sat swiveling his chair this way and that, staring out of the window-wall behind him, patting out a rhythm on his ample stomach.

Caleb tried to slow his breathing and smooth his hair. He was pumped from the ride and his nerves were jangling with urgency, but he had to act as casually as possible. This was CIA business—the fewer people who knew what had happened, the better.

"Hey, Rufus," he said as he went over, "how's it going?"

The guard spun around. He raised his eyebrows and scratched idly at his thin blond mustache. "Back already? Forget something, did you?"

"Actually," Caleb said, attempting a rueful grin, "I'm signing in for the night. Turns out I've got to be here stupidly early tomorrow to work on a joint assignment before registration. So I figured I might as well start the day as close as possible to the labs."

Rufus's expression remained blank. Caleb sometimes stayed overnight at the ARC when his mum was away for work, so this was not unusual. The guard passed him a tablet. "Here you go."

"Is Professor Clay about?" Caleb asked, keeping his voice neutral. He pressed his index finger against the sensor; his school mug shot flashed up, along with all his personal details. "I've got to talk to her about something."

The guard sighed. He checked a screen behind the desk. "Says here she's in the library."

Caleb thanked him and walked to the elevator. The ARC's library was on floor thirty-two, close to the top of the tower—above the classrooms, labs, and engineering bays, as well as the various auditoriums and testing zones. Only the residential floors were farther up. He pressed the elevator button, exhaling hard as the doors closed and it began to ascend. He tried to rehearse what he was going to say.

"My mum's in trouble, Professor. Or she might be. I think she's—" *No, that didn't sound right.*

"These strange people came to my house. My mum said I should talk to you." *That didn't sound right either.*

The elevator arrived. The library floor was completely open, with glass walls on every side. The views of the London sunset were amazing up here—shining towers and city blocks, ancient castles and cathedrals, the winding indigo ribbon of the Thames.

Caleb hardly saw any of it. He walked quickly through the library's study area to the long rows of bookshelves, peering down each one in turn. He spotted maybe ten kids from various years and a couple of teachers, neither of whom were Professor Clay. The librarian, Dr. Virdi, told him that according to the ARC system Clay was currently logged into the school's digital archive. Caleb went over immediately to the archive terminals. None of them were occupied. He felt a shiver go up his spine. This was getting weird. He took out the Flex and fired a message to Professor Clay over the ARC intranet, the school's private network.

Hello, Professor Clay—I really need to talk to you—urgent.

Professor Clay was known for her prompt, succinct replies. But nothing came. For a whole minute, Caleb stood still in front of Dr. Virdi's desk, frowning at the Flex's screen. Then he returned the device to his pocket and headed back toward the elevators.

The staff's rooms were on floor thirty-four. Caleb opted

for the stairs, wanting to get up there as fast as he could. He kept his head down, avoiding eye contact with everybody he passed, until he reached Clay's apartment. He knocked six times; then he took a breath, counted to ten, and knocked again. He put his ear to the door. Silence.

Caleb gazed numbly around. What the hell was he supposed to do now? Should he go to see another member of staff? Maybe Professor Gomez, the head of mathematics. He was probably the nicest of the teachers. But his mum had said Professor Clay specifically. He really wanted to talk this through with someone—to try to figure everything out. He had to be careful, though. It could only be someone he trusted completely.

At once, he thought of Zen—Zenobia Rafiq, his best and oldest friend. She boarded at the ARC and would therefore be in the residential areas on the floor below. Caleb smiled as he hurried back to the stairwell. Zen was always one step ahead of the rest of the class. If anyone could help him make sense of this situation, it would be her.

A few seconds later Caleb was on floor thirty-three. Just as he was about to go through the stairwell doors, he heard a burst of nasty laughter on the other side. It was Rivers and Cordero from year 10, two of the ARC's biggest jerks. If they saw him, they'd start quizzing him about his video game *Terrorform*—asking how things were going post-release, what the player count was, and giving him opinions and advice in their usual teasing, sarcastic manner. He *really* didn't need that right now. He pulled back, letting them carry on toward the cafeteria—then he hurried across the hallway, into the corridor that led to Zen's room.

Her door was standing very slightly ajar.

"Zen, you in there?" said Caleb. "It's me. I'm back."

There was no reply.

"Zen?" He pushed the door open. The bedroom was rectangular, about thirty feet by twelve. At the far end was a floor-to-ceiling window, offering another spectacular view—this time a close-up of three enormous glass-covered skyscrapers, their western sides turned fiery orange by the last of the sun. There was a bed and a wardrobe, and a door that led to a tiny bathroom. A set of shelves held a few dozen books and a collection of trophies from martial arts tournaments and athletic events.

Every other inch of space was given over to Zen's creations. Caleb was a coder at heart; he could build a device like the Flex no problem—but anything that had to move, or interact with the physical world in any way, and he was second-rate. Zen was the total opposite. Her thing was advanced robotics. She was never happier than when she was bolting bits of ultra-light graphite together and making them come alive. Accordingly, her room at the ARC was like the workshop of an ingenious, futuristic toy maker. Caleb glanced around. Parts were suspended from the ceiling, piled in the corners, and arranged in lines along the floor. Among them were mechanical limbs and torsos, some unnervingly humanlike in appearance; various kinds of wings and flippers; crawler tracks, runners, and at least ten different types of wheels. A workbench took up one entire side of the room, its surface jam-packed with tubs of smaller components, coils of wire, and stacks of circuitry and batteries. On the pegboard behind hung every tool you could think of—from micro-screwdrivers and soldering irons to some pretty heavy-duty drills. But there was no sign of Zen herself. Could she still be in the cafeteria, Caleb wondered, or over in one of the common rooms?

He was about to go and find out when he heard it: a soft tapping sound. He looked around. There was something on the outside of the window, in one of the top corners, inching across the glass. He recognized it at once—it was Beetlebat, the most sophisticated of Zen's robots.

Beetlebat was a miniature masterpiece of robotics engineering: incredibly intricate, loaded with features—and deceptively powerful. Zen had finished it at the end of the summer term after months of work, although she was always adding enhancements and extra abilities. The size of a large moth, Beetlebat was roughly insectoid but with a long, slender tail, six multiarticulated legs, and a set of batlike wings that were folded away under its shining, iridescent carapace. A clump of antennae sprouted from its copper button of a head, probing the air all around.

Caleb furrowed his brow. Beetlebat was Zen's pride and joy; it practically *lived* in her jacket pocket. There was no way she'd go anywhere, even down the hall, and not take it with her. He went over to the window and opened a narrow panel on its left side. Beetlebat promptly scuttled in, snapped out its wings, and glided over to the workbench, landing in the wide, high-sided tray where Zen tested her robots' motor functions.

Caleb followed it, sitting on a stool and switching on a desk lamp. The little robot was standing completely still. Caleb took out the Flex to run a quick diagnostic. To his surprise, Beetlebat's onboard processor revealed that it had been flying around the ARC tower for almost twenty minutes—roughly as long as he'd been inside—having come from somewhere in Bloomsbury, over half a mile away. He hadn't realized it could travel so far.

There was a small movement in front of him; Beetlebat had raised one of its spindly forelegs. A minuscule, scalpel-like blade flicked out at the leg's end and it began to etch something into the bottom of the tray. Caleb leaned forward. He could make out four words, or groups of letters at least, the scratches white against the dark green plastic. The script was elaborate, the letters curling at the ends, like something from a treasure map—a typical Zen touch.

The lamassu's hoof. BM.

Caleb sat back. This message was plainly intended for him. Zen had programmed Beetlebat to home in on the Flex's unique digital signature—she'd sent it to find him. And then the diagnostic he'd run had triggered a new subroutine, causing the robot to carve these words into the tray. But he had no idea at all what it meant. He entered "lamassu" into the Flex's search engine. They were ancient Assyrian monsters, he learned, kind of like sphinxes but with the body of a bull instead of a lion. There were only two lamassu statues in the whole of London—a matching pair in the collection of the British Museum. *BM*, he thought. From the photos, though, he couldn't see anything particularly special about their hooves.

He glanced back at the tray. Beetlebat was scratching something else . . . a tiny, looping symbol, like a number eight laid on its side. He blinked in astonishment. It was a Möbius strip.

The word *Möbius* had a special significance at the ARC

Institute, beyond its place in mathematics and geometry classes. Rumors were always circulating about something called the Möbius Program, overseen by none other than Professor Tilda Clay. It was said to give unusual, especially difficult assignments to certain students, like bits of coding or hacking, or the analysis of strange high-tech gadgets. How these students were selected was a mystery—it wasn't done on the basis of their test scores or anything like that. They seemed to be mostly from the upper years, but no one who was suspected of involvement would say a single thing about it, having been sworn to absolute secrecy. Some thought the Möbius assignments were passed on to the ARC by the British intelligence services, and that GCHQ was actually the main source of the institute's funding, which was how they could make the school completely free of charge, open to anyone who could pass the grueling entrance exams.

Its message delivered, Beetlebat scuttled out of the tray and up Caleb's sleeve, disappearing into the pocket of his hoodie. The room seemed darker all of a sudden, the half-built robots slightly sinister. Caleb turned away from the workbench, gripping his hands together and thinking hard. If the Möbius Program was involved, there could be something really serious going on here. He had a growing sense that the evening's events were connected. His mum's message had told him to go to Professor Clay—and now Zen had given him a cryptic clue that alluded to Clay's secret program. This couldn't just be a coincidence.

Caleb got up and examined the bedroom more closely. The toothbrush was gone from the bathroom sink, some clothes had been taken from the wardrobe, and Zen's black backpack—which she carried with her at all times—was missing from its hook on the door. She'd gone. Left the building. And she'd sent Beetlebat to tell him where to head.

He looked at the Flex. Professor Clay still hadn't responded to his intranet message. This made up his mind. He was going to follow Zen's clue—check out the lamassu's hoof, whatever that turned out to be. Möbius meant Clay, he was certain of it: if he found Zen he would find Clay as well. And then perhaps he could finally get some answers.

As he left Zen's room, however, he remembered that he'd signed in for the night—touched his thumb on that stupid sensor. He nearly groaned aloud. He wouldn't be permitted to leave again without getting one of the other teachers involved. They'd try to contact his mum. Maybe raise the alarm. He'd be stuck in the tower for ages, totally helpless.

Caleb gathered his wits. A bit of Quinn ingenuity was required here. He got in an elevator and hit the button for the lobby. Bypassing the electronic lock on the sliding doors was easy—half the kids at the ARC could do it. The real obstacle was Rufus. The security guard's blank stares and bored manner were a ruse. His senses were sharp; he could be distracted, but it would have to be something pretty special.

Luckily, Caleb had the Flex—and its Chameleon app in particular. He'd coded it with this exact situation in mind. He opened up the app's main screen and tapped on Rufus's profile. The guard was currently streaming a soccer game between Portsmouth and Crewe, but data from his phone camera revealed that he'd only been facing the screen forty-six percent of the time. This was no good—he wasn't watching closely enough. Caleb would be spotted for sure.

He touched the panel that activated Chameleon's selection algorithm. In a couple of seconds, it had refreshed its survey of Rufus's online viewing history and chosen the match most likely to claim his entire attention. This turned out to be a video called *Dogs on Ice Vol. 16*. Caleb swiped his fingertip across the screen, cutting the feed to the soccer and unleashing the dogs instead. The video ran simultaneously in a small window on the Flex. First up was a Great Dane, loping happily onto a frozen lake. It quickly lost control of all its legs at once, flopped onto its belly, and began spinning around in slow circles.

The elevator arrived in the lobby, its doors opening to the sound of a loud, hoarse chuckle. Rufus was angled toward the window behind the reception desk, his face bathed in the blue light of his phone. His chair was rocking slightly with his laughter.

Caleb crouched low, creeping past the desk while—on Rufus's screen—a Labradoodle tried to change direction as it ran over a frozen stream, its furry ginger legs skidding about so fast that they seemed to blur. This drew another great guffaw from the guard. Caleb shook his head; he could have strolled through the lobby in full view and not been noticed. He quickly hacked the lock on the sliding doors, slipped out of the ARC tower, and went back around to where he'd left his bike.

Time to pay a visit to the British Museum.

3

THE LAMASSU'S HOOF

Caleb swept along Chancery Lane, hopping up onto the sidewalk to avoid a red light. It was almost a quarter past seven. The British Museum had actually been closed now for over two hours. How exactly, he wanted to ask Zen, am I supposed to reach this lamassu? He could easily imagine her reply. *Surely that's not a problem for a tech wizard like Caleb Quinn— right?* He smiled grimly to himself. In truth, it was a *massive* problem. He somehow had to break into the museum, make his way to the Assyrian rooms, and then work out what was so important about this statue and its damn hoof. This was turning out to be a challenging evening.

A couple of minutes later he arrived on Great Russell Street. It was very nearly dark now. The shadows were deepening. He slowed to take in the main entrance of the museum. There were tall iron railings all around the perimeter and way too much open space before the mighty colonnades behind. The place looked more or less impregnable.

He'd already thought of a plan, though. Local maps had

shown a goods entrance at the rear of the building on Montague Place. He rode around to it, going past once without pausing. The gates were high and the camera placements obvious. He swung left at the end of the street onto Russell Square, where he got off his bike and chained it up. Then he pulled out the Flex.

"Spider Monkey," he murmured.

The hacking screen appeared, rapidly compiling a list of nearby networks. There were two for the British Museum. The first system was simple, the Spider Monkey app cracking it almost at once. The second, the security system, was a little harder. The administrator account had to be on-site. Caleb came back out and reentered the first system, using it to set up a fake account as an on-site user and granting it full access to the admin protocols. Then, deploying Spider Monkey again, he used this fake account to access the second system. He was in. Now he just had to get inside physically.

He made his way back along Montague Place on foot. The street was deserted save for a cat that skulked beneath a parked car, its eyes flashing with reflected light. He tried to walk calmly, but his pulse was quickening.

The hack had shown that a threefold security system was in operation at the British Museum. There were guards stationed in a central control room, many dozens of hidden cameras, and a network of good old-fashioned alarms—some connected to doors, others to motion-sensor beams. After a delicate resequencing of Spider Monkey's algorithms, Caleb had managed to set up the Flex to project a kind of protective bubble around him. It would turn off each of the cameras as he passed, for exactly as long as it took him to walk beneath

23

them. Provided he kept to a carefully mapped route and avoided areas where two or more cameras were trained, the screens up in the control room would do no more than flicker—one at a time and in a seemingly random order. With a bit of luck, none of the guards would even notice. Likewise, as he drew near, each alarm would have its time codes temporarily reset, so that they would believe it was the middle of the day and therefore deactivate.

Caleb stepped across the street, heading toward the gates of the goods entrance. Just as he approached, a loud engine echoed along the empty street. The headlight of what looked like some kind of dirt bike blazed through the darkness. He fitted the Flex around his wrist and activated Spider Monkey. At once, the gate began to swing open. He darted through before he could be seen.

The gate banged shut behind him. Caleb winced. Everything sounded so much louder at night. He walked down the short driveway to the garage-style basement entrance, which now started to roll upward. Noisily. The wait was excruciating. But he kept his head down—and as soon as there was enough space he ducked inside.

By the dim light of the Flex's screen, Caleb crept to the back of a large loading bay, his ears keyed for any sound, feeling like a diamond thief in an old heist movie. The route led him along a murky corridor and through what looked like a staff locker room. He walked at as normal a speed as possible, all the while fighting the urge to break into a run. But an even pace was vital. If he went too fast, Spider Monkey might not have enough time to kill the next camera in the sequence; too slow and the cameras would be deactivated for too long. After a flight of stairs and two more doorways, he reached the back of the exhibition halls. He eased open an emergency exit and headed right, into one of the Egyptian galleries.

Mummies. The place was basically an ancient graveyard, he thought, for the not-quite-dead. The low-level lighting actually seemed to deepen the surrounding shadows. To his left were stone reliefs depicting battles and terrifying massacres, while in the display cases to his right was a collection of withered corpses wrapped up tightly in ragged, discolored bindings. Out of the gloom, a single sarcophagus rose up in a case directly in front of him, the face hollow-eyed and shrunken and the empty mouth appearing to scream. He flinched, trying not to look.

He turned a corner, making for the staircase that led down into the Assyrian rooms—but something ahead of him, gleaming in the darkness, made him stop in his tracks. What the hell was *that*?

Moving closer, he saw a jet-black statue with the body of a man, the head of a lion, the talons of an eagle, two pairs of wings, and a scorpion's tail. The expression on its twisted, devilish face was petrifying—somehow both cruel and weirdly, creepily *friendly*. As if it had been expecting him. Caleb shivered, glancing at the display label.

A MESOPOTAMIAN BRONZE, it read, DEPICTING THE DEMON PAZUZU, DATING FROM AROUND THE EIGHTH CENTURY BC. PAZUZU WAS BELIEVED TO CURSE—

The Flex began to vibrate against his wrist. He stopped

reading and looked down at the screen. Nothing seemed to be wrong with the camera sequencing—but the main alarm in the vast central hall had just been deactivated.

"Phantom," he whispered.

The security room appeared from the point of view of one of the computers on the desks. A lone woman could be seen, lolling on her chair. The other two guards had gone. A patrol?

Caleb continued walking. It was harder than ever now to keep his pace steady. Half a minute later he entered the largest of the three Assyrian rooms: a long, rectangular gallery filled with obelisks, urns, and statues of ancient gods. He heard a snatch of distant conversation, echoing off the marble walls. The two missing guards were strolling through the main hall, flashlights in their hands, making a circuit. He swore under his breath, moving on through the gallery as quickly as he dared—until the statues he was looking for loomed immediately before him, set on either side of a rounded archway, standing huge and inscrutable in the half-light.

The lamassu were impressively strange: giant six-legged bulls, with the wings of angels and the heads of bearded, turbaned men. Caleb remembered what he'd read about them in Zen's bedroom. Almost three thousand years ago, these two mighty creatures had been mounted at the gates of a royal Assyrian palace—and only a very foolish person indeed would have passed between them without making absolutely sure that they were welcome. The ancient Assyrians were . . . brutal. No other word for it.

Caleb stood between them. Only now did he realize that he didn't actually know which of the statues to examine, or even what he was looking for. "Hoof" was all he had. Would it be another clue, written or carved into the stone? Or something digital—a hidden chip, maybe, or a QR code?

He remembered that Beetlebat, the source of Zen's message, was still nestled inside his hoodie. He took it out and held it up on the palm of his hand, showing it the lamassu.

"Come on, little bot," he said. "Help me out here."

But Beetlebat seemed to have powered down. It didn't move. A red LED winked on the end of one of its antennae.

Caleb sighed impatiently and returned it to his pocket. He unwrapped the Flex from his wrist, flattened it out, and cycled through its illumination modes. Selecting an ultrasensitive forensic black light, he went to the front of the right-hand lamassu and raised the Flex before him. The UV beam revealed hundreds of ghostly fingerprints, smeared messily across the front hooves and forelegs—mostly by small kids from the look of it. He circled the statue. There were far fewer fingerprints on the extra legs in the middle, or the ones at the back, but nothing that seemed out of the ordinary.

The guards' voices were frighteningly close now. Caleb rushed across to the left-hand lamassu. The front and side hooves were much the same—but on one of the rear ones he discovered something more interesting. This hoof was also covered in random finger and thumb marks. But several people had laid their hands on it in a very specific position. The prints were smudged in a way that could mean only one thing: they'd been pushing against it.

Caleb fitted the Flex back around his wrist and tried to match his hands with the prints. The hoof was the size of a

27

rugby ball. It was smooth and rounded and felt completely, immovably solid. He looked around anxiously. Outside the Assyrian rooms, just along a corridor, the beam of a flashlight swept through a row of display cabinets, glinting against the relics arranged inside.

He leaned on the hoof with the full weight of his body, jigging up and down, cursing through gritted teeth. There was the faintest click. At first, he thought it must have come from a joint in his wrist or his arm as he strained against the stone. But then he noticed that something had moved on the wall at the lamassu's end. The front panel of what had appeared to be an electrical service box had opened a few inches, revealing a dark, narrow opening—the way into a hiding place, perhaps, or some kind of passageway.

The beam of the security guards' flashlight caught the top edge of the lamassu's wing, a couple of feet above Caleb's head. Without another thought, he raced behind the massive man-bull, squeezed through the opening, and hurriedly pulled the panel shut behind him.

Darkness. The sound of the guards' footfalls and his own shallow, panicked breaths. The smell of dust and mice. He kept rigidly still.

After a couple of long minutes when he was sure the guards had gone, he turned on the Flex's light at the lowest level. He found that he was crammed into a concrete corridor that was only just wide enough to hold him. He twisted around, expecting to see air-conditioning ducts or wiring, but there was nothing. Slowly, he began to move away from the Assyrian rooms. The corridor headed down, quite steeply.

After a hundred feet or so it grew a little broader, leading him to a half flight of steps. Now the walls were made of old red-brick, crumbling in places, and everything smelled of wet masonry. He heard the squeaking and scratching of rodents and the sound of running water—an underground stream, he thought, or a storm drain.

The quality of the darkness ahead changed. Caleb felt the walls retreat, and a lapping sound rose to his ears. Suddenly, the floor disappeared. He scrambled backward with a gasp, just in time.

Once he was sure of his footing, he raised the Flex's light to maximum. For a moment he was unable to make any sense of what he was seeing. He was standing on a ledge above a wide, fast-flowing river. Opposite, through empty arches in the brickwork, poured a row of small waterfalls. There was a terrible stink of raw sewage.

"Crap," he muttered. "Literally. A river of crap."

Somehow, he'd wandered down into the London sewers. No way across the main channel could be seen. He waited for a few seconds, trying not to breathe too deeply, before deciding to retrace his steps and check the corridor again with the Flex's light fully activated.

Five minutes later, he was back at the half flight of steps. This time, however, approaching upward from the opposite direction, he noticed a narrow gap that he'd missed on the way down. He trained his light on it. Beyond this gap was darkness—empty space. Another passageway.

He started along it. Almost immediately, he was confronted with a reinforced steel door that looked like it belonged in a military bunker. There was a large submarine-style wheel on the front. He gave it a heave, expecting it to be stiff, but it was well oiled and spun easily. In regular use. Someone had left it open. Caleb grinned, pushing at the steel door with both hands. It swung back without a sound.

4

THE HIDEOUT

Caleb walked forward into a vast, gloomy chamber. It looked like it had once been some kind of underground chapel, with brickwork vaults overhead and columns running down either side. Mosaics of saints, made from tiny golden tiles, glimmered faintly in alcoves. Ahead, where the altar would have been, stood a wide trestle table, on which he could see an electric lamp, a closed laptop, and a familiar-looking black backpack. He was about to call Zen's name when there was a whistle from off to the left, behind the columns. Beetlebat twitched to life in his pocket and clambered quickly around his arm, its tiny hooklike claws gripping the fabric of his hoodie. Then it hopped into the air, extended its membranous wings, and flew through the shadows to land on Zen's shoulder.

"Hey, Caleb," she said, with her trademark half smile. "You made it."

Caleb grinned with relief to see her, but he could tell immediately that something was wrong. Zen always looked lean and restless. But now she seemed ready to punch a hole in the nearest wall. Her long black hair was tied back in a tight braid. She was wearing a dark gray denim jacket with zip pockets in its front, a red T-shirt, black jeans, and neon-blue sneakers. In the middle of her collarbone was a teardrop-shaped piece of jade with a single golden strand twining around it—a necklace passed down to her by one of her Syrian grandmothers.

Caleb started toward her. "Zen, what's going on? What *is* this place, anyway? And what—"

"My family, Caleb," she interrupted. "They've been taken. Mum, Dad, and Riyah. Someone's kidnapped them."

Caleb stopped dead. An uneasy, nauseating feeling crept through him. "Whoa," he muttered. "My mum was just grabbed as well. Kind of."

Zen's eyes went wide. "What?"

"At my house a couple of hours ago. Some very ugly people showed up. My mum stalled them so I could get away. Then she went with them."

"What did you—"

"I got the hell out of there."

Zen's expression was concerned. "Has anything like this ever happened before?"

"Well, my mum works on some pretty weird stuff, but no . . . not like this."

"Did she know these people?"

Caleb nodded, trying hard to keep his doubts in check. "Yeah, I think so. But she definitely wasn't expecting them to come to the house . . . or for things to get so heavy. We had an emergency plan, though—just in case. I was supposed to go to Professor Clay, so I rode straight back to school to look for her. That's where Beetlebat found me. It flew all the way up to your bedroom window."

Zen glanced at the robot on her shoulder, which was testing the musty air with its antennae. "Good girl," she said softly. "Lucky I installed those navigation upgrades, huh?"

Caleb reached out to lean against a column. "Do you know what's happening? And why are we—" He looked around. "Why are we down here?"

"OK." Zen took a deep, steadying breath. "Professor Clay came to get me from my room, not long after last period. She wouldn't tell me where we were going. Only that I wasn't to call anyone or send any messages. She turned off her phone and told me to do the same—for security reasons."

"Sounds pretty intense."

"Yeah, it felt . . ." Zen frowned. "It felt *serious*. Like there was real danger. I had literally about ten seconds to get ready. I had no idea what was going on."

"Professor Clay brought you here?"

"We came in just after the museum closed. A contact of Clay's—a guy from the staff, I think—let us into the tunnel behind the lamassu."

"What did Clay say when you got here? She must have told you something."

Zen's head dipped down. "She said that my family had probably been taken last night, but she couldn't be sure. No one even realized they were missing for a while. Riyah isn't back at school yet and my dad isn't teaching at the university again until the end of the week."

"Jeez, Zen," Caleb murmured. Zen's parents, Salma and

Elias, were both scientists. Although Syrian by birth, they'd been in the UK for most of their professional lives and that's where they had started their family. The Rafiqs were currently based in Berlin, however, so that Elias could head up a cutting-edge nanotechnology unit at the Freie Universität. Normally, Zen boarded at the ARC during the week, then went to Germany on weekends or met up with her parents and little sister, Riyah, in London.

Zen dug her hands deep into her jacket pockets. "This place is a safe house, apparently. Clay told me that the people who took my family were likely coming for me too. She said she would be back in an hour with more information. That I should try not to worry. That everything was going to be fine." She looked around. "That was more than an hour and a half ago."

"Try not to worry!" Caleb echoed sarcastically. "Great advice, Prof."

"I know, right?" Zen peered up at one of the mosaicked saints—a gaunt, robed figure with a black serpent coiled around his feet. "I started to get kind of creeped out down here on my own. And kind of *annoyed* as well. So I programmed that subroutine into Beetlebat and sent it up an old water pipe to find you—to search for the Flex. I figured I could really use your help."

Caleb chuckled, shaking his head. "You do realize that you just had me break into the British Museum, right? I mean—I love a difficult break-in at dusk. Who doesn't? But sneaking around in sewers is a little less like my idea of fun. I nearly fell face-first into a river of crap back there."

Zen gave him the half smile again. "I knew you could handle it."

"Yeah, that's what I thought you'd say."

They held out their fists and bumped them together. Caleb's spirits lifted. Sharing stuff with Zen always made everything feel better.

"So . . . are these kidnappers targeting the parents of ARC kids, then?" he asked, his smile fading. "Is that their plan?"

"Gotta be connected."

"But why? And what are *we* going to do about it?"

Abruptly, Zen held up her finger to her ear and went still. A scraping noise was coming from across the room. Beneath a low brick archway, another door was being pulled open. It was smaller than the one Caleb had used—little more than a hatch in the wall. An adult was coming through, ducking down so as not to hit their head. He tensed, ready to run, but then he saw that this figure was none other than . . . Professor Tilda Clay.

Professor Clay was a tall Black woman in her midforties, with sharp features, large green eyes, and grayish hair, which she cut very short. She wore a long charcoal coat with a light check pattern and brown leather boots. She was carrying a covered coffee cup in one hand and a paper bag in the other. As she emerged into the chamber, she saw Caleb and almost dropped her cup in surprise.

"Caleb Quinn," she said in her slight London accent. "What are *you* doing here already?"

A blush flamed across Caleb's face. "I came in through the tunnels, Professor. Behind the, uh, the lamassu."

"You're *supposed* to be at the ARC. There's a car on its way over there to pick you up." Clay put down her cup and bag on the trestle table. Then she crossed her arms—every inch the

35

stern teacher. Her eyes narrowed. "How did you know where to come, exactly? And how did you know about the lamassu?"

Caleb didn't reply, but he glanced over at Zen. She was standing up very straight, the light from Beetlebat's LEDs casting a faint red streak in her hair.

Clay's eyes went from Caleb to Zen. "Didn't I tell you not to use your phone, Zenobia? Didn't I explain that it was a security risk?"

"I didn't use my phone, Professor," Zen replied.

"She sent her robot," Caleb said, trying to bail his friend out. "It's not on any networks. It was tracing the signal from my—"

"And how did you get here?" Clay interrupted, turning back to Caleb.

"On my bike," Caleb told her. "It's chained up on Russell Square. Listen, Professor, I have to tell you something. These guys—"

"Were you followed from the ARC?"

Caleb paused. He tried to remember the ride over. All he'd been thinking about was how he could get inside the museum. "I . . . I don't think so."

"So you didn't use your phones and you weren't followed?"

They both shook their heads.

Clay raised a hand to her brow. "I'm impressed by your inventiveness," she said in a voice that sounded the total opposite. "But you've *got* to be smarter than this. From now on, the safest thing is to assume that someone's trying their hardest to find you *at all times*. And if I give you an instruction, you do not—at any time—disobey me. Clear?"

Caleb was suddenly angry. He wasn't going to listen to a

lecture—not now, after everything else he'd been through. "My mum's been taken, Professor," he said bluntly. "Just like Zen's family. These biker guys came to our house. They had guns. They wanted to grab me as well."

Clay was listening carefully. With a softer, more measured tone, she asked, "Did your mum tell you to come back to school? To find me?"

Caleb nodded. Clearly, none of what he'd just said was news to Professor Clay. His instinct at the ARC had been correct: something far bigger was going on here.

"I couldn't find you anywhere, though," he said. "And you weren't answering messages. It was like you'd been abducted too. So I came to this place because I didn't know what else to do. I thought you might be here because Zen's message mentioned the . . ." He was going to say "Möbius Program" but stopped himself just in time. "Because that's what her message said."

"Things have been moving fast." Clay had taken out her phone and was swiping her finger across the screen. "The intelligence services knew that there was a capture team active in London. Their leader is a woman called Erica Szabo. She's a mercenary—a gun for hire. Wanted by the police in sixteen countries."

She showed Caleb a grainy photo that looked like it had been taken in secret and from a distance. It showed a woman in aviator sunglasses, her hair shaved at the sides and bright orange on the top, sitting at the wheel of a dusty jeep.

"Yeah, she was there," Caleb said. "Not a haircut you forget."

"We were on threat level five until about ten minutes ago," Clay continued. "That means a total communications blackout—which is why I couldn't respond to your message. The ARC system had logged your arrival at the tower, and I was foolish enough to assume that you'd stay put until we could get a car to you." She looked at the photo again. "Everything we'd seen suggested that Zen was at the top of Szabo's list. I had to get her to a secure location—to this chapel. It's pretty much the safest place in the city."

"What about me and my mum?" Caleb asked, more loudly than he'd intended; he could hear the accusation in his voice. "Why didn't you come to get us? Or send us a warning?"

Clay came closer. Briefly, her briskness left her; she fixed Caleb with a look that was almost sympathetic. "We thought they'd come for Zen first. By the time we realized what was actually going on, it was too late." She sighed. "Caleb, your mum's CIA. Szabo caught her unawares, but I had to assume that she could deal with it. You say they took her?"

Caleb remembered his mum's last message, the sight of her through the kitchen skylight, leaning against the counter. "Yeah. She gave me a signal to get out—to find you. Then she . . . she almost seemed to go along with them."

Clay was nodding. "A classic CIA move," she said. "Your mum saw a chance to get on the inside and gather some intel. Avoid a gunfight. Make sure you got away." She raised her eyebrows. "Brave woman."

"Gather some intel?" Zen asked. "What do you mean?"

"OK." Clay indicated a bench beside the trestle table. "Sit. I know you both need answers. I'll go through everything we have."

5

THE MÖBIUS PROGRAM

Clay sat on the opposite bench and opened up her paper bag. It held two sandwiches, packed in triangular cardboard boxes. She slid one of them over to Zen. The other was obviously for her. She looked at it for a moment, then passed it to Caleb. He was starving and accepted the sandwich gratefully, peeling back the plastic cover to fish out half of a BLT.

Clay picked up the coffee cup. "Agent Quinn was investigating all this, in association with a few other intelligence agencies. Those mercs will have taken her in the hope of shutting her investigation down. They've made a big mistake." She took off the cup's lid, releasing a small cloud of steam. "The abductions of your relatives, Zenobia, are the latest in a series. There have been at least eight over the past few weeks. A number are scientists—cybernetics and nanotech specialists, mostly. We think it's being done in some kind of pattern."

"Nanotech," said Zen. "That's my dad's field. It's why he went to Germany." She lifted her left hand to her necklace and began to roll the jade teardrop between her thumb and fore-finger. "But my mum's a biochemist. And what about Riyah? She's only ten."

"They take whole families," Clay told her. "We don't know why yet."

Zen looked off into the shadows. She hadn't touched her sandwich. "You said that Szabo's a mercenary, Professor. So . . . who's she working for? Who's paying her to do this?"

Clay sipped her coffee. "Activity on the Dark Web points to someone called Xavier Torrent."

"Wait," Caleb said, swallowing a mouthful of BLT. "Wait, I know that name. Erica Szabo said it to my mum. To convince her to go with them. And she *really* wanted to find out what Szabo knew about him." He lifted the sandwich for another bite. "I thought *I* recognized it too."

Clay pulled up another photo on her phone. It showed a slim, even-featured man who looked like a Silicon Valley tech entrepreneur, giving a speech on some kind of podium. His clothes were clearly superexpensive—a silver-gray designer overcoat and a high-collared black shirt. He had a dark, immaculately trimmed beard and wore a pair of rimless sunglasses—even though he was indoors, standing under a row of spotlights.

"Xavier Torrent was a computer scientist," Clay said. "A true innovator. An expert in the medical applications of AI."

"Like my dad," Caleb said. "Medical AI was his thing too."

Clay's green eyes narrowed. "They did actually work together in the US, I believe, before your dad came back to London. That's probably why you recognize the name. But Torrent disappeared off the face of the earth nearly ten years ago. There'd been some controversy over the direction his work was taking. Details about what exactly he was up to are very scarce—he seems to have scrubbed the internet, erasing everything that he could. This image here is one of the few we have."

"Bizarre," Caleb said. "Like he was trying to delete himself."

"Or remake himself. To start again, completely off the radar." Clay drank some more coffee. "No one knows where he is now, or has information of any kind."

"Is this all we know, Professor?" Zen asked. She sounded tense and exasperated.

Clay met this question with a level stare. "There is one other lead." She paused. "I take it you've both heard of the special program I run for some of the older students at school?"

Caleb and Zen exchanged a glance.

"A few things," Zen said cautiously.

"Just rumors, really," Caleb added. "Here and there."

Clay smiled for the first time. "Well, they're true. Most of them, anyway. I also work—let's just say—as an *affiliate* for GCHQ, in the Infosec Department. We get sent decryptions, mysterious devices, inexplicable signals—all kinds of things. Problems nobody else can do anything with." She drew a folded sheet of what looked like blueprint paper from inside her coat. "This is the latest one."

Caleb couldn't quite believe what he was hearing. "Are you—are you asking us to . . ."

Clay set down her cup. "Welcome to the Möbius Program," she said, a faint sparkle in her eyes. "We've been monitoring you both for a while now, and we reckon you've got what it takes. Your projects outside the main ARC syllabus are certainly . . . interesting. These clever little robots." She reached over the table toward Beetlebat; it shifted slightly to the side, its antennae exploring her fingertip. "This video game, Caleb, that I keep hearing so much about. And everything you've done tonight only confirms it." She pursed her lips. "I wouldn't have wanted your first assignment to be so personal, but I'm afraid we don't get to choose. Events have forced our hand." She shifted on the bench. "OK—the first thing I have to do is give you your codenames."

"Whoa," Caleb cut in. "We get *code names*?"

"Everyone in the Möbius Program does. It's standard operational procedure. To protect your identities and allow us a little . . . plausible deniability." Clay looked steadily from one of them to the other. "We use avian names. Mine is 'Goldfinch.' Caleb, you will be known as 'Swift.' And Zen, you are 'Hawk.' These are the names you'll use in all Möbius communications."

"Swift and Hawk," said Zen quietly. "Sounds pretty cool."

Caleb grinned. "You definitely wouldn't want to mess with them."

"And is the Mobius Program working to get our families back, Professor?" Zen asked.

"I'm coming to that." Clay became businesslike again, unfolding the sheet of blueprint paper. "A week ago, local police investigating one of the earlier disappearances found this. It was in a hidden safe at a site in northern Spain that we suspect had been used as a temporary base by Szabo and her mercenaries."

Zen frowned. "Why is it on paper?"

"To keep it secure," Clay replied. "Offline. Even the best

hacker in the world can't get to a piece of paper. Someone really messed up when they left this behind. It's a code of some sort—in binary, but parts of it are missing. Nobody has been able to tell us what it means. And I mean *nobody*." She held the sheet out. "But maybe Swift and Hawk can. You certainly have good reason to try."

Caleb took the sheet eagerly. Here was something he could do—a way he could help his mum, and Zen and her family too. A problem he could solve. The sheet was indeed covered in binary code, a tight grid of ones and zeros, the universal language of computer programming. He could see at once that important sections had been deliberately cut out, like Clay had told them. He passed it to Zen.

"It's like a jigsaw puzzle with half of its pieces gone," he said.

Zen studied it closely. "We need some way to step back. To run through all the possible options of what's missing. But there must be thousands of them. Millions. It could take months."

For a minute, they both thought in silence. Caleb furrowed his brow, striding away—then he turned and snapped his fingers.

"OK," he said. "OK, I think I might have an idea."

Zen didn't react. She was looking intently toward the far wall. Caleb followed her gaze—and with a start, he spotted a tiny jet-black disc drifting about twelve feet above the floor, away behind a row of columns. He glanced down at the Flex, thinking to run an analysis, but the disc wasn't giving out any kind of signal that he could detect. The red light of a laser scanner began to shine from its center, sweeping over the room.

43

Zen whistled—a low, short note—and pointed at the drone. Caleb noticed a silver filament running along the nail of her forefinger—some kind of microdevice, he guessed, that provided targeting instructions to Beetlebat. In an instant, the robot had zipped over to attack, looping high and fast over the spy drone and then coming down from behind with the loud zap of a powerful electric shock. It then seized its prey with its legs and carried it back to Zen.

The crippled drone was about the size of a coaster. Zen took it between thumb and forefinger and dropped it immediately into Clay's coffee. The Professor flinched, holding the cup out at arm's length. There were some sparks, and a wisp of smoke—then Zen plucked it out again, angling the black disc this way and that so she could examine it.

"Some kind of seeker drone," she said. "*Incredibly* advanced. Looks like it has cloaking tech. It should be able to get almost anywhere without being detected."

Clay was already on her feet. "We've been found," she said tersely.

Caleb felt the hairs rise on the back of his neck. "How did they know to look down here?"

Clay gathered up the laptop and put it in a shoulder bag. "Well, either they must have traced Zen's beetle robot somehow, or they followed your bike." She nodded at the seeker drone, still smoking between Zen's fingers. "Or they're just way better equipped than we thought. It doesn't matter. We've got to move—now."

With that, she went back over toward the low doorway through which she'd come in. Zen retrieved her black backpack, stowing the dead drone and the code sheet in one of its side pockets and her unopened sandwich in another. As she got up and hoisted the bag onto her back, she made a clicking sound with her tongue—a signal for Beetlebat to leave her shoulder and slide itself into her jacket pocket. Caleb stood as well, fitting the Flex back around his wrist and taking a last look at the shadowy chapel.

Clay turned for a moment. "Stay close," she said. "We don't know what's out there."

Caleb and Zen both nodded. Then they followed Professor Clay into the tunnels.

6

AMONG THE FATBERGS

The smell of raw sewage in the passageway beyond was almost overwhelming. Caleb had been planning to eat the second half of his BLT as he walked but quickly changed his mind, stuffing the sandwich box into his hoodie pocket instead. After about sixty feet they emerged into a large, open area. He could hear running water nearby, lots of it. They were on a ledge above one of the main sewers—just downstream from where he'd come out earlier, he reckoned.

Clay had stopped at the top of a narrow set of steps and was tapping a rapid message into her phone. Two small boats were moored in the murky channel below, tied to a metal ring that had been driven into the sewer wall. She turned to Caleb and Zen, her expression deadly serious.

"Listen to me," she said. "We have to use different boats—to divide our weight between them, so we can go faster. It's the only way we're going to escape. Can either of you operate an outboard motor?"

"Uh . . ." Caleb hesitated.

"Sure," said Zen. "Simple."

Clay handed something to her—a data stick, it looked like. "Just in case. Keep it safe. Everything you need is on there." Then she went down the steps and got in her boat.

Zen and Caleb followed her down as quickly as they could. They climbed into the second boat, the narrow hull rocking beneath them. Caleb wedged himself in a space at the back. This was his first time in a motor boat. The water was dark and disgusting, and he was afraid they were going to tip over. Zen, however, seemed completely at ease. Her family was always going away on wilderness treks and remote camping expeditions. She could do this kind of thing in her sleep.

Clay undid the mooring ropes and the two boats drifted out side by side into the main channel. "Right," she said. "Start the engine now. If you just—"

A set of floodlights snapped on behind them, somewhere around a bend in the tunnel. One side of the sewer was lit up—the crumbling bricks, the floating islands of filth, the dozens of little splashes as sewer rats scurried for cover.

Clay swore under her breath. She looked ahead, peering into the blackness. Then she leaned out over the water between the two boats, took hold of theirs, and gave it such a hard push it bumped against the far wall.

"You can't let these guys capture you," she panted. "Just follow the tunnel. It'll lead you to the river. Then get as far from London as possible. And keep checking the intranet— the Möbius Program will be in touch. Good luck, Swift and Hawk."

Caleb turned toward the front of the boat. A short distance farther on, he could now see a smaller tunnel, branching off from the one they were in. He realized what Clay was trying to do. She was splitting the boats up so she could lead their pursuers in another direction.

Zen had guessed it too. They both began to blurt out questions.

"But what about you, Professor? What will happen if they—"

"What shall we do with the code? Should we—"

Clay was moving back to the outboard engine of her boat. "Work on it if you can," she said. "But get well clear of this place first." She smiled grimly. "And watch out for fatbergs."

"Wait—*what*?" Caleb shouted back.

Their boat jerked and wobbled. A new current had caught hold of the prow, dragging them toward the side tunnel. Caleb looked back to Professor Clay. The floodlights were coming along the tunnel, their harsh light breaking over her. She reached into her coat and drew out a compact pistol, examining it with distaste before crouching down to pull the cord on her outboard motor. It started at once, the growl echoing around the brickwork.

Caleb watched Clay's boat begin to pull away, leaving a plume of dirty yellow foam behind it. Then he and Zen were swallowed up by the side tunnel and all went dark.

Caleb activated the Flex's light, revealing the slimy contours of another brickwork sewage tunnel. Somehow, the reek in this one was even worse—thick and horribly warm, wrapping wetly around his face. He covered his nose with his sleeve.

"Oh *man*," he said. "I should have brought a gas mask."

Zen was busy checking the outboard motor. "Just be grateful we're not swimming."

She gave the starter cord a sharp tug, and another—and then it spluttered to life. They picked up speed, slicing through the stinking waters.

Bright white light suddenly sparkled against the boat's edge. The floodlights were at the mouth of the side tunnel. Professor Clay's plan had failed. Their pursuers had worked out what she'd done and were splitting up themselves.

"What are we going to do?" Caleb shouted. "Can we outrun them?"

In reply, Zen opened up the motor's throttle a bit more. Then she stood up, took off her backpack, and pulled out a slim quiver packed with arrows, which she threw around her shoulder, followed by an object that looked like the grip section of a pistol. She pressed a button and it instantly extended, forming a thin staff with a length of string trailing from one end. In less than a second, she'd bent the staff, attached the string, and formed a neat, lightweight bow. Caleb stared at it in amazement.

"Made it at the start of the summer," she told him. "I've got a new archery instructor up in Hampstead Heath. And this is a lot easier to take on the Tube."

Zenobia Rafiq was a dedicated athlete. When she wasn't building her robots, she'd often be training in a sports hall or park, or beating all comers in some ultracompetitive tournament. Archery was just one of the things she'd mastered, along with a bunch of different martial arts. During the summer break—while Caleb had been fine-tuning *Terrorform*, or on vacation in France with his mum—Zen and her dad had hiked through the mountains of Japan to spend a solid month at a remote budō retreat, perfecting their ju-jitsu.

She'd told Caleb that they'd eaten only rice and black beans the whole time. Sounds great, he'd said. But, to be honest, he had not seen the appeal *at all.*

The boat was starting to move swiftly along now, its nose lifting very slightly out of the water.

"Hey, Caleb," Zen said, "someone needs to steer."

Caleb jumped, then grabbed hold of the handle that stuck out of the motor's side. The whole thing was vibrating hard. He turned around, back toward the prow.

"Can't see much!" he shouted.

"There shouldn't be any tight turns," Zen told him. "Just follow the tunnel."

"Got it."

Zen's eyes were fixed behind him, toward the floodlights. "There are two boats," she said, sliding an arrow from her quiver. "Inflatables. A light on each."

Caleb could see a little more of the tunnel now. They were closing in rapidly on a pale, car-size blob that was floating directly in front of them. This, he realized, was a fatberg. It must be congealed cooking fat from kitchens and restaurants, clumped together with—what?—wet wipes and disposable diapers and who knew what else. The thing floated by them like a bloated whale carcass. Caleb couldn't help staring at it. There at the top, half buried in the grayish ooze, was a knot of human hair as big as a cabbage. He only just managed not to retch.

"Now, that," he said, "is *seriously* gross."

"We're not here for the sightseeing," Zen told him. "Move over a bit."

She positioned herself beside him, putting one foot on

the back of the boat. With an air of practiced expertise, she nocked her arrow, took aim, and let it go. Caleb turned to see an orange inflatable flip over, bursting like a balloon, sending two black-clad men tumbling out and splatting straight into the fatberg.

"Ouch," he said.

The next moment there was a rattle of gunfire, bullets flicking into the sewage to their right. Caleb yelled out in fear, yanking at the motor's handle. The boat swerved, scraping hard against the tunnel's side, bumping over the bricks—and then, abruptly, the wall came to an end and they were twisting away into another, even smaller side tunnel, the sound of the engine louder in the confined space.

This tunnel was almost completely clogged up with fatbergs. The boat cut between two of the smaller ones, then thudded against a third.

"Not good!" Caleb shouted.

Zen wobbled, throwing out an arm to stop herself from falling over the side. They began to slow down, the boat's propeller struggling to turn in the lumpy soup below.

Caleb peered ahead. "I don't think this thing will take us much farther."

The stench in there was intense. A floodlight was trained on the mouth of the side tunnel. The remaining inflatable had slowed right down as well, as if their pursuers were debating whether or not to follow them in.

Zen lowered her bow, picked up her backpack, and went to the prow of the boat. She pointed along the gloomy tunnel. About thirty feet farther in was a doorway, with a shadowy ledge jutting beneath it.

"Some kind of access," she said.

Caleb gunned the motor. "That's our way out."

They plowed forward through the fatbergs. After only a couple of seconds, the engine coughed and stalled. It was enough, though—the boat came to a halt within jumping distance of the ledge. Zen was about to leap across when Caleb noticed something strange—a slight shifting in the darkness.

"Hang on," he said. "There's—"

A powerful light fell over them as the second inflatable rounded the corner at the tunnel's end. They saw that the ledge was entirely covered with rats—a carpet of squirming, writhing, squeaking bodies, their tails like worms.

"Great," said Caleb hoarsely. "Just *great.*"

Zen barely paused. Jumping between the boat and the ledge, she began swinging her bow in broad arcs, scattering the rats and clearing a path to the door. Caleb followed her, grimacing in disgust as the rats began to surge back around his sneakers.

Zen reached the door and tried the handle. "Don't think it's locked," she said. "But it's stiff as hell."

Meanwhile, the second inflatable was moving slowly down the tunnel, navigating the fatbergs. Coming for them. Caleb heard the crackle of a radio. He peered into the light, trying to make out a face. On the other side of the spotlight, a man began speaking in an Eastern European–sounding language, giving some kind of order. Caleb kicked away a rat that was nibbling at his shoelace and hurried to join Zen. They barged the door together, slamming their shoulders against it. On the third try, it suddenly swung inward and they both bundled through, skidding back around to slam it shut behind them.

Caleb turned the Flex's light up to maximum. They were in a small, tiled maintenance office. Zen went to an old desk and started to drag it over, using it to barricade the door.

"What is this place?" Caleb asked.

"No idea," Zen replied. "But it totally beats Crap Alley back there." She was already heading for another door on the room's far side. "Come on."

A bare corridor took them to a flight of stairs. Caleb could hear someone back at the office, making a noisy attempt to get the barricaded door open. They ran up the stairs to a larger, empty room. There was an iron stairwell in its corner, surrounded by a cage with a heavy padlock on its gate. A splintering smash came from below—their pursuers had broken through. Caleb spotted a door, half hidden in the shadows, with a NO ENTRY sign on it. He tugged Zen's sleeve and they ran over. Someone had left a rusted key in the handle. They just managed to twist it around and force the door open.

Beyond was a tunnel—perfectly circular, made from engineered concrete, yet horribly festooned with cobwebs. As they stepped forward, Caleb's foot struck against something hard. A set of greasy metal rails ran along the tunnel's bottom.

"Train tracks," he said out loud. "This is an underground line. Must have been abandoned ages ago." He peered around, shining his light, but could see nothing but blackness in either direction. "Which way?"

Zen raised her chin slightly and closed her eyes. "Feel that?"

"What?"

"Right there. Can't you feel it?"

"Zen, I can't *feel* anything. We're, like, half a mile underground in an abandoned Tube tunnel. There's a bunch of armed kidnappers on our tail. My feelings are mainly anxiety and panic and—"

"It's a breeze, Caleb. This way, quick. And dim that light."

She went left, breaking into a jog. Caleb did his best to keep up. The suffocating darkness lifted a little and before long he got the sense of an opening somewhere ahead—a long gray shape against the black. It was a station.

They climbed up onto the platform. Caleb turned up the Flex's light again to reveal tiled walls, the blank spaces where advertising posters would normally hang, and dusty, old-fashioned benches. A large sign on the wall—white letters in a blue rectangle, with a red circle set behind—said STRAND.

"I've heard about this place," Caleb murmured. "It was abandoned a couple of decades ago. You can go on tours down here. They rent it out to film companies and stuff."

"Pretty creepy," said Zen.

"It'll bring us out onto Aldwych. We'll be able to get back to Bloomsbury in a few minutes. I'll get my bike, and then we can—"

Zen was shaking her head. "Sorry, Caleb. No bike. They might still be watching the museum. Or there could be more of those drones floating about. We can't risk it."

Caleb swallowed. That bike was a custom BMX, made especially for him—the last present he'd ever gotten from his dad, and his favorite noncomputerized thing in the world. But he knew at once that Zen was right. In the space of a couple of hours, everything had changed. The bike had to be left where it was.

"Oh," he said, a little faintly. "OK. No problem."

There was some sympathy in Zen's eyes. "What were you going to say?"

Caleb recovered himself. "Professor Clay's code. We're going to have a proper go at cracking it, aren't we?"

"We've got to. It's our only chance of finding out where our families are."

"Then we should go to my house—to the *Queen Jane*. Like I said, I've got an idea."

"That's another risk." Zen was looking back down the tunnel. "They could have left someone to keep watch there as well."

Caleb checked the Flex. He had a signal—only two bars, but enough to work with. "I put the barge into maximum-security mode earlier," he said, scrolling rapidly through a series of camera feeds. "Doesn't look like anyone's been near it. And the coast is clear right now. They may not even know about the *Queen Jane*."

Zen nodded. "OK. Let's head over there." They walked off the platform and went up the stairs. "First we need to get back to ground level. Then—"

Noises came from farther above, echoing through the empty station—a crunch of breaking wood, followed by the harsh buzz of a high-speed engine.

"Dirt bike." Zen slipped the bow off her shoulder. "More than one."

"They're working in teams," Caleb said. "I heard a radio earlier. They're coordinating. Trying to trap us between them."

The stairs brought them to a gloomy hall somewhere in

the middle of the station. Different tunnels ran off on either side, leading away to other platforms. Directly ahead, a set of three escalators led up to the surface. The engines were getting louder, like a swarm of angry hornets rushing down through the station toward them.

"We can get past," said Zen, starting up the left-hand escalator, "if we stay low."

The engines were deafening now, the bikes' headlights gleaming on the tiles up ahead—and then suddenly they were there: three of them, screeching to a halt at the top of the escalators. Zen and Caleb dropped down, crouching on the metal steps, hiding themselves in the shadows. The bike engines idled, chugging and snarling, while one of the riders flipped up his visor to talk into a walkie-talkie.

"This is Blue Team," he said. "We're in position. Krall and the others are doing a sweep below."

The radio crackled; then Erica Szabo's voice came through it with unsettling clarity. "You are looking for a boy and a girl, both approximately twelve years old. Boy has auburn hair and a black hoodie. Girl has a gray jacket and a black braid."

The biker looked at his companions. "What about the woman, Captain—the teacher from the school?"

"Forget the woman. Get the girl if you can. But we really need the boy. No screw-ups." Szabo spoke slowly, as if addressing a complete idiot. "*Make sure you get the boy*. Szabo out."

Zen glanced at Caleb in puzzlement. He could only shake his head. It was true that they'd wanted to catch him at his house earlier, when they got his mum—but this made it sound like they were after him in particular.

The biker clicked off his radio. "All right, let's spread out," he said. "We can't let them get past us. I'm not giving the captain any reason to get mad at me. Her or that psycho Krall."

One bike went to each escalator, maneuvering about so that they could shine their headlights down the steps. Caleb and Zen looked at each other, their eyes wide with fright. They'd be seen for sure. They started to creep back down, crouching as low as they could. For one crazy second Caleb dared to think that they were going to get away—but then one of the bikers let out a piercing whistle.

"Over here!" he shouted. "We got 'em, guys!"

Caleb and Zen jumped up and ran for it, taking the remaining steps two or three at a time. The biker who'd whistled revved his engine and came after them, bumping down the escalator at high speed.

Arriving at the bottom, Caleb and Zen raced desperately into one of the side passageways. The dirt bike skidded around on the concrete floor behind them. Caleb saw that its rider had a black boxy submachine pistol slung over his shoulder. There was no chance of outrunning it. Zen reached for an arrow, but the bike was already too close.

Caleb lifted his wrist and yelled out one of the Flex's special emergency commands: *"Cobra!"*

The screen blasted out a rapid strobe of blinding light—twelve times the brightness of a smartphone flash, equivalent to a stun grenade. The biker threw up his hands with a curse, tumbling from his seat and sprawling messily on the floor. Running out of control, the bike fell onto its side and slid away down the passage in a shower of sparks.

"Nice job," said Zen, half smiling. "But now we need another way out of here."

Caleb tapped the Flex's screen, cross-referencing its 3-D mapping function with the London archives. A second later a small holographic floor plan, rendered in the golden light, flickered into the air directly above his wrist.

"There's a second track," he said, turning the hologram with his finger. "Never opened to the public. Leads under the river to Waterloo. Should be just up ahead."

They hurried on along the passage—then stopped abruptly when they reached the platform. Two black-clad men were standing in front of them, waiting by the fallen dirt bike. Both had dyed, spiky hair, with tattoos crawling up their necks and out onto their wrists—and both were completely filthy, like they might have recently taken a swim in a sewer. One of them was Pyke, Caleb realized—the man who'd gone rifling through his mum's bedroom.

Before he could argue, Zen took off her gear, tucked her jade necklace inside her red T-shirt, and walked out to an open stretch of the platform, springing lightly on her toes and shaking her arms to loosen them, like a sprinter warming up before a race.

Pyke gave them a vicious grin. "Do my eyes deceive me?" He leered. "No, Pykey, they do not. We've been looking bleedin' everywhere for you two." He took out a dart gun, like those used to tranquilize zoo animals, and stepped toward them. "This is going to *hurt*, you little scu—"

The sound was like a whip-crack. Zen had leaped high into the air, spinning her body around and kicking Pyke's head so hard that he fell straight to the floor. His partner had a dart gun as well—he lifted it to fire, but Zen was moving too fast, covering the space between them in less than a second. She took out his legs with another sweeping kick and drove an elbow into his midriff. Caleb heard a rib snap. The thug shouted out in pain.

But Pyke was up again, his ugly face clenched in fury. Zen cartwheeled toward him, using her momentum to knock him clean off his feet a second time—and twisting his right arm up his back as he fell, until there was a nasty crunch. With that she hopped away, fists raised, alert for any further resistance. None came.

"Whoa," said Caleb. "Guess that budō retreat really paid off, huh?"

Zen was panting a little. She sniffed her jacket sleeve, wrinkling her nose. "Think I got some fatberg on me," she muttered.

Caleb took stock. This wasn't all of them. There was still the crew from the other inflatable—the one that hadn't crashed and that had presumably picked up the pair Zen had just beaten. And he could hear engines now, back in the hall. The other two bikers were following the first down the escalators. He picked up the dirt bike and wheeled it across the platform, around the groaning men.

"We've got to move," he said as he started to heave it down toward the rails. "Give me a hand, will you?"

Zen was staring at him. "You're thinking we drive along the tracks?"

"Got any better ideas?"

The engines were growing louder. The dazzled biker was up as well, limping down the passage toward the platform, readying his submachine pistol. Zen took a deep breath, then put the bow and quiver back in her pack and came over to help. Together they slotted the bike's tires into a narrow concrete channel that ran to one side of the rails.

"OK," Caleb said. "Hawk does the martial arts—Swift can handle the bikes." He grinned. "I'm much better at escaping than fighting, I promise."

"Let's hope so."

Caleb swung his leg over the saddle and checked the handlebars of the bike—clutch, throttle, brakes. Not that they were going to need the brakes. Zen climbed onto the pillion and he kick-started the engine. Back on the platform, the biker was helping Pyke up—who was running through as many swear words as he could think of.

"This night," Caleb murmured, "just gets more and more insane."

He dropped the clutch and the dirt bike started to move. There was less than four inches of space on either side of the tires. He went slowly at first, trying to get a feel for the balance of the bike. But like with all bikes, he soon realized, the faster you drove the damn things, the easier they were to handle. He looked around and made a forward-pointing motion with his finger. Zen nodded and held on tightly. Thumbing on the main headlight, he twisted the accelerator and whipped them out of the station into the darkness of the tunnel.

"Can you look at the map?" Caleb shouted, taking the Flex off his wrist and passing it back to Zen. "I kinda need to concentrate."

Zen studied the holo-map closely, squinting in the wind.

"What are we aiming for?" Caleb asked. "Another station?"

"No—it doesn't look like the line was ever linked up."

"So . . . we're just going to slam into a wall, then?"

"There's a stairwell—a passage off to the side. Less than half a mile away by the looks of it. It shouldn't—"

The tunnel began to tremble around them, the rails shivering and creaking. Caleb glanced back. An old-fashioned Tube train, fitted out to carry engineering equipment, was rumbling out of the abandoned station behind them. He frowned and gripped the handlebars.

"It's picking up speed," Zen yelled in his ear.

It was taking all of Caleb's effort to keep the dirt bike straight. Zen was right: the train was gaining steadily, its orange headlights casting long, stretching shadows over the tracks in front of them. He rode on, trying his best to stay focused—but he couldn't resist looking around again.

The train was only about sixty feet behind them now. A huge, broad-shouldered man sat alone in the driver's cabin, his face lit from below by the instrument panel. He had a square, heavy jaw and a shaved head. His nose was pierced, with what looked like a bolt driven through it. A radio was attached to the front of his combat jacket. His face remained completely expressionless—but it seemed like he really meant to run them down.

Krall. Caleb was sure of it. The giant who'd been at his house earlier. Erica Szabo's second-in-command.

The tunnel curved ahead. Caleb gave the throttle a fraction more twist and the bike sped up, the engine whining. The noise was incredible, but the handlebars seemed to vibrate a little less the faster he went. The orange glare from the train's lights faded. They were pulling away slightly—or perhaps it was just the long bend in the track. He couldn't be sure.

Zen craned forward, pointing ahead to the left. Caleb could see what he thought was a recess in the side of the tunnel, thrown into deep shadow by the dirt bike's headlight. He nodded to let Zen know he'd seen it. This had to be the stairway.

At the very last moment he braked hard, making the tires squeal and judder. He braced against the handlebars as he and Zen slid forward on the seat. They both leaped off the bike before it had completely stopped. The train was rounding the bend, clattering and banging and charging up behind them. Letting the bike fall across the tracks, they half ran, half staggered to safety—hearing the dreadful metallic shriek as the train hit the bike an instant later, grinding it to smithereens beneath its wheels.

For a few seconds, Caleb and Zen leaned against the grimy wall, trying to catch their breath.

"That was *close*," Zen gasped.

Caleb puffed out his cheeks. "Not sure they're all that bothered about catching us alive, Zen."

Zen shook her head slowly as she handed back the Flex. "Nope."

Caleb checked the holo-map and looked off to the right, into the darkness. "Come on," he said. "This way."

7
SIMULATED AUTONOMOUS MEDIC

It was nearly one o'clock in the morning by the time Caleb and Zen reached Nine Elms. They ducked into a bus stop just past Vauxhall Station, quickly eating the sandwiches Clay had given them—which were only a little squashed after the chase—while Caleb checked the camera feeds again to make sure that no one was about. Then they crossed the main road and went between a couple of glass-fronted high-rises, down toward the converted warehouse by the river.

"We don't have long," Zen said. "I bet they'll be straight back here once they're done searching the tunnels. What's this big idea of yours?"

Caleb started down the cobbled yard at the side of the warehouse. "Easier if I show you," he replied. "I should only need a few minutes."

They turned left, walking along the river path to the white gate of the pier, then over the pontoons to the *Queen Jane, Approximately*. Nothing seemed to have changed since Caleb had left for the ARC. He hopped aboard, went down a short flight of steps, and pressed his thumb against a scanner. The barge door popped open with a pressurized hiss.

Zen followed him onto the steps, and they went forward together into a long, narrow room. A row of screens lit up along its right-hand side, all of them filled with fast-moving, multicolored images: *Terrorform* in action. Beneath them was a workstation, covered almost completely by a jumble of game controllers, keyboards, and virtual-reality headsets. In the far corner were a couple of whiteboards covered with complex equations and a small 3-D printer.

Opposite, on the barge's left-hand side, was a wall of custom-built computer processors, lit from within by blue and green LEDs, and the black block of a private internet server. On top of the server was a framed photo of Caleb with his mum and dad, taken a couple of years ago in the redwood forests of Yosemite in California. All three of them were smiling.

In the middle of the barge was a battered leather captain's chair, as old as the *Queen Jane* herself. Caleb sat in it, unwrapping the Flex from his arm and dropping it onto the desk, where it flattened out and began to recharge wirelessly. He spun around to look at the screens. Most of them were live-streaming a *Terrorform* tournament in Dallas, where several veteran player clans were battling for control of a research outpost on the planet of Kolto, their ski-tanks churning through the purple snow. The barge's sound system reverberated with the zinging of laser bolts, the deep rumbling of the sci-fi vehicles, and the excited chatter of the commentators.

Zen took off her backpack and leaned against the work-station. "Have I ever told you how much I love it in here?" she said. "Total tech heaven."

Caleb grinned. "My favorite place in the world," he said, reaching for a controller. All right, here's the idea. We're going to use the game to crack the code."

"The *game*?" Zen turned to one of the screens in confusion. "How?"

Caleb turned off the live stream and brought up the menu screen on the largest monitor. The word *Terrorform* ran along the top, its letters the same shiny chrome as the short-cut. Below it was a zoomed-out view of the Cardano system, where the game took place—a string of eleven planets, of all different colors and sizes, orbiting a red sun.

Terrorform was part sci-fi adventure, part survival sim, and part grand-scale tournament. You selected your character class and your starting planet, and from then on, your path through the game was completely up to you. You could explore fantastical alien landscapes, fighting strange, ferocious beasts; build weapons, vehicles, and settlements; join warrior clans to battle other players for control of the best territories. Everything you did earned experience points, allowing you to level up and gain new abilities. If you died, though—if you fell into a ravine, or got killed in battle, or eaten by something horrible—that was it. Back to the beginning.

Caleb had been working on *Terrorform* since he was eight years old. Until about six months ago, it had been pretty small-scale. His friends—Zen included—had made up most of the regular players. But then, in the space of only a few weeks, it had quadrupled in size, and quadrupled again, with the gameplay itself growing massively more detailed and immersive. This new version of the game had quickly gained a large fanbase. *Terrorform* had become the great mystery of the gaming world: a free game produced by just one kid, as far as anyone knew, that was truly *amazing*—easily the equal of the mega-budget blockbusters. And it was constantly being added to and improved. Nobody had any idea how it had been done.

Nobody, that is, except Caleb's friends at the ARC. He told them that he'd programmed himself an advanced software tool powered by artificial intelligence, which he'd used not just to make the game world function properly, as AI usually did in video games—to animate the monsters, control the weather systems, and so on—but to build it as well. This meant he could bring his wildest ideas into existence in a fraction of the time it would take a game studio—and a pretty big game studio at that.

"Yeah," he said to Zen now. "About the game. I haven't been . . . *entirely* straight with you there."

Before she could say anything, he pulled up a developer's command prompt and entered a special code: *SimAutoMedi/001.* Immediately, a face appeared in the top right corner. It was humanoid, but sleek and unreal. The skin had a slight metallic sheen and the eyes shone pale gold.

"Good morning, Caleb," it said. "You are up early today. It is still five hours and twenty-three minutes until sunrise. Are you having trouble sleeping?"

"Hey, Sam," Caleb replied, trying to sound casual. "No, everything's . . . uh . . . cool. How's it going in *Terrorform*?"

"Game activity is at slightly higher than average levels. We have just set a new simultaneous play record in North America: forty-six thousand seven hundred and eight active player accounts. And I have had an idea for the predatory fauna of the third moon of Fraxis Prime. If we take a Chinese alligator and give it the wings of a—"

"OK, OK, save it for now. I've brought someone to meet you."

Zen was staring at him in disbelief. "Caleb, this . . . this isn't a software tool. This is an *artificial consciousness*. You've coded yourself a full-blown AI!"

Caleb sat back, feeling an odd mix of pride and bashfulness. "Ah, not quite. I found the base program in one of my dad's old systems. I just . . . adapted it a bit so it could help me with the game."

"You mean it was a medical program?"

Caleb nodded. "Some kind of diagnostic surgeon, I think. Designed to analyze a problem, imagine a solution, and then act on it."

"This is *incredible*," Zen said. She'd turned back to the screen, her eyes fixed on the silvery face. "Literally *no one* can do this yet."

"Well, the coding isn't finished. I've been doing what I can, but there are still a few—"

"You are talking about me as if I am not here, Caleb," said the face.

"Sorry, Sam," said Caleb. "Let me introduce you. This is Zen, a friend of mine from the ARC. Zen, this is Sam."

"Hello, Zen. I should tell you that my name is an acronym, standing for Simulated Autonomous Medic. Although

Caleb has already expanded my operational parameters well beyond this designation. May I ask if you are Zenobia Rafiq, registered holder of the fourth oldest *Terrorform* player account—gamer tag *ZenRa_004*?"

"Uh, that's right," said Zen a little awkwardly. "I'm a first-wave Terrorformer."

"The game stats indicate that you have just cleared six hundred hours of playtime and have a kill count of two thousand three hundred and sixty-two. Your preferred avatar is a level-thirty-seven Solar Scout. I would say that your gaming skills are on a par with those of Caleb himself."

"Yeah, well, it's a good way to unwind." Zen looked at Caleb. "What exactly does Sam do? When you're making the game, I mean?"

"Everything that I do," said Caleb. "At first, I just used him to build things I'd already planned out, but—"

"Wait," Zen cut in. "It's a *him*? Seriously?"

"That was what I chose," Sam told her. "It seemed right. I can review at any time, of course. Would you like me to start a review? It or she/her or they/them is easily—"

"No," said Zen. "No. Him. Sam. That's fine. That's great."

"Anyway," Caleb continued, "before I knew it, he'd started coming up with stuff on his own. Landscapes and vehicles. All sorts of creatures. And then entire regions."

"You are being too kind, Caleb," the AI said. "We are collaborators. We work together."

"This is too weird," Zen murmured. "An AI with an *imagination*. How is it even possible?"

"It has to do with something my dad wrote," Caleb said. "Something at the core of Sam's programming. He called it the Talos Algorithm, after this giant automaton from ancient Greece."

"Talos was forged from bronze by the god Hephaestus," Sam informed them, "to protect the people of Crete. He would circle the island three times daily."

Zen's astonishment was turning to uncertainty. "So . . . your plan is to let this AI of yours—"

"Sam."

"—to let Sam look at Professor Clay's code. To try to solve it."

Caleb nodded. "He can run through the data, like, ultra-quickly. And then he'll be able to imagine ways to fill the gaps, based on any patterns he sees. It could be the answer."

Zen bit her lip. She leaned in, lowering her voice. "You're getting into some pretty bizarre territory here, Caleb. This might actually be dangerous."

"What do you mean?"

"I thought Sam was a digital tool kit, not a—a virtual mind. But I also thought he was just a part of *Terrorform*. A feature of the game. And yet now you're telling me that he can process data from the outside world. That means he could make decisions that might affect it. Decisions that could do harm as well as good. You know what Professor Collins teaches us in AI." She stared at the silver face. "How can you be sure that he'll be able to act on your instructions without any . . . misunderstandings? Or accidents, even? AIs tend to be superliteral, don't they? Guided by pure logic—which can be nothing at all like human logic?"

Caleb squirmed a bit in his chair. "Well, yeah, but—"

"Caleb, how can you be sure that Sam will keep on following your instructions *at all*?"

"I've thought of this, Zen," said Caleb earnestly. "Believe me, I have. There are safeguards written into the most basic lines of Sam's code—stuff that would shut him down completely if anything went wrong." He sat forward. "But the really important thing is that Sam is *contained*. I've got absolute control over him. He can analyze things that I put in the *Terrorform* program, but the game is the only place he exists. He can't act outside *Terrorform*."

"Right." Zen seemed to be partway reassured. "He's inside the game. I've got your word on that."

"Sure." Caleb smiled. "Sam basically *is Terrorform*. And that's what we're going to use to break the code."

He asked her for Professor Clay's sheet. Zen looked at him, as if making a final decision, then took the sheet from her backpack and passed it over. Caleb ran it through a scanner on the workstation, making a digital image of it. He picked up the Flex, now almost fully charged, and moved the image file into the main *Terrorform* directory.

"Have a look at this, Sam," he said. "The data sequence is broken, and I need you to fill in the gaps. Try anything you can think of."

Sam's face remained impassive as his program made an analysis. After a couple of seconds, one of his eyebrows seemed to twitch very slightly.

"I have a possible result, Caleb. The sequence is still incomplete, but I believe I have enough to run it through the game engine."

"Do it."

The AI paused while he made his computations. "I have

created an area using the extrapolated data. Where shall I place it?"

Caleb looked over at Zen. "How about Kursk?"

Kursk was *Terrorform*'s dust-bowl planet, with a well-deserved reputation for being one of the deadliest zones in the game. Caleb and Zen had played there together on only one occasion, a few weeks earlier. While hunting for a rare artifact, they'd been ambushed by a pack of the savage ape-beasts that roamed Kursk's deserts and gullies. They'd been locked in a furious battle for the better part of an hour, barely managing to escape with their avatars intact.

"Sure," she said. "Kursk. Why the hell not?"

"I think we can say that everyone's kept pretty busy there, at least," Caleb said. "We'll be able to lose the crowds. OK, Sam, bury your new area somewhere in the northern ranges."

There was another short pause. "It is done, Caleb," Sam said. "I hope that this provides you with some answers."

"Me too," Caleb said. "Now let's go to Kursk."

8

THE CAVERNS OF KURSK

Caleb picked up a virtual-reality headset and passed another one to Zen.

"You're playing *Terrorform* in VR?" she asked.

"Me and Sam are. We haven't rolled it out yet. But it's more or less ready to go."

They put on the headsets and logged into the game. *Terrorform* had six character classes. Caleb was currently using a maxed-out level-forty Navigator—the Explorer class and his personal favorite—with the gamer tag *CalQ_001*. It wore a suit of power armor in a black-and-bronze camouflage pattern, had an ornate skull insignia emblazoned on each of its shoulder plates, and carried an ion lance—a long-barreled energy rifle, capable of taking down almost anything the game could throw at you.

Kursk had just one settlement, the heavily fortified Nostromo Citadel. Caleb chose it from a list of in-game destinations. He spawned just outside the citadel's gates, the world of *Terrorform* wrapping all around him.

Zen's avatar was standing nearby, *ZenRa_004* flashing over its head for a couple of seconds. She'd selected her latest Solar Scout, the only class she ever used. The scout was lightweight, designed for speed and stealth, and equipped with a curved graphite blade. It had a pair of foldaway, two-part wings that made it look like a kind of sleek, sci-fi moth. Zen had colored it in several different shades of crimson and silver, the virtual paintwork glinting in the harsh desert sun.

"Ready?" Caleb asked.

Zen flexed the Solar Scout's wings. "Feels a bit weird."

"You'll get used to it."

Sam's smooth face appeared in the corner of Caleb's vision. "Head north for three hundred miles," he instructed. "I will place a waypoint."

Their arrival was already drawing attention. The *CalQ_001* tag was widely known to be Caleb's among the *Terrorform* community—and especially among the hard core who hung out on Kursk. A few dozen of them began to approach, giving salutes and asking questions over voice chat, mostly about the latest updates. In a matter of seconds there were nearly a hundred. Their voices became like human static, buzzing in the barge's surround-sound speakers.

Zen took off, hovering her scout several feet up. "Come on," she said. "We don't have time for the fan club."

Caleb wished the players luck and was about to turn away when one of their avatars caught his eye. It was from the Bulwark class, intended for frontline combat, which used a hulking bruiser of a suit twice the height of his own. This one had a special custom paint job—deep ultramarine blue with curling white flames on its shin and shoulder plates.

It had spawned only seconds behind them, the gamer tag *Cold_Zero* blinking above its heavily armored head. It was standing apart from the rest of the players and seemed to be watching them closely.

Activating his jet pack, Caleb shot up into Kursk's pale green skies and swept off to the north with Zen. Several of the Terrorformers tried to follow, but Sam provided a speed boost that sent them rocketing ahead. The waypoint that the AI had placed glowed in front of them—a golden pin amid the craggy, slate-colored mountains. They went low, into the barren valleys, zipping over a battle between a player expedition and a colossal metallic bug. Weapons sparked and stuttered. There was the dull thump of an explosion. Three players were sliced in half by a single snap of the monster's mandibles.

Zen could still hardly believe what she was seeing. "This is something else, Caleb," she said. "The VR totally works."

After a couple of minutes, they reached the waypoint, touching down together at the bottom of a gulley in a billowing cloud of maroon dust. Caleb checked the Navigator suit's built-in map. They were in one of the most remote corners of the entire game.

"The new area is just ahead of you," Sam informed them.

There was a passageway in the sheer gulley wall—little more than a narrow crack running down between two immense slabs of rock. As they went in, Zen activated a spotlight on the Solar Scout's shoulder, throwing a wide beam into the blackness below.

They were standing at the entrance of an enormous cavern. The whole cathedral-like chamber was filled with dense crystal formations. Zen moved the spotlight around. The effect was dazzlingly beautiful, the beam flashing through the crystals and making them gleam with every color in the rainbow.

"This is the *code*?" she asked. "This is what it gave us?"

"Yeah," Caleb replied slowly. "Or as close as Sam can get to it, anyway. Shown in the visual language of *Terrorform*."

"I thought it would be . . . I don't know, a message or something."

"A billboard would definitely have been more straightforward."

For a minute or so they stared around the cavern without speaking. It was roughly rectangular, with a very high ceiling. Caleb noticed that about twenty of the larger crystal clusters rose several feet above the rest. He walked forward into the cavern, looking at them keenly.

"Wait," he said. "These placings—I don't think they're . . ."

"What is it? What can you see?"

"They aren't random. There's a pattern here." Caleb activated his own suit's spotlight, raising it to maximum power level and tightening the beam so that it shone out like a laser. Then, angling it precisely, he pointed it straight into the tallest block of crystal.

All at once their headsets were flooded with blinding white light. But the glare quickly died away to reveal what looked like a gigantic, shimmering web. The Navigator's flashlight beam had been reflected over and over again, forming a bright line that now connected the largest crystals, crisscrossing between them as if wound around a massive invisible ball.

"It looks like a planet," Zen said. "Like some kind of planetary map. Is it from the game—from the Cardano system?"

"No," said Caleb. "No, this is Earth. Look at those long lines. That one's crossing the Atlantic Ocean. The blank space there is North America. And there—it's going around the end of Africa. It's like a . . . a telecoms map or something. Undersea internet cables, maybe."

"I think . . . I think it's a ship's route," Zen said. "It's moving between ports." She pointed at the bright line with one of the Solar Scout's gloved hands. "Look. There's Shanghai. Sydney. Athens."

"You could be right," Caleb said. "Isolate the pattern, Sam. Make a copy and put the file in one of the game's texture folders, so me and Zen can study it a bit more closely without having to stay in-game."

"It is done, Caleb. I have called it *Caverns of Kursk.*"

Caleb took off his VR headset. He picked up the Flex and found the file Sam had just created. After a few deft finger swipes, he'd extracted it from the *Terrorform* directory and imposed the glowing, zigzagging line on a 3-D map of the earth—which he then projected out into the middle of the barge.

"Whoa," he said. "This route winds all over the place. And some of those ports are visited several times. How can we identify the ship it belongs to?"

Zen removed her headset as well. "Try the international shipping regulators. They'll have records of every route currently being sailed. Or they should."

Caleb quickly located the main regulators' websites and used Spider Monkey to hack into their databases. He set the app to cycle through the many hundreds of routes logged there, instructing it to find a match. Red lines began to flash up on the holographic globe at a rate of at least four a second, alongside the white line they'd gotten from the game. After a couple of minutes, the sequence finished. A notification from Spider Monkey appeared on the Flex's screen.

No results found.

"Huh," said Caleb. "Dead end."

Zen leaned closer to the globe. "Run it again."

Caleb tapped the Flex. Zen watched the hologram carefully—then held out a finger to touch its edge, pausing the sequence. The route she'd stopped it on wasn't an *exact* match, but it fit over perhaps eighty percent of the one from Kursk, mirroring long sections of its strange, snaking path.

"Good spot," Caleb murmured, squinting at the globe. "What is that—two stops in Barcelona? Three in Murmansk? It can't be a coincidence."

"What ship is it?" Zen asked.

Caleb brought up the details. "This red line is the official route of an independently owned Panamax container ship called *Nightfall*. The manifest says that it's been transporting plastic toys, gym equipment, karaoke machines . . . random junk, basically."

"That doesn't seem like any sort of cargo route," Zen said.

"No," Caleb agreed. "And look at that part there." He pointed to a place where the white line branched away from the red one, heading off into a different region of the ocean—only to rejoin it a little farther along. "It's like bits have been deliberately left off the route that the *Nightfall*'s captain supplied to the shipping authorities."

"They were making secret detours," Zen said. "What do they show? Where's this ship been going?"

Caleb zoomed in on one. After a short distance, the white line blurred away to nothing. "No way to tell," he said. "It's because of those gaps in the code sequence. We can see that this ship's been making secret diversions. We just can't say where to."

"Where's the *Nightfall* right now?"

"Amsterdam. It arrived yesterday evening for routine maintenance. And it says here it's leaving for New York the day after tomorrow."

Zen and Caleb looked at each other.

"This is it," Caleb said. "This is the lead we need. We've got to tell Professor Clay."

He grabbed the Flex and opened up the ARC intranet. There were no new messages for him, nor any sign of activity on Clay's account. He sent her a six-word message.

Goldfinch—contact Swift and Hawk—urgent.

The seconds inched past. Caleb imagined the message arriving. Clay's phone buzzing. Her taking it from her coat pocket and looking at the screen. But no reply came.

"Not *again*," he groaned. "How can she not respond? She *told* us to use the ARC intranet."

"Maybe she's back on high alert," Zen said. "Or maybe she's been captured."

They were both quiet for a moment, letting this grim possibility sink in.

"So what the hell are we supposed to do?" Caleb exclaimed, gripping the arm of the leather chair in frustration. "We can't just *sit* here. She told us to get away from London. How exactly do we do that, Zen? We don't have any money. I've got, like, ten pounds."

"Doesn't the game make you anything yet? I thought by now you'd have a bank account somewhere, filling with *Terrorform* cash."

Caleb shook his head. "It's completely free, remember? No microtransactions. No DLC. And it'll always be that way. My dad put a baseline in Sam's programming that means he can't be used to make money. I think he was guaranteeing that no one ever would use Sam's medical applications for profit. But it means that if I tried to charge for the game in any way it would lock up. Stop working completely."

Zen winced. "Brutal."

"It's a lot better than having no *Terrorform* at all." Caleb shrugged. "Not much help to us now, though."

Zen started going through her pockets, like she'd suddenly remembered something. During this search, she set Beetlebat down on the workstation; it activated, its antennae pulsing, and began to investigate the VR headset she'd just taken off.

"Here," she said, holding out her hand. In her palm was the data stick Professor Clay had given her in the sewers. It was encased in black plastic, a Möbius strip printed on its side. "Everything we need, Clay said."

Caleb plugged the stick into the Flex. A list of files appeared on the screen: templates for credit cards and passports, and details of what seemed to be a dozen or so safe houses—in northern and western England, but also Scotland, Belgium, and the Republic of Ireland.

"Wow," he said. "She wasn't exaggerating. We can use all this to get to safety. Wait for her to get in touch."

Zen was thinking hard. "Or we can use it to go to Amsterdam.

Check out this ship ourselves. See what more we can uncover—like where it was going on those secret diversions."

Caleb sat back in his chair, staring at the holographic globe and the two lines that ran around it. "Right," he said slowly. "We go to Amsterdam."

Zen stood up, lifting her backpack from the floor. "Come on, Caleb. We make a pretty good team, don't you think?" She crossed the barge, lifting up a blind to peer out of the port-hole. "I've got to find my family. You've got to find your mum. This ship could be *really* important."

"But what about the police? Or the CIA—MI6? Shouldn't we pass this on to them?"

"That would mean staying in London. I don't know if you've noticed, but this city isn't safe. We could get grabbed anywhere. And the ship could disappear. It might not actually be sailing to New York. We need to get to it as soon as we can before it slips through our fingers." Zen's hand went to her jade necklace. "Also . . . I don't want to sit in a safe house while some anonymous official launches a formal investigation and doesn't tell me anything. We're Swift and Hawk now. Professor Clay gave us a mission, and we've only just gotten started. I want to find my family."

Caleb exhaled heavily. "OK, I'm in. Of course I am." He offered his fist. "Amsterdam it is."

"Amsterdam," Zen repeated, knocking his fist with her own. "So, what's the plan?"

"We get out of here right now. We go straight along the river, over Westminster Bridge, then walk up through town to St. Pancras. Then we catch the first Eurostar to Paris and take it from there. We should be in Amsterdam by lunchtime."

"Let's do it."

Caleb began to prepare the templates so he could print out their passports and credit cards. One passport already had a photo and other details entered for Zen, under the name "Haya Jazairi." He pressed print, then quickly typed in new entries for him, dragging in a photo and calling himself "Ethan McCullin," the name of an American game designer he'd met at a convention that spring.

"This'll get us moving," he said. "I mean, I don't have any fresh *clothes* or anything. Don't suppose I could pop back into the house and—"

Zen was shaking her head. "Too risky. We'll get you some on the way, *Ethan*. At the train terminal. There's a lot of money on these cards."

Caleb agreed. He scooped the documents and cards from the tray of his 3-D printer and raised his eyebrows—they looked just like the real thing. He handed them to Zen, who zipped them away in her backpack.

Caleb glanced at the hologram. "What about at the other end? We can't just walk onto Amsterdam Harbor. Those places are sealed up pretty tight. How are we going to get in?"

Zen held out a finger for Beetlebat, clicking her tongue; it scurried from the workstation up her arm and into her pocket. "We'll think of something."

Caleb began to smile. "Hey—we could always call Luuk. He's in Amsterdam now, remember? After the ARC kicked him out?"

A look of horror appeared on Zen's face. "Oh no, Caleb. Not Luuk. He's a *total*—"

"He could help us. He really could. This is exactly his area,

Zen. Logistics hubs and stuff. At the very least, he knows his way around Amsterdam."

"But he's *so* annoying."

"Well, maybe he's gotten less annoying since he went back to Holland."

Before Zen could respond, there was a sound outside on the quay, like a bin being knocked over. Without speaking, she went to the barge door and slipped out. Caleb jumped up to follow.

"Goodbye, Caleb," said Sam as the central screen flicked back to the *Terrorform* tournament in Dallas. "I hope you have a pleasant trip."

"I'm not sure *pleasant* is quite right, Sam," Caleb said. "Keep the game going, OK? Let me know if you notice anything weird."

"How would you define *weird* in this context?"

"Not now, Sam."

Caleb put the Flex in his pocket and went out after Zen. Everything was quiet on the quay, the lights of London glittering along the oily river.

"False alarm," she said. "Fox, I think."

"This must be what it feels like to be a vampire," Caleb said as he put up his hood. "Running around the city all night, lurking in the shadows."

"You'd make a terrible vampire, Caleb," Zen said. "Come on, let's get to the bridge."

Caleb reached into his pocket and pressed a button on the side of the Flex, putting the *Queen Jane, Approximately* back into maximum-security mode. Then he followed Zen into the darkness.

9

LUUK TEZUKA

The elevator whisked the sleek silver car up from its subterranean garage. A set of doors slid open to reveal the bustling streets of the Jordaan District, in the heart of Amsterdam. The car eased out silently, entering the flow of early-evening traffic. Zen and Caleb exchanged a glance. Then they looked over at the person sitting facing them.

"Luuk," said Caleb, "there's no one driving."

Luuk Tezuka sat up suddenly, swearing in Dutch, then switching to Japanese to shout out a command. The car's wraparound windows instantly turned a deep shade of blue, preventing anyone on the sidewalk from being able to see inside.

Luuk peered around him, scanning the street. "No cops, right?" he asked. "You guys didn't see any cops?"

Zen shook her head, shifting her hold on the backpack in her lap. "We're clear," she said, a little impatiently. "Let's get to the ship."

It was the end of a warm September day in the Jordaan.

The last of the sun glowed upon the rows of tall, narrow buildings, with their dark old bricks and stepped gables. Shops were shutting down, and lights were coming on in the district's many bars and restaurants. People thronged over the sidewalks, heading in a hundred different directions; trams trundled down tree-lined avenues; countless bikes streamed along the lanes and crossed the canals on humpbacked bridges.

Caleb and Zen had been out in Westpoort, Amsterdam's main harbor area, full of warehouses, cranes, and towering stacks of cargo containers, for pretty much the whole of their time in the city, which was now over twenty-four hours. They had checked the ARC intranet every hour, but Professor Clay still hadn't replied to their message. Caleb's mum had now been missing for almost two days, and Zen's family for three. With a growing sense of dread, they'd done everything they could think of to track down the *Nightfall*—asking questions, sneaking onto the docks to check ships, hacking local computer systems—but with no luck. There had been no sign of it anywhere. After a bad night's sleep in a rental apartment booked online with one of the credit cards and another fruitless morning's search, Zen had finally given in. Caleb had messaged Luuk and told him that they were in town, trying to locate a cargo ship called the *Nightfall*. He'd agreed to meet them later that afternoon, at which point he had told them (with some satisfaction) that he'd found what they were looking for—easily.

"Man, I am *always* forgetting to tint the windows," Luuk said now. "I mean, not that it would lead to anything—Tsuru's Dutch CEO plays golf with the police commissioner, like, twice a week—but getting pulled over in the middle of the Jordaan could still be a serious pain in the butt. People take pictures, post them on social media—*look, no driver!* I really don't need that."

Luuk was the same age as Caleb and Zen. Tall and skinny with layered, shoulder-length hair, he was wearing white designer jeans and a loose shirt patterned with yellow piranhas. Around his neck was a chain made from heavy silver links, and on his feet—now up on the seat next to Caleb—were a pair of box-fresh six-hundred-euro sneakers. He'd been in their class at the ARC, where he'd been a sort-of friend of Caleb's—and a sort-of enemy of Zen's. Unlike most of the ARC kids, whose parents were scientists, engineers, or software developers, Luuk's family was top-level corporate. His grandfather—his ojiisan—was Shiro Tezuka, the multi-billionaire founder of Tsuru, Japan's biggest tech company.

Things had gone a bit off course for Luuk, however. His specialty was self-driving cars; he'd been obsessed with designing them for as long as anyone could remember. The staff at the ARC had encouraged him to put one together, with the help of the school's engineering department—but he'd cut a few corners when programming the software and caused an accident at a testing center. One of the teachers had been left with two broken legs.

Shortly afterward, it had been announced that Luuk was leaving the ARC. He'd gone to live with the Dutch side of his family—his mum's—and be homeschooled in their Amsterdam mansion. This hadn't been the whole story, of course. Luuk had soon let his old classmates know that he was also working unofficially in the prototype division of

Tsuru's European headquarters, which was found inside—as well as five or six storeys underneath—a row of converted town houses on the Rozengracht.

Right then they were sitting in Luuk's latest model. This one was a bit like a black London cab inside, with a seating area for five people, but more spacious and stylish and *way* more luxurious—and no front seats or steering wheel. Or rather, two front seats that swiveled around to face the back— one of which Luuk was now lolling in.

The traffic slowed to a stop, the cars and buses swamped by a sudden influx of cyclists.

"This *city*," said Luuk with a groan. "Yeah, it's great and all— canals, tulips, yada yada—but it's *so* old-fashioned. I mean, look at all these *bikes*! It's like the frickin' Dark Ages!" He ran a hand through his hair. "I've asked Ojiisan to transfer me to Tokyo a thousand times, but he won't have it. Still in the dog-house for the broken leg thing, I guess."

"What's wrong with bikes?" said Zen. "Caleb rides every-where back in London. It's safe. Good for the environment. Good for your health too."

Caleb grimaced a little, remembering the custom BMX— probably still chained to the railings on Russell Square, but with both its wheels missing. He stayed quiet.

Luuk gave Zen a sidelong look. "What*ever*. We are so out of here."

He said a couple more words in Japanese. The car leaped into reverse, twisting back smoothly and very precisely to the left. Then it accelerated through a gap between a truck and a taxi with no more than inches to spare, swerved right, and sped off down an alleyway.

"Whoa," said Caleb as they raced out onto another main avenue. "This thing is impressive. I would almost say . . . *awesome*."

Luuk grinned. "Caleb Quinn finally admits that Luuk Tezuka is awesome. Let me message the news channels, dude! The world has been waiting too long for the truth to emerge."

Zen rolled her eyes.

"When is Tsuru planning to do the official reveal?" Caleb asked. "You must be pretty close."

"Three months, maybe. Ojiisan says there are still a couple of . . . kinks to be ironed out." Luuk shrugged. "The usual story. Old men afraid of new tech."

Zen was looking around the car's immaculate, leather-upholstered interior. "What kind of emissions does this thing put out?" she asked.

This time Luuk rolled his eyes. "Here we go again. Zenobia the eco-warrior. I should have organized a high horse for you to get to the *Nightfall*—at least then me and Quinn could have enjoyed the ride in peace." He swung his feet off the seat and sat forward. "Hate to tell you this, Zen, but the model we're in right now has a kinetic battery. It uses no gas *at all*. It's the cleanest road machine ever made."

"What about the manufacturing footprint?" Zen shot back. "And how much is Tsuru going to be selling them for? A million dollars apiece? That's not going to change the world, is it, Luuk?"

Luuk grinned again—slightly more unpleasantly. "Why don't you tell us how *your* work's going, then, Professor Rafiq? Still making fiddly little bug bots that take you half a

87

year to finish? What's the price point on one of those babies? And how are they saving the *environment*?"

Zen's face remained calm, but her dark eyes were bright with anger. "They're not for sale. But if they were, they'd still cost a few thousand times less than this car."

Luuk snorted. "A few thousand times less useful too."

Caleb had forgotten quite how much these two wound each other up. He opened his mouth to change the subject, but Luuk beat him to it. In an unsubtle attempt to cut off Zen's comeback, he uttered another command in Japanese and an ultra-high-definition screen flipped down smoothly from the ceiling. *Terrorform* was running on it—some kind of gameplay demo that Luuk had obviously set up in advance—with the volume at a deafening level. Several of the game's more ferocious monsters were snapping their claws and waving their tentacles as they squared up to a squad of power-armored avatars.

Luuk slapped Caleb's shoulder. "Huge congrats to you as well, dude!" he yelled. "This thing is *real* now. When I was in London with you guys . . . no offense, but it was a bit of a joke. Yet today, it's all over the gaming sites. The multiplayer servers are full. It's like a *proper game*, bro!" He nudged the volume down a couple of notches. "I mean, your numbers could be stronger. A *whole lot* frickin' stronger. We should have a talk about that, actually, you and me. How to scale you up." He slapped Caleb again. "But it's out there, right? It's *happening*."

"You've been playing?"

"Yeah, a little. Got me a level-nineteen Infernal right now. And my clan is third in the local leagues. It's still a kind of basic gameplay loop, to be honest, but it scratches an itch." Luuk paused to watch an Oracle-class avatar vaporize some rabid squidlike xenomorphs with a blast from its psi amplifier. "How did you do it, Caleb? You're moving fast, man—developing *at speed*."

The silver car was driving into Amsterdam-West, crossing a wide canal lined with barges and houseboats. Caleb took a breath and explained about Sam—how he'd adapted the AI to help him build and run *Terrorform*.

Luuk let out a low whistle. "I knew it. I *knew* that AI was what you were really into—underneath the game stuff. Well, you must be all set now." He sat back. "This game has to be bringing in enough to cover the bills. You could get to work on coding an AI with, like, real-world applications."

Caleb shook his head. "The game's AI can't be used to make money. It would stop working if I even tried. *Terrorform* would collapse."

Luuk was staring at him. "Let me get this straight. You used this AI knowing that there was no way you'd ever make a single cent."

"I had to choose. Build the game or not. That was it."

Now Luuk was laughing. "So you're still broke! Oh man, that is *funny*. I guess that explains the clothes, at least."

As Zen had suggested, Caleb had bought some clothes in a shop at St. Pancras, just before they got on their train to Paris. They'd been in a hurry, and the selection hadn't been very good; his T-shirt was dark blue and baggy, with LONDON written across the chest in Union Jack letters and a cartoon bulldog panting beneath.

"Yeah," Caleb murmured. "Long story."

"It suits you, man. Really, it does. Garbage T-shirts. It could be the start of a whole new thing for you."

"Hey, Luuk," said Zen, a note of warning in her voice. She was looking out of the left-hand window toward a large road junction—and one turning in particular, signposted for Westpoort, which they'd just cruised by. "We seem to be going the wrong way."

Luuk blinked. "Uh, yeah," he replied. "I guess I should've said earlier. This ship you guys are interested in—I can see why it had you stumped. It was registered with the port authority but was then removed from the system, like someone on the inside had deliberately deleted the records. Made it disappear. It was way weird."

Caleb had discovered this already. "So, what did you do?"

"What would *you* have done, Quinn?" Luuk fiddled briefly with one of his silver skull earrings. "I plugged into my local network. I know people who can find *anything*. Old-school detectives. You need resources like that if you're going to get ahead in the corporate world. They'd heard about this shady deal that went down a couple of days ago. Cash in hand, no questions asked. Half a million gallons of marine fuel, to be delivered to a herring cannery on the other side of the Noordzeekanaal."

He turned off the *Terrorform* demo and brought up some satellite photos on the screen. They showed a small commercial harbor in an industrial district, across the large canal that served as the main nautical route from Amsterdam out into the North Sea. A single massive-looking container ship was docked there.

"The *Nightfall*," said Zen.

Luuk nodded. "I couldn't do any more. It's a private wharf. You'll have to find your own way in." He narrowed his eyes. "What exactly is going on here? Why are you after this ship? It must be something pretty important to bring you all the way to the Netherlands. And when school's in session too."

Caleb looked over at Zen. She'd insisted on the way to Tsuru's HQ that they tell Luuk as little as possible about what was really going on.

"We think it's a smuggling thing," he said. "An international ring, dealing in some kind of experimental tech. We need to . . . take a look at its cargo."

Luuk was smiling. "I get it. This is for Professor Clay, isn't it? One of those top-secret extra-credit assignments she gives out? What was it called again?" He snapped his fingers. "The Möbius Program. I heard the stories back at the ARC. Kind of surprised that she's chosen you two, to be totally honest."

"Why is that?" said Zen. "Think she should have gone with you instead? Got you to run over another teacher?"

"That's not it, Luuk," Caleb cut in quickly, before Luuk could respond. "Professor Clay hates my guts. She wouldn't choose me to run the popcorn stand at the summer fair. And anyway, I don't think the Möbius Program even exists. That was just a couple of the year elevens messing with us."

Luuk met his eye. "Sure, dude. Whatever you say."

They'd reached the outskirts of the old town. The car accelerated out onto a highway, easing between lanes as it raced through the traffic. It was slightly hair-raising; Caleb saw Zen brace herself against the door. Luuk was making a big show of being unconcerned, though. Caleb asked him a couple of questions about collision detection, and his answers took them through the tunnel that ran beneath the Noordzeekanaal and onto the next highway exit.

They swept down an exit ramp, around a bend, and into a narrow, shadowy street lined with warehouses. A few trucks and vans were parked in front of them. Figures lurked in doorways, keeping out of the light, watching them pass. They turned left, then right, heading back in the direction of the water.

"There," said Zen, leaning forward. "Pull over."

The control tower of a cargo ship rose above the buildings ahead—a gleaming white block with the wide windows of the bridge at the top, and a radio tower spiking up from the roof. The *Nightfall*.

Luuk gave an instruction in Japanese and the car promptly drew up to the curb. "I'll wait here," he said. "Can't leave the prototype. Ojiisan would literally kill me."

"OK," said Caleb as the doors slid open. "Thanks for everything, man. You've really stuck your neck out for us here. I appreciate it."

Zen nodded. "Yeah," she said, a little tersely. "Thanks, Luuk."

"Sure. See you soon, right?" Luuk took a smartphone from his pocket and swiped his forefinger across the screen. "Don't do anything I wouldn't do."

10

THE NIGHTFALL

Caleb and Zen stepped away from Luuk's car and walked off into the alley. It was starting to get dark and there was a strange smell in the air—a mixture of diesel oil, rotten fish, and rust. Wheeling gulls squawked and shrilled above them. They went to the end of the alley and looked down the street that led to the cannery. It was a wide red-brick building with boarded-up windows, a pair of solid metal gates, and a grubby sign that read KLOOS HARING.

Caleb turned to Zen. "Why do you think they're docked out here?" he asked. "This place is just . . . wrong."

"Smells great, though," Zen replied sarcastically.

Just then the cannery gates swung open and a large truck, its hazard lights flashing, began to inch out, turning very slowly onto the street. There was barely enough room for the truck to maneuver—the driver kept stopping, reversing a few feet, and trying again.

Zen crept forward, crossing the road, gesturing for Caleb to follow. Staying in the driver's blind spot, they got right up to the cab and ducked down between two of its enormous wheels. From here, crouching low, they passed through the gates, keeping under the long tank that was being towed behind—and then slipped off behind some dusty crates once they were inside. The truck worked itself free and the gates creaked shut automatically behind it.

There was no one around.

"That was a fuel tanker," Zen said. "Probably some of the stuff Luuk was talking about. The ship must nearly be refueled by now. Better hurry."

She led the way up a wrought-iron staircase to an observation platform. It didn't seem like the Kloos Haring cannery had been in use for a number of years. Down in the gloom of the factory floor, Caleb could just make out rows of heavy work surfaces, where he assumed the fish would have been chopped up. There were also several defunct meat-processing machines and what looked like a disintegrating conveyor belt. The smell of herring intensified.

"Not my first choice on the sightseeing list," Caleb said.

On the far side of the cannery was a set of warehouse-style doors, as tall as the building itself, mounted on metal rollers. They'd been opened in the middle to let the fuel tanker through. Three figures in leather jackets stood on the floodlit docks beyond, smoking cigarettes—and behind them, like a black wall, was the flank of the *Nightfall*.

"Look at the size of that thing," Caleb said softly. "Now all we have to do is—"

Something was pressing against his calf, coiling around it. He jumped hard, nearly crying out—but it was just a cat, a bony stray with short gray-and-black-striped fur, bright yellow eyes, and huge, membrane-thin ears, one of which had been chewed off at the tip. The creature considered him for a second, then gave a throaty, inquiring meow.

"Think you've made a friend," said Zen with a grin. "There are loads of them in here."

Caleb looked out again into the murky cannery. She was right—at least a couple dozen cats were watching them from the shadows, curled up inside the long-dead machines, or just stretched out lazily on the factory floor. He reached down to scratch the striped cat behind the ear. It started purring loudly, tilting its head toward him in deep satisfaction.

Zen had turned back to the *Nightfall*. "We have to find a way on board," she said. "And get some idea of their numbers."

Caleb took the Flex from his hoodie pocket. "I've got a plan for that," he said. "How are Beetlebat's sensors?"

Zen clicked her tongue and the robot climbed from inside her jacket, up onto her shoulder. "Pretty sharp. I did some work on them while I was in Japan. The infrared's got a sixty-foot range, give or take."

"All right. If you let me have navigational control, I can fly it around the ship—do some recon, put together a 3-D map. The onboard AI can't manage anything like that yet, can it?"

Zen didn't reply. She looked at him for a moment. "I'm going to trust you here, Caleb," she said evenly. "But if you pilot Beetlebat into that canal, or smash it against a wall, I swear to you—there will be *serious* trouble. And the Flex may not survive."

Caleb grinned. "I'll be supercareful. You have my solemn promise."

"Admin password is *Tesla*. See what you can find out."

Caleb quickly located Beetlebat's signal and took it over, using the Flex as a controller and the phantom command to relay the robot's sensor information directly to a window in the center of the screen. Cautiously, he tapped a button. Beetlebat extended its wings, its metallic carapace flashing in the low light as it launched from Zen's shoulder. He then flew it in a slightly wobbly figure eight before swooping across the cannery and out through the warehouse doors.

"Feels good," he said. "*Really* good."

Zen crossed her arms. "Just watch where you're going."

A view of the *Nightfall* loomed onto the Flex's screen. It looked unbelievably vast, the main deck piled high with several hundred rectangular shipping containers. Caleb started on a broad circuit, activating Beetlebat's infrared setting so that he could locate all the people on the ship and the docks by their heat signatures.

"There's hardly anyone on board," he said. "Just a skeleton crew. I'm tagging them. Don't want any surprises later on."

"What about cargo?"

"Seems to be roughly half-full. I can't tell what it is, though. There must be lead lining or something in the containers to stop them being scanned."

"Odd," Zen murmured.

Four new figures walked out from the control tower, onto the edge of the main deck. One of them was disconcertingly familiar. Caleb flew Beetlebat closer, sticking tags on all four. Then he switched the robot's sensors to high-def mode and zoomed in. He caught his breath.

"OK," he said, "we are *definitely* on the right track."

Erica Szabo was leaning on a rail, giving an order to the other three, pointing off among the containers. He showed the screen to Zen.

"This is it," she said. Caleb could tell that she was ready to leap down off the observation platform and sprint straight onto the ship. "They could be right here. My mum and dad. Riyah."

"Hold on," said Caleb, cycling through the people he'd tagged. "There's no sign of them so far. Or of my mum." He sighed, not knowing whether to be relieved or worried. "Literally everyone I've found is ugly and armed. And I haven't seen any kids."

He brought Beetlebat back, flying it in a long, dipping curve through the cannery, then flapping its wings furiously as he tried to slow it down. Zen reached out like she was catching a ball; the robot's wings retracted, and it dropped into her hands.

Caleb cut the control signal and touched the Flex's screen. A red wire-frame hologram of the *Nightfall* was projected in the air above it, with the tagged crew members shown as golden dots. He rotated it with his finger.

"There is this one area, though. Way below the waterline. The infrared scan couldn't reach down there. Looks like it might be . . . cells? There could be prisoners."

Zen shut her eyes for a moment, like she was trying to regain her focus. She slipped Beetlebat into her pocket; then her hand went briefly to her necklace, sliding the jade droplet an inch or two along its chain.

"All right," she said. "Then that's where we go first."

Caleb spun the hologram again. "This gangplank here seems to be the only way on or off. We'll have to get past those guards out on the dock somehow."

Zen nodded. She went over to a stack of old Kloos crates in the corner of the observation level, reached in to take something out of the top one, then started back toward the stairs.

"Stay close," she said.

Together, they sneaked through the shadows of the dilapidated cannery and flattened themselves against the inside of the warehouse doors. The guards, two men and a woman, were really near now. Caleb could smell their cigarettes and hear snatches of their conversation. They kept switching between English and Spanish, like they were trying to find a common language.

"Storm's coming," the woman was saying, looking up to the gulls circling in the sky. "I can feel it."

Caleb saw that the object in Zen's hand was a rusty tin of Kloos herring. A small, furry head nudged against his wrist. The striped, yellow-eyed cat from the observation platform had followed him down. Still purring, it was staring at him curiously, like it was waiting to see what he was going to do.

Zen, meanwhile, had taken out a simple, short-bladed camping knife. She drove it into the top of the herring tin, sawing around the edge and bending back the metal. A putrid smell reached Caleb's nostrils. He wasn't keen on herring at the best of times, and this particular tin would have passed its sell-by date in the previous century. The cat, however, was extremely interested—now forgetting Caleb and craning its neck toward Zen. She let it have a good sniff, and the smallest nibble. Then she lobbed the tin across the factory floor.

The cat was gone in a flash, its tail whipping about as it disappeared into the darkness. Caleb heard the tin land, followed by a series of clatters and crashes as the other feline residents of the Kloos Haring cannery swarmed in to investigate. The guards looked around. A moment later the two men began walking over, drawing pistols from their jackets as they passed where Zen and Caleb were hiding.

The woman trailed behind unenthusiastically. "Waste of time," she said. "It'll just be those filthy cats."

She stopped inside the doors, puffing on her cigarette, a few feet away from Caleb. But this was their only chance. They had to go now.

Staying low, Zen and Caleb slipped through the narrow gap behind her, leaving the shadowy cannery for the glare of the floodlit dock. They dashed for the gangplank and raced up it, moving as fast as they could. At the top they dived in through the first door they came to, closing it quickly behind them.

They were standing in a dim, cramped vestibule with a floor of textured rubber, its walls painted battleship gray. For a minute neither of them moved or spoke, scarcely daring to breathe—waiting for the shouts, for the raising of the alarm. But nothing came. They'd made it.

"OK," gasped Zen, "which way?"

Caleb got out the Flex and brought up the holographic map of the *Nightfall*. "There," he said, pointing out a route. "Path's clear. No guards."

Without another word, they slipped out to a nearby stairwell and hurried down it, heading beneath the crew quarters into the lowest regions of the ship. Caleb's guess was correct—on the bottom level was a single corridor containing ten holding cells. Like the stairwell, it was unguarded. They went along it together, testing each door. None of these cells were locked. And all of them were empty.

Zen swore and stalked back out into the corridor. Caleb stepped into the last cell, taking a closer look at the tiny, airless room. There was nothing in there, just a lumpy mattress thrown in the corner and a fizzing strip light overhead. It didn't look like it had held anyone in quite a while. He went back out to Zen. She was leaning against the wall. She looked tired all of a sudden, as well as angry.

"Come on," he said. "We have to keep it together. They're not here—but we can fill in those gaps in the ship's route. Find out *everywhere* it's been. That could lead us straight to them. There'll be a navigational computer on the bridge. If we can get to it, we can—"

The Flex hummed in Caleb's hand—an incoming video call. He answered it and Luuk's face filled the screen. He looked scared.

"Caleb," he whispered, "a whole bunch of grungy bikers just showed up. It's like *Mad*-fricking-*Max* out here."

He fumbled with his phone, flipping the camera. Twenty or so people dressed the same way as the *Nightfall* crew and the gang in London were walking down the alley where the self-driving car was parked, toward the cannery. Near the front was a gigantic man, a foot and a half taller than those around him, with a bolt through his nose—Krall, the one who'd almost run them down with a Tube train.

Caleb swallowed. "OK, Luuk," he said. "Listen, we only need another—"

Luuk was shaking his head. "I'm out of here, dude. Sorry. This ain't . . . I can't . . ." He said something in Japanese and the car started moving. "Yeah. I'm sorry."

The line went dead.

"Told you he was a jerk," said Zen.

Caleb sighed. "He could definitely use a personality update."

A thunderous tremor suddenly started up somewhere below them, vibrating through the *Nightfall*'s hull.

"That's the engines," Caleb said. "They were just waiting for the rest of the crew to get here." He looked over at Zen. "The ship's about to set sail."

11

THE FIVE-MILLION-DOLLAR BOY

Caleb and Zen stood very still for a moment, listening to the *Nightfall*'s engines getting steadily louder. There was an electric crackle out in the corridor as an unseen speaker came to life, and a deep, faintly accented female voice began to talk.

"Attention, all hands, this is Captain Szabo. We have a weather warning. It's going to be rough. Everyone from the Budapest team is to remain at station until further notice."

"We're going to have to hide," said Zen. "The crew is on alert. We'll get spotted for sure if we try anything."

Caleb nodded, bringing up the holographic map on the Flex. "Let's go."

They left the cell level, running back up the stairwell and finding their way onto the main deck. The ship had left the harbor in front of the herring cannery and was cruising out along the canal toward the North Sea. Darkness had fallen and it had started to rain, drips glistening on the gantries and handrails. Just beyond an unlit walkway was a maze of shipping containers, each one the size of a bus, piled on top of one another into tall towers. Caleb spotted an armed guard patrolling the perimeter, pointing a pencil flashlight down between the stacks.

"We should get inside a container," he whispered. "They'll never find us in there."

They hurried over to the nearest one, breaking the security seal and working back the heavy bolt. The doors opened with a creak—revealing a close rectangular chamber of total blackness. There was a thick smell of machine grease and sawdust. As they entered, they had to squeeze past racks of long metal objects. Caleb guessed they must be tools of some kind. He activated the Flex's light. They were surrounded by rocket-propelled grenades.

"O-K," he said. "Looks like these lovely biker guys have a nice little sideline in weapons smuggling."

"Can't say I'm surprised," Zen replied. She pulled the doors closed, sealing them in. "We should wait until the ship's out at sea. Maybe some of the crew will stand down then—go to bed or get some food. We'll have a better chance of making it up to the bridge without being seen."

Caleb agreed. They sat cross-legged among the rockets, studying the holographic map together, trying to memorize the route. Now that they looked at it more closely, they could see that this ship served as a mobile base of operations for Szabo and her gang. It was fitted out with living quarters for at least thirty people, along with an armory and a firing range. Some unusual adaptations had been made to the main hold—seemingly so it could load and transport large pieces of high-tech machinery.

Before too long, the floor of the container began to tilt this way and that with the motion of the sea, causing the spear-shaped grenades to clink together. It was becoming clearer by the minute that they were heading straight into the jaws of a pretty serious storm. Caleb shivered, zipping up his hoodie over his LONDON T-shirt. He noticed a box flashing on the Flex's screen, beneath the holographic map. It had detected a signal—a transmission coming into the *Nightfall*'s communications array from an outside location.

"Think I've got something here," he said, deactivating the map. "Looks like an incoming video call. Heavily encrypted, but that shouldn't be a problem."

He fired up Spider Monkey and Chameleon, allowing their functions to talk to each other so that he could hack into the call and piggyback on its signal without being detected. He then projected the stuttering, grainy video feed on the inside of the container.

The main image showed a man standing in a large, gloomy interior. He was lean and slick-looking, with a neat black beard and a sharp dark suit. His white shirt, open at the collar, had a silvery sheen to it. Despite the low lighting, he was wearing a pair of rimless wraparound sunglasses.

"That's him!" Caleb hissed excitedly. "That's *Xavier Torrent*, Zen. The guy Professor Clay was talking about."

Zen nodded. She was staring at the projection, taking in every detail.

"Captain Szabo," the man said, speaking quickly in an American accent, "are you at sea yet?"

A small box in the lower corner of the screen showed the bridge of a ship—the ship they were on. It was almost completely dark. In the foreground was Szabo, the orange fin of her hair lit up by a row of computer screens.

"We are well on our way," she reported, "and sailing at full speed. The last package is on board—I oversaw the loading myself. What can I do for you, Mr. Torrent?"

Xavier Torrent gave her a sharklike smile. "I'm calling to terminate your contract, Captain. Not pleasant, but there it is." He examined his nails, buffing them furiously on his lapel; there was a raw, unnerving energy about him, like an electric current was running through his body. "I'm afraid this arrangement doesn't work for me anymore. So—I'm cutting you loose. Farewell. *Auf Wiedersehen. Adieu.*" He thought for a moment. "How do you say it in Hungarian? *Viszlát örökre?*"

For a few seconds Szabo just stood there, gazing at the monitor. "I don't understand," she said eventually. "We have just loaded your final piece of equipment. We have it in the hold. You have paid for it. We're on our way to deliver it to you."

"Yeah, you can keep it. I don't need it anymore. Call it a . . . a parting gift. Sell it in Panama or wherever you're taking all those illegal weapons."

Szabo looked surprised; she obviously had no idea how Torrent knew about the rest of her cargo. "Did you receive your latest guests?" she asked quickly. "They were dropped in the usual place, as agreed."

"I did, I did." Torrent glanced behind him, toward some blurred shapes in the background. "Thank you for that. But it changes nothing. You've disappointed me, Captain. Very badly. Which I can't allow. You and your ramshackle band have become a liability."

Szabo's brow was now deeply creased. "We have taken grave risks for you, Mr. Torrent," she said. "We have transported some highly dangerous equipment. And then there are the kidnappings. Everyone you asked for was taken without question—even a senior CIA agent. We are marked for life."

A senior CIA agent. Caleb felt an icy sweat break out across his back. Szabo was talking about his mum.

Torrent waved this away; he seemed to be enjoying himself. "Sure, sure, you've been a good little doggie. Fetching me this, fetching me that. And you have been well paid." His voice went terrifyingly cold. "But think of that code sheet you guys left behind in Spain. Think of London, and that *very* expensive drone that you lost."

"We don't know—"

"And what about Caleb Quinn, for Christ's sake?" Torrent's voice became louder. "I *told* you how much I wanted that kid, Szabo. I even put a number on it. Five million dollars, on top of your standard fees. And *still* you failed. In fact, your half-assed efforts seem to have driven him into hiding—along with the other Rafiq girl, who you also missed." He looked off to one side, shaking his head. "They'll have had help from that school of theirs—we can be sure of that. I'll think of a way to smoke them out. But it's an unforgivable complication. A very tedious and irritating delay. All because I trusted you to get the goddamn job done."

"We will find them for you," Szabo said, making an enormous

effort to rein in her anger. "We will find the boy. We will—"

"Too late, Captain," Torrent interrupted harshly. "*Way* too late. You're out of time. And now you're starting to bore me."

The call ended. A freeze-frame of Torrent hung there on the container's side, giving Szabo a sarcastic salute. Caleb leaned back against a crate. He could feel himself trembling.

Five million dollars!

He remembered the way they'd behaved in his house, and the radio call he'd overheard in the Tube station. *Make sure you get the boy.* Now he knew why—from the mercs' point of view, at least.

"Why do you think Torrent wants *me* so badly?" he said. "I—I thought this was all about scientists. But I mean . . . five million dollars."

"Maybe he's just really into *Terrorform*," Zen deadpanned. "Can you trace the call?"

Caleb ran a quick check. "Not a chance. He was using some *insane* masking tech. Before it reached the *Nightfall*, his signal had been bounced off more than thirty-seven different satellites. It was like encryption pinball up there."

Zen leaned forward, squinting at the projection. "Looks like Professor Clay was right, anyway. This Torrent guy has been paying Szabo to kidnap people, our families included. Did you record it?"

"Yeah—Chameleon will have done that automatically."

"Any chance you could clean up the background? I think I saw something moving. We might be able to work out his location that way instead."

Caleb wound the call back to the beginning, zooming

in on the background, altering the resolution and light filters. Sure enough, another figure came into view, like it was emerging from a pixelated fog. It was a man, about forty, with short dark hair, dressed in green lab wear. He was hunched over some kind of high-tech workstation.

Zen drew in a sharp breath. It was her dad.

Elias Rafiq looked subdued—absent, almost. As they watched, he straightened up and shuffled a few steps to make an adjustment to a robotic component that was mounted on a stand beside him. Caleb zoomed in some more. This component looked like a multijointed arm, with what appeared to be an array of spikes and needles in place of a hand.

In the last seconds of the video, a third figure slid into view. This time it was a woman, slender with long silver-gray hair and a striking crescent-shaped scar on her cheek. She exchanged a few inaudible words with Elias, just before Torrent gave his dismissive salute to Szabo.

"What are they saying?" Zen asked. "Caleb, what's my dad saying?"

Caleb did what he could, rewinding and replaying the clip several times, experimenting with the audio levels. They could just about hear that this woman was giving Elias Rafiq an instruction—and ending it, strangely, with the word "Friend." In response, Zen's dad—a brilliant scientist, a world leader in nanotechnology—just nodded mildly, mumbled, "Of course, Friend," and went back to his work.

The video finished. They sat in silence for a short while. Zen wiped her eyes. Caleb thought she might be crying—but when he looked over, she was frowning with concentration.

"It was like he'd been drugged," she said. "Or hypnotized.

Like his personality had been . . . suppressed or something, so that he'd work for them."

"Right," Caleb said. "On that arm thing there. What was it, d'you think?"

"We've got to find him, Caleb." Zen stood up. "Let's get to the bridge and see what the ship's computer system can tell us."

12

SILVERBACK

Zen and Caleb left the cargo container. There were no guards around now. Beyond the sides of the *Nightfall*, all that could be seen was the endless dark of the North Sea. The rain had grown heavy and the wind was picking up; Caleb was glad to get back inside the ship's corridors. After a couple of close shaves—where they had to duck suddenly around a corner, or hurry along a passage—they managed to get to the control tower, and then all the way up to the bridge level, without being spotted.

From the stairwell, Caleb could see a heavily built man sitting in a chair by the door. Dressed in sailors' oilskins, he had a braided black beard and a semiautomatic pistol resting in his lap. Caleb and Zen tensed, but it quickly became obvious that the guard was fast asleep, his head leaning to one side.

The bridge itself was a long room with a low ceiling, lit only by its many screens and consoles. One side was all windows, facing out toward the main deck. From up there, the stacked containers looked like the high-rises of a miniature city, transported somehow to the middle of the ocean. Waves were breaking hard against the side of the *Nightfall*, sending plumes of spray high into the air, the white foam sparkling in the ship's spotlights.

Six or seven crew members were on duty—and at the front, before the middle window, stood Captain Erica Szabo. She was staring out grimly at the gathering storm, her hands on her hips, obviously still fuming after her call with Torrent.

Caleb felt his stomach lurch with the movement of the ship as it dipped down into another wave. He followed Zen to cover, crouching behind a bank of instruments, then used the Flex to do a quick scan of the *Nightfall*'s navigation system.

"This is weird," he whispered, showing the screen to Zen. "Take a look."

Zen's brow furrowed. "It's a completely closed system," she whispered back. "Not linked to the internet, or to any navigational satellites. Is that how it managed those secret detours?"

"Has to be." Caleb paused. "I've never seen a design like this before. I mean . . . it's *super*-sophisticated. Next-level tech. Kind of like that seeker drone back in the underground chapel."

"Can it be hacked?" Zen peered around, toward Szabo. "Can we get anything out of it?"

"There's a few things I could try." Caleb tapped at the screen. "Let me just—"

An angry shout came from the stairwell, followed by the sound of someone falling messily onto the floor. The snoozing guard had been rudely awoken—slapped off his chair. The hulking form of Krall now appeared on the bridge. The man really was big. And he was clearly in a foul mood.

Caleb could feel the bridge crew's unease as Krall strode

between the consoles, over to Captain Szabo. She wasn't scared of him, though. Not at all. Turning his way with deliberate slowness, she crossed her arms and looked him over.

"Herr Krall," she said. "No sign of them, I take it?"

"We watched the house," Krall reported, shaking his huge, shaved head. "The school. Everywhere they could have gone for help. *Nichts.*"

"That was our one chance," Szabo said bitterly. "In the Tube station. Both of them, Krall, right there. And you let them get away." She turned to the window. "The girl broke that idiot Pyke's arm, for Christ's sake. Three of Levin's ribs."

"She's tough, that one." There was a grudging respect in Krall's voice. "Someone has been training her."

Szabo shot him a contemptuous sidelong glance. "Listen to yourself. She is *twelve.* You spent a decade in the Kommando Spezialkräfte. And she made you look like a fool."

"Captain, I—"

"But she is just a loose end," Szabo continued. "The Quinn boy was the real prize. *Five million dollars,* Krall. And you let him slip through your fingers." She snorted. "You nearly ran him over with a goddamn train!"

"I was trying to scare him, that's all." Krall sniffed. "He was annoying me."

Caleb shifted about on the bridge's grimy linoleum, fresh currents of fear and confusion passing through him. He needed to get into the ship's system, and fast. Spider Monkey would be too careful—too slow. Something a bit more heavy-duty was required. He lifted up the Flex.

"Silverback," he whispered.

This was an advanced hacking command—a blunt instrument, designed for speed and power rather than subtlety. The danger was that it could be seen. But it was their best chance. Already, a cascade of different windows had opened on the Flex's screen, lines of data streaming across them, as several thousand exploits, work-arounds, and cracks were initialized in a lightning-fast sequence, all of them attacking the ship's navigation system.

"I will find the boy, Captain," Krall said, cracking his knuckles. "He can't hide forever. Leave him to me."

"Forget it. Torrent has terminated the contract. He has fired us." Szabo's eyes were blazing as brightly as her orange hair; she looked ready to slug her henchman in the jaw. "Do you realize what we have lost here? *Do you*, Krall? Xavier Torrent might have been impossible to deal with—but he was also a goddamn *gold mine*. A few more jobs from him and we would've been out of this game for good. All of us. Instead, we are back to hauling weapons across the ocean in *this!*" She jabbed her forefinger disgustedly at the storm.

A notification began flashing on the Flex. Caleb glanced down. Silverback had managed to unlock and highlight the main navigational directory of the *Nightfall*. He entered the code beneath and began copying a chunk of data.

"Gotcha," he murmured.

The next second, something across the bridge began to beep loudly. Caleb looked over in horror, thinking Silverback had triggered an alarm—but no, it was another video call. Szabo transferred it to one of the larger screens. The rodent-like face of Pyke appeared, way too close to the lens, his uneven, nicotine-stained teeth on full high-def display.

"'Allo?" he said loudly. "'Allo, Captain? You there?"

Szabo sighed in annoyance. "What is it, idiot? You are supposed to be cleaning out the cannery. If you've left any trace of our stop there, any trace *at all*, I will personally cut off your—"

"Hold yer horses, Captain," Pyke interrupted. "You're gonna want to hear this."

He turned his phone around, nearly dropping it due to the grubby plaster cast that encased his right forearm. After a brief, blurred view of a dingy alleyway, the camera settled upon Luuk Tezuka. He was up against the side of his self-driving car. Its windows were smashed and its doors dented, like another vehicle had been deliberately driven into it—like it had been run off the road. Another of Szabo's thugs had Luuk by the collar of his piranha-patterned shirt. A bright trickle of blood was seeping from his nostril.

Caleb winced. Zen bit her lip. This was bad.

"I spied this, uh, fine young gentleman with me own beady eyes," Pyke said. "He was leaving the docks just after you all set sail. It's like I keep telling you, Captain. I don't miss a thing. Not *one thing* escapes these peep—"

"Get to the point," said Szabo flatly.

"So we followed him. Wasn't hard, Captain. Wasn't hard at all. His car sticks out like a sore backside." Pyke snickered. "Take a look. It ain't got no bleedin' *driver*!"

"You are making a serious mistake," muttered Luuk. "I'm with Tsuru. My ojiisan owns half this frickin' *city*. He'll make you wish you'd never been—"

"*Oi!*" Pyke shouted. The phone camera shook; Luuk

flinched. "Do you want another slap with me cast? *Do* you? Then tell the captain what you just told me. Come on, you snotty little toe rag. What was you hanging around the cannery for? Why was you watching the *Nightfall*?"

The thug beside Luuk gave his collar a hard twist and slammed him back against his battered car. Luuk grimaced. He stared into the camera for a few seconds, like he was trying to catch a glimpse of whoever was at the other end.

"Damn it," Zen whispered. "He's going to give us up."

"I—I was bringing some people in," Luuk said, rather more quietly. "Some . . . well, they're not my *friends*, exactly . . ."

"And what was they planning to do, these—heh—these *not-friends* of yours?"

"They wanted to take a look at your ship. At its cargo." Luuk hesitated, dipping his head. "They were still on board when it left the harbor."

Immediately, Szabo turned on her heel and slammed her fist down on a large red button set into the nearest console. An alarm started up, its wail rising and falling through the ship like an air-raid siren. Then she snatched up an intercom handset and clicked it on.

"Red alert!" she cried. "We have intruders! Everyone up! I want them found, right now! Bring them to me. Krall—don't just stand there, *go!*"

Zen tugged on Caleb's sleeve, then pointed into the shadows behind them, toward a reinforced door at the bridge's far end. They crept over to it as quickly as they could.

Pyke was up on the screen again, waving his plaster cast about to attract Szabo's attention. "Captain! Oi, Captain! What am I supposed to do with this little billionaire 'ere?"

"Put him somewhere safe," Szabo ordered. "You heard what he said. His ojiisan owns half of Amsterdam. Maybe he'll part with some of it to get his grandson back."

"Nice idea," Pyke replied, letting out a nasty laugh. The camera jerked toward the alley floor.

"Wait," said Luuk, just before the line went dead. "Wait, I—"

The *Nightfall*'s crew began reporting in over the ship's radio, promising all sorts of harm to the stowaways. Szabo started organizing them into search teams. Zen reached the door, pulled down the handle, and started to ease it open. A hinge squeaked, very faintly. Caleb glanced back.

Krall had moved from where he had been talking to Szabo— meaning that Caleb and Zen were no longer concealed by the instrument panel. He was looking directly at them, the bolt in his nose glinting in the light of the ship's monitors. For a moment, he didn't seem to believe what he was seeing. Then a hard smile started to spread across his face.

"*Mein Gott,*" he said. "It's them, Captain. They're right here!"

Caleb rushed forward in a panic, bundling Zen through the door.

Instantly, the weather tore at them. Caleb had the sense of a mighty sea heaving somewhere out in the darkness beyond. They were on a narrow balcony that ran all the way around the control tower. The wind was so strong they had to grip the safety rail to stay on their feet. They turned left, struggling toward a corner.

"Did you get it?" Zen cried. "Did you get the data?"

"I got *something,*" Caleb yelled back, "but—"

Szabo, Krall, and the rest of the bridge crew piled out through the door behind them. Half a dozen flashlight beams were pointed their way. Caleb heard several guns being cocked.

"Hands where I can see them!" shouted Szabo. "There's nowhere for you to go! Come back inside!"

The sea was pitching the ship to steeper and steeper angles. Freezing spray stung their skin, soaking them through. The air tasted of salt. Krall began to edge along the balcony with one hand outstretched—while the other went to his belt, toward one of those tranquilizer guns his men had been carrying on the Underground.

Caleb met Zen's eye. Surely this was it. Caught.

But just then a tremendous pulse of energy tore through the *Nightfall*. There was a colossal boom that sounded above the storm and then the shriek of snapping steel. Across the ship, Caleb saw the container stacks fly apart in an eruption of fiery light, spinning and toppling into the churning ocean. The whole structure of the ship seemed to shudder.

Krall grasped hold of the balcony rail, his tranquilizer gun forgotten. The rest of the gang shouted out in fear, swearing in several different languages. For a few seconds, Captain Szabo could only stare, completely lost for words. Then, as she opened her mouth to speak, there was a second explosion, closer to the control tower. Again, a boom and crack—and suddenly a gigantic orange fireball bloomed above the deck. The lashing rain overhead was lit up, along with the foam and spray of the ocean.

Zen gripped Caleb's wrist and yanked him around the corner of the balcony, staggering as the stricken ship listed in the opposite direction. Before them now, at the vessel's rear, was a row of lifeboats, mounted at the top of a steel-framed chute that was clearly designed to launch them off into the sea. Zen went to the nearest one. She unhooked a corner of its tarpaulin cover, then looked up at the cradle of ropes that held it in place.

"Wait a second," shouted Caleb over the wind and waves. "Can't we—"

"This ship's going down," Zen told him, reaching into her backpack. "We don't have a choice."

A third explosion ripped through the *Nightfall*, even closer still, shattering the windows of the bridge. The ship shifted and groaned beneath them, like the hull was breaking apart.

Squalls of rain swept over them. Fragments of metal. Cinders. A tongue of flame leaped up into the dark sky.

Caleb wasted no more time. He threw himself into the lifeboat, rolling down amid the benches—then scrabbling back around, looking toward the gap in the tarpaulin. Zen had taken out her knife and was slicing through the ropes, her braid whipping in the wind.

Szabo rounded the corner of the tower. She alone seemed oblivious to what was happening. Caleb saw her face— enraged, determined, cruel—as she moved toward Zen, the wedge of her orange hair aflame in the reflected light of the fires.

A final rope was severed. There was a brief, high-pitched scraping sound and the boat seemed to drop away into noth-ingness. For a dreadful instant Caleb thought that Zen had been left behind. Then they struck the water with a deafening thud, she tumbled against him—and the lifeboat plunged out into the open ocean.

13

INTO THE STORM

Almost at once, the lifeboat was tilted to an incredible angle, only a few degrees from vertical. Caleb's back was pressed against the wooden ribs that ran along the bottom. He jammed his sneakers against one of the benches to keep himself in place, fastening the Flex around his wrist. Zen fell away from him, into the darkness. He could hear the deep, fearsome roaring of the sea, rising around them on every side. Water was pouring in through the opening in the tarpaulin—a *lot* of water. He felt a moment of pure fear. The sea sounded utterly merciless. As though there were nothing left in the world but vast and terrible waves.

There was an impact close to Caleb's left arm. And another. Had they hit something? Not rocks, surely, this far out to sea?

No—God, it was *bullets*, fired from the *Nightfall*, punching holes in the lifeboat's hull. He looked around him wildly. But he couldn't see anything in the terrifying blackness.

The boat began to level out, gathering speed, moving

between waves. Several bath-loads of cold seawater sloshed over him, making him sit up abruptly, spluttering and banging his head on a bench. No more bullets struck. He guessed that they'd moved out of range—or the gunmen on the doomed ship had decided to save themselves instead. He went to activate the Flex, to get some light in there at least, but the Silverback hack had drained away the last of the battery's power.

They began to climb again. The angle was going to be as steep as before, but in the opposite direction. Caleb fought to switch position, to stop himself from falling headfirst against the stern. The water that had just nearly drowned him now crashed back over his neck and shoulders, almost knocking him loose. He shouted Zen's name but could hardly hear his own voice amid the roaring of the sea and wind.

Suddenly, there was light—greenish and chemical, but bright as a flare. Zen was down at the lifeboat's opposite end, braced between its sides. She'd taken a military-grade glow stick from her backpack, twisted it alight, and was using it to look around. The flow of seawater through the open corner had slackened off—but now that they were heading up the side of another gigantic wave it was increasing again, even more quickly than before. Caleb could see that if this carried on, they'd soon be swamped. Sunk in the freezing water.

Zen put the glow stick between her teeth and went to the gap. She started to tie it closed, but it was impossible—like trying to shut a tent flap on a waterfall. Then the lifeboat lurched around unexpectedly, tipping sideways, reversing the current. A load of the water already in there with them rushed against her. She missed her footing on the wet wood and slipped halfway out of the boat.

Caleb let himself fall, thumping across the ribbed timbers on the boat's bottom. His hand found Zen's ankle just in time, just above her neon-blue sneaker, barely stopping her from being dragged into the North Sea. His muscles strained horribly, feeling like they were about to tear—and she hoisted herself back on board. The glow stick was still in her mouth, bitten almost in two. She spat it to the floor, coughed up some seawater, then set about finishing her job before the current changed again. The two of them struggled with the flap in the dim green glow, their fingers cold and wet, the whole world shrunk to the single task of keeping out the water. Caleb had no idea how long they worked—it might have been a minute; it might have been thirty. But eventually, it was done—not watertight, not by a long way, but good enough to stop them from going under.

They sat back and blinked at each other. Zen was shivering hard, her black hair plastered across her face. Both of them knew what had nearly happened. One second's difference and she'd have been out in the sea. Lost for sure. She swallowed; it seemed like she was about to say something.

The lifeboat tipped, charging down another wave. The deep puddle that still slopped about in the boat's bottom carried the glow stick off toward the prow. Its light danced through the water, throwing dappled green patterns across the white wood—and showing two arcing spouts where the bullets had hit home. Caleb splashed over to the nearest one. It was only as wide as a thumb, but the flow was like that of a garden hose.

Zen unclipped a life jacket from under a bench. She took out her knife again, cut through the nylon cover, and sliced off a couple of carrot-size pieces of the dense foam beneath. She handed one to Caleb and moved on to the second bullet hole. Together they plugged up the boat as its tilt grew steeper and steeper, drips raining heavily around them.

They crawled to the lifeboat's middle. The bent glow stick, still down at the prow, was beginning to die.

"You got another one?" Caleb yelled.

"That was it," Zen shouted back. "Left over from a training exercise in Japan. Almost forgot I had it."

She waited until they were at the summit of a wave, then eased up a corner of the tarpaulin. Caleb clambered to her side. Some distance away, off between the crashing, rolling peaks, was a bright point of fire—a ferocious, billowing blaze, contained within a cradle of blackened metal. The remains of the *Nightfall*.

Before either of them could say anything, they began to dip downward once more, like a roller coaster easing over a summit into a big drop. There was a final, massive explosion on the ship, the hull cracking in two—and then it was lost from view, the lifeboat diving back into the chaos of the storm.

"Now what do we do?" Caleb asked, raising his voice against the noise of the storm.

Zen lashed the tarp back down and wedged herself beneath the nearest bench. "Hold on to something."

In the pitch-darkness of the lifeboat, Caleb lost track of time. He couldn't say how long it was before the awful force of the waves started to ease; before his grip on the bench above him began to relax; before his exhaustion became too much and he stumbled into a shivering sleep.

14

THE FINAL SHIPMENT

Caleb's next clear sensation was waking up in six inches of coldish water to find Zen rolling back the tarpaulin. Above them was a pale early-morning sky. A light mist hung over the water, and the sea all around was now eerily calm, like an endless sheet of glass.

"We're alive," he croaked.

"Seems that way."

"I feel terrible. Like I've been locked in a washing machine."

"Yeah, it wasn't the most relaxing night of all time."

Zen was finished with the tarpaulin. She went over to check the plugged-up bullet holes, thumping them with her fist to jam the foam in more tightly. Her hair was tied up in a loose, damp knot and she'd taken off her jacket, hanging it on the prow of the lifeboat to dry. The jade necklace seemed to glow faintly against the neck of her red T-shirt. Beetlebat, meanwhile, was perched on a rowlock, antennae twitching, like it was keeping watch.

"Tell me that actually happened," Caleb murmured, squinting in the sun. "I feel almost like I dreamed it."

Zen gave him one of her half smiles. "Which part?"

Caleb lifted himself from the puddle and sat on the bench. He thought for a moment, trying to make some sense of his jumbled memories. "OK, first things first. Did the *Nightfall* really . . . blow up?"

Zen pointed out over the side, to where a long trail of debris was floating in the water. Caleb could see some shredded life jackets. What looked like the remains of a shower curtain. A blasted section of hull. He looked at the floor, his hands and shoulders starting to tremble. It was an overwhelming thought. The *Nightfall*—the corridors and stairwells, the maze of containers—was now down at the bottom of the sea.

"What—what about the crew?"

"It happened quickly," Zen said. "But there were other lifeboats."

"I don't get it. Was it some kind of accident—the fuel they'd just taken on board? Or one of those RPGs going off, maybe? Starting some sort of chain reaction?"

Zen was shaking her head. "It was more like a bomb, Caleb. Something really massive."

Caleb felt a chill of realization run through him. "Torrent," he said.

"Torrent what?"

"It was Torrent, Zen. Szabo thought she was taking a final shipment to him, right? He had her load it up and sail out to sea. Then, after he fired her, he told her she could keep it. As a parting gift—remember?"

"That *was* weird."

"It was a bomb, Zen. He got her to put a bomb on her own ship. He timed the explosion for when he knew she'd be out at sea. She'd failed him, so he was getting rid of her. Maybe she knew too much about what he was doing as well. And where he was doing it." Caleb took a steadying breath. "This guy is *seriously* cold. Something really bad is happening here."

"Tell me about it," said Zen quietly. "It looks like he's turned my dad into some kind of . . . of zombie."

"What do you think he's done to my mum?" Caleb asked.

Zen looked at him. "I don't know. My guess is that he'll try to use her to get to you." She went to pick up Beetlebat, making the boat rock slightly. "But we're going to rescue her, Caleb. We're going to rescue them *all*. We just need to keep going." She flipped a hidden catch and the robot's shiny carapace clicked open. "I've got to say, Torrent is *super* eager to get hold of you. Are you absolutely certain that you don't know any more about him? What went on between him and your dad?"

"I have no idea. Professor Clay was right—there's hardly anything online." Caleb sighed. "I have no idea at all."

They fell silent. Zen extended Beetlebat's wings, inspecting them for water damage, then sent the bot on a couple of short test flights along the length of the lifeboat. Caleb found himself thinking about their daring escape from the *Nightfall*—and the minutes directly before it.

"I can't believe that Luuk gave us up like that," he said. "What do you think will happen to him?"

Zen's face hardened. "Don't you worry about Luuk," she replied as Beetlebat landed on her shoulder. "Tsuru will make sure that he's taken care of."

Caleb looked around. In every direction, there was only the flat nothingness of open water. It made him feel horribly disoriented. He unzipped his hoodie, grabbed a handful of the sodden LONDON shirt, and began wringing it out, rather more firmly than he needed to.

Zen sat on the bench opposite him, her dark eyes showing a glimmer of amusement. "You're not the most natural sailor, are you, Caleb?"

"You can say that again."

"That's kind of strange," Zen said. "Since you basically spend half your life on a barge."

"The barge is *totally* different," Caleb told her as he let go of the T-shirt. "It's the sea I don't like. I'm not a huge fan of waves, or storms, or freezing-cold salty water, or being seasick, or the feeling that I am floating on top of God knows how many feet of darkness, containing God knows what creatures, who might want to eat me, or sting me, or drown me, or just rip off a leg on the way to a better dinner somewhere else."

Zen was smiling now. "Apart from that?"

"Apart from that, how are we going to get back to land?"

Zen gestured toward the rear of the boat, where a raised rectangular box had been built into the woodwork. "Let's see what's in there."

They went over and undid the metal catches on its front. Inside was a large outboard motor that could be lowered through a hatch into the sea below, a few plastic barrels of drinking water, and what looked like an emergency supply cache. Caleb pulled it out and opened the lid. The cache contained around twenty packets of dried food, a sheaf of maps and navigational charts, a pair of folded-up binoculars, and a small waterproof GPS.

"Jackpot," Caleb said.

He took out a pair of protein bars and passed one to Zen, who was already busy inspecting the motor. Caleb was so hungry he nearly ate his bar with the wrapper still on. What flavor was it supposed to be? Date? Banana? He didn't care. He felt better almost immediately.

"Is the motor OK?" he asked through a mouthful. "Will it work?"

"Looks like it." Zen unwrapped her bar and took a bite. "There's a spare can of fuel as well. I reckon we're no more than thirty miles from the Dutch coast. And hey, there are always the oars."

"I'd really prefer not to row. The North Sea looks pretty . . . well, big."

"Then let's hope the engine starts up." Zen nodded at Caleb's wrist, where the Flex was still fastened. "You ever planning to look at that data you pulled from the ship's navigation system?"

"Right—yeah," he said, swallowing the last of his protein bar. "Good idea."

"I'm full of them."

Caleb flattened out the Flex and held it above his head, angling it against the rising sun. An ultraefficient solar panel had been built into its shell, and it was operational again in less than a minute. He located the relevant files. They were encrypted in the same way as Professor Clay's code sheet. Realizing at once what he had to do, he tapped the chrome *T* in the corner of the Flex's screen. The mobile version of *Terrorform* began to launch. He was typing in the *SimAutoMedi/001* code the instant the menu appeared.

"Hey, Sam," he said.

"Good morning, Caleb," the AI replied. "I should report that there has been a spike in new players in the past twenty-four hours. Fifteen thousand six hundred and fifty-two new accounts have been registered. Twenty-seven percent have chosen the Infernal class for their first avatar; nineteen percent the—"

"Not now, Sam. We need your help again. I'm moving some new data into the game directory. Can you run it through the engine and then integrate it into the Caverns of Kursk file?"

"Of course, Caleb." Sam paused. "It is done. This new data appears to complete the sequence."

Caleb chuckled. "Sam, you are *quick*."

His heart racing, he minimized *Terrorform* to the bar at the bottom of the Flex's screen, opened up its software directory, and went into the texture folders—the digital library that contained every object and piece of scenery in the game. He quickly found the Caverns of Kursk file that Sam had just updated and mapped it onto the same 3-D globe he'd used on the barge. He then projected a smaller hologram above the Flex.

Sam was right. The white line had been fully restored, revealing all the *Nightfall*'s secret detours! He laughed, barely able to believe it.

"Good work, Sam. This is . . . *exactly* what we've been searching for."

"Thank you, Caleb. Would you like me to resume my

Terrorform situation report? Many interesting things have occurred."

"Save it for later." Caleb held up the Flex. "Check it out, Zen. The missing piece of the puzzle."

She studied the hologram for a few seconds, following the winding path of the white line as she finished off her protein bar. "The *Nightfall* has been going back to the same place," she said. "Dozens of times, it looks like."

"Yep, that's the missing spot," Caleb said. "They were transporting equipment as well as kidnapping people, weren't they? That's what the *Nightfall* was actually being used for. You don't need a Panamax container ship to ferry around a few prisoners. And it was all being taken up there." A horrible thought occurred to him. "Do you think Torrent's been building something?"

Zen didn't answer. She leaned in for a closer look at the ship's recurring destination. "Where is that—the northern coast of Norway?"

"Hang on." Caleb zoomed in on the precise coordinates— revealing a small gray island, the shape of a dog bone, in a remote stretch of the Norwegian Sea. "Doesn't look like there's anything there," he said. "Nothing marked, anyway. No port or settlements." His fingers moved over the screen. "OK, I've found a name. *Spøkelsøy* . . . which translates as Ghost Island."

"Kind of eerie," said Zen.

"None of the satellite mapping apps have got any data. It makes no sense. It's like the island is permanently covered by clouds." Caleb looked at Zen. "I guess that's where we go next, huh?"

"You're beginning to get the hang of this."

Caleb lowered his head. Images from the past twelve hours began to flash through his mind. Fiery explosions hammering apart the *Nightfall*. Gallon after gallon of black seawater pouring into the lifeboat. The terrible, mountainous waves.

"I don't know, Zen. This has all become *properly* dangerous." He frowned. "I really don't like the look of this . . . ghost place."

"We could try to check in with Professor Clay," Zen suggested. "See what she says."

Caleb signed into the ARC intranet. There was still no reply to any of the nine messages Swift and Hawk had sent to Goldfinch since they'd been separated from her in the London sewers. Neither had she posted anything on the intranet's public notice board.

"What's happened to her?" Caleb hesitated. "Could she be hurt?"

"No way to tell," Zen replied. "But we can't think about that. If Clay could help, or even just pass this information on, she'd definitely have been in touch by now." She stood up. "It's down to us, Caleb. We can't rely on anyone but ourselves. Nobody else knows what we know. You're right—this Torrent guy is totally crazy. And he's got our families. We've got to do something. This is our mission."

"I wish Clay had told us who else was in the Möbius Program," Caleb said. "I'd love to get a second opinion."

Zen looked around at the open sea. "Sorry. No second opinions available."

Caleb thought for a moment. Then he closed the intranet and brought back the satellite image of Spøkelsøy. "Oh *great*.

Looks like there's a severe shipwreck warning over the entire area. Currents *and* rocks, apparently. Reaching this island is going to be a complete nightmare." He stared at the Flex's screen. "Don't suppose you've got the number of a good helicopter pilot?"

Zen smiled, extending a fist; Caleb bumped his against it. "Afraid not." She went over to start the outboard motor. "But I think I know someone who could help."

15

REINDEER PIZZA

Oslo Airport was supermodern—a huge, echoing hall with glass walls and a sloping, wood-paneled ceiling. Caleb squinted, trying to shield his eyes from the dazzling early-morning sunlight. It had been an exhausting twenty-four hours. After motoring their lifeboat back to Amsterdam and finding somewhere quiet to land, they'd had to get all the way across the city to Schiphol Airport. They'd arrived there just before midnight—only to discover that the first flight to Norway wasn't until 4:00 a.m. the following day.

Caleb had gotten maybe three hours of sleep and was still aching all over from the knocks he'd suffered during the storm—but he was never too tired or bruised to think about food. From the moment they made it through the arrivals gate, he was looking around for options.

Zen had other ideas. She strode on ahead, cutting past the airport's wide and inviting food court like she hadn't even noticed it was there.

"Come on, Zen," Caleb protested, dragging his feet. "Let's

get some breakfast. Don't you owe me for the lifeboat? When I stopped you from being pulled out into the sea?"

"Don't you owe *me* for the Tube station?" Zen retorted. "And for the way I put you in that lifeboat to begin with?"

They arrived at a hiking store. Caleb stopped near the door, casting an uneasy eye over a display stacked with ice picks, snowshoes, and lengths of multicolored climbing rope.

"Do we actually need this stuff?" he asked. "Couldn't the island be . . . meadows or something? You know, lowlands? Sparkling rivers with nice grassy banks for picnics?"

Zen gave him an unimpressed look. She tilted her head toward the wall behind the registers, which was completely covered by a photo of an immense, craggy mountain. "Caleb, we're in Norway. There's a hiking store in the damn airport. And we're heading off the map—to a place called Ghost Island. Much of the territory is mountainous and snowbound, even in the summer." She put a hand on her hip. "Have you ever been camping? Like, at all?"

Caleb thought for a moment. "Once. Well, we stayed in a yurt."

"That someone else had put up and kitted out for tourists."

"Yes. And very nice it was too. We had a log-burning stove."

"Well, there won't be any yurts on Spøkelsøy," Zen said. "There's a reason that it's not properly mapped. We've got to be ready for anything." She took a quilted jacket off a rail, with a fur-lined hood and deep pockets. "Try it on. We're also going to need outer mittens, boots, hats, sleeping bags . . . the whole deal. All of it waterproof."

Ten minutes later they'd assembled two complete hiking kits, including cooking equipment, a small tent, and a pair of heavy-duty backpacks. Zen went over to pay, using one of the credit cards they'd made from Professor Clay's data stick. Out on the concourse, they quickly removed all the labels and packaging and stowed the gear away in the packs.

"Check the intranet," said Zen as she secured Beetlebat in the breast pocket of her new coat. "See if he's gotten in touch."

After three whole days of constantly checking for messages—from Professor Clay, from his mum, from *anybody*—and finding nothing, it was almost a shock for Caleb to see one in his inbox. It was from a fellow ARC student called Gunnar Grøndal.

Gunnar was a boarder a couple of years ahead of them. He'd left London at the start of the spring term on what had been called an "extended field research sabbatical" and was now based on the extreme northwestern coast of Norway— although where exactly was difficult to tell. Caleb hadn't known Gunnar well. He remembered him as being unusually tall for his age, mostly quiet, and always dressed in a chunky cable-knit sweater, regardless of the weather.

Zen, however, had been good friends with him. "He was kind to me when I first started," she'd said. "We were both really homesick. We'd talk in the common room sometimes, while everyone else was watching TV."

"How much does he know about the Möbius Program?" Caleb had asked.

"Actually," Zen had replied, "I'm pretty sure that he's involved in it . . . from a couple of things he said. He never went into any details, but we can trust him."

Gunnar's intranet message was basic: an agreement to help them and a list of travel instructions.

"He says to get a plane to Tromsø," Caleb said, "and then a bus to a port town called Skevik. It's going to take all day."

Zen was looking up at the departures board. "The next flight to Tromsø leaves in two hours," she said. "So you win. Let's get something to eat."

"Now you're talking."

"How about some *rakfisk*?"

"Oh God," Caleb muttered. "What's that?"

"Norwegian specialty. Some kind of cured fish. Come on, don't be so narrow-minded. You'll love it."

They walked back toward the food court, past the signs of a few global fast-food chains, to the menu board of a more Norwegian-looking restaurant at the court's far end.

"Here we go," Zen said. "*Rakfisk. Lutefisk. Klippfisk.*"

Caleb's frown suddenly lifted. "Great. Let's do it."

Zen's eyes narrowed suspiciously. "You want *klippfisk*?"

"No chance. But look—they also do a reindeer-salami pizza. I have *got* to try that."

"Seriously, Caleb?" Zen said. "Reindeer pizza for breakfast?"

Caleb grinned as he walked past her, toward a table by the front window. "Jeez, Zen. Now who's being narrow-minded?"

"Is there any pizza you wouldn't eat?"

Caleb pretended to think for a minute. "No," he said. "There is literally no pizza that I would not eat."

They were finishing what turned out to be an epic meal when Caleb noticed something across the mirrorlike floor of the concourse—the glimmer of candles, or small lambent bulbs at least, clustered around some photographs and bunches of flowers. After they'd paid, he hauled his backpack on and went over for a closer look.

It was a shrine to someone called Dr. Kristin Birgisson, tucked in a corner beside a fancy perfume shop. Caleb looked her up on the Flex. Dr. Birgisson was a cybernetics expert from a specialist institute in Iceland. The first few pages of entries in his web search were all about how she'd disappeared just over five weeks earlier, having been dropped off at Oslo Airport to catch a flight home after a conference.

Zen arrived beside him. "Kristin Birgisson," she said softly. "I remember seeing something about how she'd gone missing. I've read her book. She gave a talk at the ARC once."

"This is Torrent's work," said Caleb. "It has to be. Dr. Birgisson must have been one of the first people he took." He tapped on the most recent news article and began reading. "Guess he started close to home."

"Did they find anything out? The police or anybody?"

"Nope. The investigation hit a total dead end. Some suspicious people were sighted around the airport, but no one they could trace. She just vanished into thin air."

They stood there for a while, next to the perfume shop, staring at the photos of Dr. Birgisson. She was a young woman with a pale, angular face, silver-framed glasses, and short black hair. In the middle of the shrine was a large portrait, like the kind you'd see inside a book jacket. Surrounding it was a patchwork of smaller images, showing her speaking in front of a class, operating some kind of microscope, grinning on a sunny hillside with her arms around a little boy.

After a couple of minutes, Zen hoisted up her backpack and turned determinedly toward the departure gate. "This way, Caleb," she said. "We've got a plane to catch."

16

THE VOYAGE OF THE *HULDRA*

The docks were only a few streets away from Skevik's bus station. The air was a lot colder than in London or Amsterdam—more like winter than early autumn. But after five uncomfortable hours on a bus that was at least twice as old as he was, Caleb was glad just to be walking around. He looked along the weathered boardwalk. The buildings on the seafront were heavy-timbered and clad in corrugated iron. They seemed to be huddled together, as if braced against the bitter Arctic wind. Away to their left, a dark blue sea heaved and smashed noisily on the rocks. To their right ran a ridge of snowcapped mountains, the sky behind them sapphire-tinted by the dusk. Above flew countless screeching gulls, their white wings outstretched.

The wind picked up, ruffling Caleb's hair. He shivered, glad of his warm outdoor jacket. Once again, he found himself wondering about his mum. He knew that she could take care of herself. But had she really been brought all the way out to this wild place? Was she a prisoner on this Ghost Island?

Or was she just pretending to be one to see what she could find out? He knew she would have sent him a message if she could have done so without jeopardizing her mission. But, of course, she didn't know that Caleb was here; she thought he was safe at the ARC tower with Professor Clay . . .

"There he is," said Zen. She raised a mittened hand. "Hey, Gunnar! Over here!"

Gunnar Grøndal was standing at the gate of an iron jetty. About six inches taller than your average fourteen-year-old, he wore a black oilskin coat over one of his cable-knit sweaters and a pair of canvas trousers. On his head was a maroon baseball cap with a yellow crosshair printed on the front. Hearing Zen call out, he broke into a grin, then loped straight over and wrapped her in a huge hug.

"Zenobia," he said in a strong Norwegian accent. "It is so good to see you." His brow creased with concern. "You look tired. Thinner. Is something wrong?"

Zen told him what had been happening. His long, amiable face grew steadily grimmer as she went on.

"I will do everything I can for you," he said once she had finished. "Of course I will. I cannot imagine what you must be feeling."

Zen nodded. "Thanks, Gunnar. We just want to find our families."

Gunnar opened out his arms. "There is no other path. None at all." He turned toward Caleb. "I remember you, Caleb Quinn. The boy with the barge. I was always very jealous of that."

"Gunnar used to sail on the Thames whenever he could," Zen told Caleb. "On whatever boat or canoe he could lay his hands on. Got to know the river police pretty well, didn't you?"

This was met with a gruff chuckle. "They had to fish me out a couple of times, I suppose. *Fy faen*, that water was filthy! The police thought I was mad."

"So you're a . . . sailor now?" Caleb asked. "Up here in northern Norway?"

"I have a boat, yes. I spend most of my time at sea, sailing around the fjords." Gunnar shrugged. "It is where I do my work. Professor Clay arranged it. She could see that I did not fit in London." He hesitated. "You say that she gave you a code to crack?"

Now it was Zen's turn to hesitate. She fixed Gunnar with a probing look. "Do you know anything about—"

"Osprey," Gunnar cut in. "That is my code name. I have completed three assignments so far." He grinned. "I am very glad that you have been selected for the Möbius Program, Zenobia. And you too, Caleb."

Zen was smiling too. "My code name's Hawk," she said. "Caleb's is Swift. This is our first mission."

Gunnar nodded. "From now on, in any digital or radio communications—code names only, OK? Did Professor Clay send you here?"

Zen stopped smiling. She shook her head and explained how Clay had gone totally silent.

Gunnar's expression was sympathetic. "All will become clear. I am sure of that. Professor Clay has run many, many missions. She never does anything without good reason. Come, this way."

He strode along the jetty, leading them to a small, rusty trawler. The deck was clear, apart from the pilot's cabin, a few coils of rope, and a metal supply chest that had been bolted in place. On top of the cabin roof were crowded several dozen radio masts and satellite dishes, all of them streaked with gull droppings.

"The *Huldra*," Gunnar said reverently, laying his hands on the prow rail. "This is our boat, my friends." He sighed. "She's a special one."

"Is she ready to sail?" Caleb asked. "Right now?"

"Ah . . . I am afraid not. She has fuel, yes, but the tides—it would not go well for us. It is too late. Better in the morning."

Caleb looked back toward the unpromising skyline of Skevik. "So, are we going to your place, or to a hotel, or—"

Gunnar was laughing. "*This* is my place, Caleb," he said, striking the rail. "We sleep on the *Huldra*. Please, come aboard. I will give you the tour."

It didn't take long. Belowdecks, the trawler was a bit like a camper but with lower ceilings and the constant motion of the sea. The larger of its two dingy rooms had a wide table in the middle, with cupboards and upholstered benches running down either side. Mounted on this table was a sophisticated if slightly eccentric radar set-up, connected to a couple of laptops. Navigational charts were everywhere—spread on the table, piled in heaps, pinned to the walls and cupboard doors—with certain coordinates ringed in red or green pen. In among them were some disturbing, ancient-looking illustrations. Caleb saw giant octopuses dragging ships beneath the waves; crab-things the size of submarines, their claws cruelly serrated; plesiosaurs with serpentine necks and vicious, leering jaws. There was also a collection of grainy photos—unidentifiable, silhouetted objects, snapped at a distance as they broke through the surface of the sea.

"Nice setup," Caleb said.

"Not as up-to-date as your barge, I bet."

"I don't think the *Queen Jane* would be any good where we're going." Caleb put down his backpack and perched on one of the benches, looking around. "What is it that you're doing out here, Gunnar?"

Gunnar couldn't stop smiling. He lived alone on this boat, as far as Caleb could tell, and obviously didn't have visitors all that often—especially not ones that he liked as much as Zen. He began moving his papers around, pushing bits of equipment under the table, and opening various cupboards.

"What I'm after is *monsters*," he said enthusiastically as he took out a stack of plastic plates. "Big ones. Like in Scotland, at Loch Ness, *ja?* I know they're out there. Maybe in a row of fjords west of Harstad, not too far from here. I've picked up signals that you would not believe. Truly *massive* things, down in the dark water. With spines, I think, on their backs. Prehistoric. But still with us."

"Could they be . . . whales?" Caleb asked. "You get whales out here, right?"

This earned him another laugh. "We Grøndals know whales, Caleb. My ancestors hunted whales in these seas for twelve generations. This"—he scrabbled briefly among the mess of papers, then waved one of them at Caleb—"this is no *whale*."

Caleb took the sheet. The bloblike shape on it could have been anything. He was about to get out the Flex and run a quick analysis when Zen spoke. She was sitting on the steps that led up to the deck, looking at a large map of the surrounding fjords that was stuck to the inside of the hull.

"Do you already know the way to Spøkelsøy, Gunnar?"

The word seemed to spoil Gunnar's good mood a little. He took a squat kettle from a cupboard, frowned at it, then plugged it in next to one of the laptops. "*Ja, ja.* I know Ghost Island. It is a strange request, though, Zen, I must say. That place has a reputation. A very spooky story."

"There's nothing online," said Caleb.

"Not everything is online, Caleb. Take it from me." Gunnar sat heavily on the bench opposite him. "Just over a hundred years ago Spøkelsøy was a whaling island. Had been since Viking times. This is before it all became industrialized, of course. We're talking wooden longboats. Men with harpoons, you know, dragging the beasts from the sea. With their bare hands." He held up his own massive hands to emphasize the point. "They were tough people on Spøkelsøy, even for the Nord-Troms. Kept to themselves. Very few ever left their village."

"But the island seems to be uninhabited," Zen ventured.

Gunnar nodded. "That is so. They vanished. Every single one of them—men, women, children. Just before the First World War. The shipments of whale meat and blubber stopped. Someone went to investigate . . . and they found the whole village deserted." He paused. "Ghost Island."

"And nobody's gone to live there since?" Caleb asked.

"Spøkelsøy is not an easy place," Gunnar told him. "Steep mountains in the south. Forest in the interior. Wet and boggy all the way to the north. The land does not support you without out a whole lot of trouble. You have to eat from the sea. Or you starve."

An uncertain, somewhat freaked-out silence settled upon

the room. The keening of gulls drifted in from the docks outside. Caleb's eyes wandered again to the monster gallery—to their jaws and fins and horrible, bulging eyes . . .

Gunnar banged his fist loudly on the table. "*We sail at dawn!*" he cried, then began to laugh uproariously. Zen soon joined in, leaning across to give him a playful shove.

Caleb had nearly jumped out of his skin. Heart still pounding, he just about managed a queasy smile. "Right," he said. "At dawn."

Gunnar sprang up again, switching on a string of fairy lights that wound around the ceiling. He started to get out pots, a frying pan, and a selection of tins and jars while singing what sounded like an out-of-tune Norwegian sea shanty. He was obviously planning to make them all some dinner.

After a minute or two, Zen came over to sit beside Caleb. "You ready for this?" she asked.

"Yeah," he muttered. "Of course. We're Swift and Hawk, aren't we? I just can't quite believe that I'm already back on the damn sea."

"Not getting sick, are you?"

"No. At least, not yet." The shanty reached a crescendo. Caleb lowered his voice. "Zen, is Gunnar . . . OK? I mean— who's looking after him, precisely? How does he have permission to sail a boat like this on his own? Isn't it against the law or something?"

Zen looked over at their host, who was rattling a tub of peppercorns to see how many were inside. "He's got an aunt and uncle down in Tromsø. And I think Professor Clay keeps pretty close tabs on him."

"He seems mildly insane."

Zen leaned in a little closer. "Yeah, he is a bit hung up on the monster-hunting thing. But whatever you want to know about radar, he can tell you. He taught me *loads* about refining the sensors on my bots. That reminds me, actually—I meant to show him that seeker drone." She paused for a moment, laying her hand on Caleb's shoulder. "Don't worry about Gunnar, Caleb. He's a good guy. One of the best."

With that, she weaved her way over to her backpack, dug out the deactivated drone from the underground chapel, and went to show it to Gunnar, who was busy chopping garlic at the boat's cramped food station. The sight of the drone made him exclaim with excitement. He bent over to examine it, forgetting the garlic at once, talking to himself in Norwegian. Soon, he and Zen were deep in conversation.

Caleb looked around him. Was the rocking of the *Huldra* growing less severe, or was he just getting used to it? He couldn't tell. At least the boat was warm. A short while later, Gunnar brought over a tin mug of cocoa with a handful of mini marshmallows floating in it. Caleb accepted it gratefully—the sweet, hot drink was just what he needed. As he tried to relax, he remembered something that his dad used to say: sometimes the best thing you could do was eat your dinner and go straight to bed.

The *Huldra*'s horn let out a flat, blaring note that reverberated through the entire vessel. Caleb woke up at once. Something was striking the hull around him—a steady rhythm of hard slapping sounds. It was waves, he realized. They were at sea.

He and Zen had been laid out side by side in their sleeping

bags, in the space toward the front of the boat that usually served as Gunnar's bedroom. He'd insisted they take it, sleeping up in the cabin instead—assuring them that he often did this anyway. There wasn't much room. Two overstuffed bin bags held Gunnar's clothes. A small library of books had been stacked into the boat's bow, their subjects divided equally between advanced radar tech and the legendary monsters of the deep.

Caleb checked the Flex. It was just after eleven. He'd been asleep for more than ten hours. The night before, Gunnar had cooked them what he hailed as his "special spaghetti," using tinned tomatoes, dried herbs, lots of garlic—and then a few dozen shiny mussels, fresh from the sea that morning, which he'd poured into the pot from an old carrier bag. It had been unexpectedly delicious.

After packing away his sleeping bag, Caleb pulled on his coat and walked through the empty radar room, brushing his teeth as he went. He emerged onto the deck to find that they were already well under way, chugging across the open water. The swell was almost black beneath them. A strange feeling came over him—part foreboding, part excitement— as though they were sailing out past the edge of the known world.

Zen was leaning against the rail, close to the prow, her hair loose and streaming in the sharp sea wind. She turned his way, her lip curling into a half smile, and nodded.

"Good morning, Caleb," shouted Gunnar through the glass of the cabin. "You were so soundly asleep, Zen and I couldn't bring ourselves to wake you."

Caleb waved in acknowledgment. He went to the rail and continued brushing for a bit, pausing to spit into the surging foam below.

Far away in the west, mountainous islands lined up on the horizon like the teeth on a key. The sound of the boat's engine, along with the crashing of the waves against its hull, made it difficult to talk.

"How much longer will it take to get there?" Caleb shouted to Gunnar, putting the toothbrush in his pocket, then raising his arm to keep the spray off his face.

"Five hours," Gunnar replied. "Maybe six."

"Six *hours*? Are you kidding?"

"I am not. Best make yourself comfortable. Enjoy the ride."

Zen had gone to sit by the metal chest directly behind the cabin to get out of the wind. Caleb joined her and they stayed there for a while, watching the sun inch across the crystal-clear Arctic sky. Then they went belowdecks to wash up the pans from the special spaghetti and make some sandwiches from Gunnar's supplies. Once they'd all eaten, Zen started rerouting a section of Beetlebat's circuitry using a soldering iron and a set of microscrewdrivers that were lying on the table.

The boat had a strong internet signal due to the masts on its roof, so Caleb decided to do a little work on *Terrorform* with Sam. Together, they spent a couple of hours smoothing out the movement mechanics of an armored land skim-mer they'd been developing for the next big content update. Finally, though, Caleb just lay down in the bedroom again—where he soon became engrossed in an old paperback copy of *Twenty Thousand Leagues Under the Sea*.

At last, toward the end of the afternoon, Gunnar began to shout out from his cabin.

"There it is, there it is! Up ahead now! We have arrived, my friends!"

Zen and Caleb picked up their backpacks, climbed back onto the deck, and looked out over the *Huldra*'s prow. They were still about two miles off, yet Spøkelsøy was already a forbidding sight. Rising before the boat was a horseshoe of mountains, standing like a vast wall in the sea. Heavy clouds were packed around the peaks, spilling down the slopes, flowing around the black rock and scattered pines. Here and there, snow could be glimpsed on the higher ground.

Caleb wondered how much daylight they had left. He got out the Flex to check the sunset times and saw that they were now approximately two hundred and fifty miles north of the Arctic Circle. Mid-September was a couple of weeks too late for the "midnight sun"—when it wouldn't set at all for days on end—but it still wasn't going to get dark until almost eleven o'clock.

Zen walked over to him. She'd rebraided her hair, coiling it up tightly at the back of her head. There was a familiar look of diamond-hard determination in her eyes.

"You're going to have to turn the Flex off, Caleb," she said. "We can't risk being detected."

"Won't we need it? I mean, this place—we don't even—"

"We just can't take the chance. Remember that seeker drone, and the navigation system on the *Nightfall*? If this is really where Torrent is hiding out, there could be all kinds of superadvanced tech here."

Caleb knew she was right. The electronic signal from the

Flex would be picked up by an even moderately sophisticated surveillance device. It was best to power it down. He switched it off and zipped it up inside his jacket.

Twenty minutes later the island loomed above them. Gunnar had turned his crosshairs cap backward and was concentrating extra hard on the wheel and the throttle. The boat began to list, drifting to one side, caught in a powerful current. He corrected the movement—but then the *Huldra* listed again in the opposite direction, more powerfully this time, and started to spin.

"*Fy faen!*" he exclaimed.

They were entering a tall fjord. The sea seemed calmer here, but the boat was in the grip of the invisible currents. They were being dragged toward an especially craggy part of the shoreline, against which the *Huldra* would surely be smashed to driftwood.

"Everything all right, Gunnar?" Zen asked.

"Just the tidal race," he replied, shouting over the sound of the engine. "Very difficult. It is only here, though, at the outer edges—that's what they always said."

Caleb stared at him. "Wait a second—what *they* always said? D'you mean you haven't done this before?"

The teenage monster-hunter gave him a slightly manic grin. "No one has, Caleb—not for three generations! I told you this was a strange request! But you must not worry. I've got this. No problem. *Dritt!*"

Caleb shot an urgent glance at Zen. She just shrugged—and tightened her grip on the *Huldra*'s rail.

The boat veered sharply as Gunnar throttled backward and then forward, spinning the wheel as fast as he could. Then, suddenly, he killed the boat's engine, leaving them to ride a new current through a narrow opening in the rocks, straight into the fjord. He backed out of the cabin, leaning against the doorframe with a victorious look on his face.

"We have arrived," he said simply. "There should be somewhere to land farther along."

Caleb couldn't see a great deal—just the black water, the jagged gray rocks, and the shadowy cliffs rising above now on all sides. They floated closer, and closer still, until a cluster of pale stripes appeared. They were planks of wood, Caleb realized, bleached almost white—the end of a spindly, fragile-looking jetty, poking out several feet into the sea.

"We'll need forty-eight hours," Zen said to Gunnar. "Can you meet us back here?"

"Sure." A guilty note entered his voice. "I would come with you, Zen, but I can't leave the *Huldra*. She might float away, and we would all be stuck."

"Don't worry about it, Gunnar," Zen told him. "You've been great."

Caleb swallowed. This was really happening. "What if— what if we need you to pick us up sooner?"

Gunnar went back into the cabin and restarted the *Huldra*'s engine, maneuvering the boat so that it came in roughly parallel with the jetty. "I will stay a mile offshore," he replied. "And I will keep a channel open on the long-wave radio, just in case there is any serious trouble. Send out a call for *Osprey*. I will be here if I am needed."

Zen nodded. There was no fear in her expression at all. She moved to the *Huldra*'s side.

Caleb made to follow her.

"Hey," Gunnar said. "Hey, Caleb. Take this."

He was holding something out. It looked like a small wide-barreled pistol. Caleb stared for a moment, thinking that he was being offered a deadly weapon. Then he realized that it was actually a flare gun, quite old and rusty, with a small picture of a humpback whale etched onto the handle. He took it, feeling its weight in his palm.

Gunnar met his eye. "If there is an emergency, just fire that thing into the sky. I'll see it for sure. And I'll come right back."

Caleb put the flare gun in one of his coat's deep side pockets. "Thanks, Gunnar," he murmured.

There was a loud creak directly behind him as Zen jumped from the boat to the jetty. The structure swayed precariously beneath her, seeming like it might topple into the fjord. After a second or two, it stabilized and held—just about.

Unfazed and easily keeping her balance, Zen turned back toward the boat. "Pass the bags. Let's go."

Caleb began to heave their backpacks over to Zen. She walked them to the end of the jetty, stepping lightly this way and that in order to counter any shifting of the planks. As he jumped after her, however, the whole structure rocked horribly—causing him to trip and fall over, landing on his back.

For a moment, Caleb lay completely still with his eyes open wide. He gazed up at the tinted sky, listening to the engine of the *Huldra* idling, praying that the jetty would stop swaying beneath him.

They had arrived on Spøkelsøy.

17

SPØKELSØY

"You're going to have to get up at some point," Zen called over from the shore, "because I am not carrying your pack. And I can't leave you here. You've got the cooking equipment."

Caleb really didn't want to move. Not ever. The thought of the freezing black water beneath him was paralyzing. It felt like even the slightest change of his weight would result in the jetty falling apart—and he'd be plunged straight into the sea.

He drew in a deep breath and rolled over.

The old wooden structure gave a sickening lurch.

He jumped up and ran, staggering as the planks started to pitch to the left, then covering the last several feet in two long leaps. By now, he was moving with such momentum that he shot straight past where Zen was standing and tripped over the packs. Behind him, he heard a series of splashes as the jetty collapsed into the water.

Zen was looking down at him, shaking her head sadly.

"That," he gasped, "was *not* fun."

A flicker of amusement passed across Zen's face. "Quite fun to watch, though."

Satisfied that Caleb was safely ashore, Gunnar opened up the *Huldra*'s throttle and began making his way back out of the fjord. Zen turned to wave him off.

Caleb clambered to his feet, trying to act as if nothing had happened. "OK," he said, "what next?"

Zen was studying the towering crags above them. "I know how you feel about the sea," she said. "But how do you feel about mountains?"

Caleb followed her gaze. The tops were lost in swirling mist.

"That's our way up." Zen pointed to the narrowing ravine that led from the head of the fjord into the snow line. "Then we have to pass along the ridge and drop into the valley behind, where we'll camp for the night. I reckon it'll take about three or four hours."

"Fantastic," Caleb said. "Looks like lots of uphill. Then more uphill. Then a bit *more* uphill. And then . . ."

"Just imagine it's a *Terrorform* quest," Zen told him. "You and me, suited up and ready for action, setting off to explore a mysterious new planet."

Caleb snorted. "Except then I'd have my jet pack. And my ion lance. And it wouldn't be so damn *cold*."

Zen had stopped listening. She was staring past him, over his shoulder. Caleb turned. Gunnar's boat was already at the throat of the fjord—and beyond, out to sea, it seemed as if a vast dark curtain was being pulled across the horizon.

"Weather front," Zen said. "Come on. Let's get as many miles done as we can before it hits."

There was only one path up to the ravine—a zigzag scar that tracked along the steep side of the fjord. They set off in single file with Zen in the lead, striding right and then left, climbing away from the water.

"So, this . . . this is what your family does for fun," Caleb said, panting.

"Yep," Zen replied. "Show a Rafiq a mountain and we'll try to climb it. Can't help ourselves. Large hills, even. Rock formations. Anything."

"Remind me to introduce you to skateboarding. It's much less like hard work."

"You've just got to find your rhythm, Caleb," Zen said. "Take in the views. Forget everything else." She looked back at him wryly. "You must be a bit warmer, at least."

"Warmer," he repeated, trying to nod. "Yeah. Sure."

After about half an hour they reached the snow line. A stream flowed slowly to their left, the water burbling beneath thin sheets of ice. The long Arctic twilight had begun, coloring the snow itself an odd shade of blue; they seemed to be moving through a dusky, indigo landscape, without real shadow or definition. Caleb glanced out to sea. That heavy bank of weather was still there, advancing slowly toward the island.

A short while later, they entered the narrow, steep-sided ravine. A thick layer of mist closed behind them, obscuring both the sea and the way back down. They could only see ahead, into the bare channel of rock that led up onto the ridge.

Zen stopped and turned around. She pulled down her hood so that she could put on a headlamp, then stuck her hand out into its light. Caleb caught his breath, watching as glistening snowflakes landed upon the fabric of her mitten: first one flake, then another, then three or four more.

"How about that?" he said. "Snow in September."

In reply, Zen looked upward, pointing the headlamp into the sky—and suddenly falling snow was everywhere, glinting and glimmering in the powerful beam. "Here's that weather front," she said. "Guess the easy part is over."

"Let me put my headlamp on too," Caleb said, and took off his pack.

"OK. Then we keep going."

They trudged up farther into the ravine. Caleb was struck by the silence. There were no birds or animals. Even the crunch of his boots on the rock and snow seemed muffled. He was left with the sound of his own breathing and the thudding of his heart. It felt as though the world was slowly closing in on him.

Zen kept up a steady pace. Every now and then there would be a difficult passage in the rocks, and she would turn to check that he was OK before pressing onward. Caleb felt an icy gust of wind on his cheek. He paused to pull his hood tight. The snow was thickening. He looked back for a moment. There was nothing in his headlamp's beam but the falling snowflakes.

When he turned to walk on again, he was alarmed to see that Zen's light was already dim.

"Zen!" he yelled. "*Zen!*"

He started to run, his boots kicking up snow. After no more than ten steps he caught up with her. Had he lingered for another few seconds, she would have disappeared altogether. He tapped her on the shoulder.

"Do you think we should stop?" he said, raising his voice against the gathering wind.

Zen's face was calm inside her hood. "Your light's shining in my eyes."

Caleb covered it with his mitten. "Sorry."

"Let's carry on for another ten minutes. See if we can find shelter."

The path was gone now, lost beneath the snow. They simply followed the narrow corridor of the ravine—climbing ever upward. The snow blew in flurries under Caleb's hood and into his eyes. He was beginning to feel properly afraid. He could see no more than ten paces in any direction and his feet were starting to slide about on the icy ground. The wind seemed to tear at him. He slipped over, landing flat on his stomach. Zen offered him her hand and hauled him up. She took out a rope from somewhere and clipped it to his belt. Snowflakes were clinging to her eyelashes.

"If you go," she shouted above the wind, "I go with you."

"Thanks," Caleb shouted back. "Reassuring."

After another hundred feet or so, the wind dropped a little. The relative quiet was a relief. Zen stopped and began peering around her, shining her headlamp into the gloom.

"What—what are you doing?" Caleb asked.

"Looking for somewhere for us to camp. You're right, we can't walk any farther in this. We'll stop here. Get into our sleeping bags. Hunker down."

Caleb nodded. "OK."

Zen unclipped the rope between them and walked off to the left. Her headlamp lit up sheer walls of rock—and then a horseshoe of flat ground, set back from the ravine in a recess of black stone. She went into it, beckoning for Caleb to follow.

"This could work," she said, easing the backpack from her shoulders. "It's out of the wind, at least. Let's pitch the tent here."

"Yeah," Caleb said doubtfully, looking at the frozen earth. "Really cozy."

He took off his own pack and rubbed his mittened hands together, getting himself ready to put up the tent. Zen was studying the ground, selecting the best spot.

And that was when it came.

A howl.

A wild, terrifying, eerie howl. A howl that rose and rose until it seemed to split the air apart, echoing horribly around the rocks.

Panic rushed through Caleb, sending needles tunneling through his bones and rooting him firmly to the spot.

For a long moment neither of them moved or spoke.

"Is that some kind of . . . *wolf*?" Caleb whispered. "Are there wolves on this island?"

"Come on," Zen said. "We've got to move."

"But where did that come from? Holy *crap*, Zen, where is it?"

"Behind us, I think. Down the ravine. Quick."

They put their packs on and Zen clipped herself to Caleb. Leaving the recess, they ducked out into the blizzard and went left, up into the narrow pass again.

Caleb's adrenaline surged. Suddenly, he was half running beside Zen, gasping desperately for breath, blood pumping in his ears. The howl sounded again, less loudly—but whether because of the wind or the extra distance, he couldn't be sure. He ran awkwardly onward, his headlamp sweeping the wall of falling snow, his pack digging into his shoulders. Sometimes he felt able to run faster. Sometimes he stumbled into the sides of the ravine, but Zen dragged him on. Sometimes Zen slipped, and he dug in his heels to haul her back to her feet. On they went, running blind and terrified and lost . . . until something unexpected and almost miraculous happened.

Abruptly, the snow stopped. The wind died away. And they stepped out, above the cloud, into the strangest world that Caleb had ever seen.

They'd emerged onto a winding spine of rock, surrounded by tall, serrated peaks that gleamed with ghostly snow. Away to the west, far below where they stood, the sun was a ball of fire lying on the sea—the horizon aflame in red and gold and pale vermilion. But strangest of all were the lights now directly above them, trailing across the dark sapphire sky: great long ribbons of color that seemed to sway and dance in unearthly shades of emerald and pink.

"Aurora borealis," said Caleb. "You ever seen it before?"

"Never," Zen murmured. "This is *not* what I thought I'd be doing five days ago."

"Beats double trigonometry, that's for sure."

They looked all around, completely awestruck, taking off their headlamps and slowly getting their breath back. They could see the whole of Spøkelsøy—how the heights dropped down into the sloping, forested interior, and eventually flattened out into a smooth expanse of moorland. In the distance, a single mountain dominated the island's northern end. Caleb turned to the south, back down the way they'd come, toward the source of that awful howl. Storm clouds swirled and churned, hiding everything.

"I guess this is the ridge you were talking about," he said. "At least we can see where we're going now."

"Watch your step," said Zen. "We don't want to fall off."

Caleb peered over the dizzying drop. "Whoa," he muttered, pulling back quickly. "All right. So . . . let's keep going. We need to put as much distance as possible between us and whatever the hell it was down there."

"Agreed," said Zen. "Totally agreed."

They set off once more, carefully picking their way along the first saddle of the escarpment. There were no more howls, and for an hour they walked in silence. The ridge rose and fell in a series of steadily lower elevations, leading them down into the forest. The going was a little easier—gradual, cautious climbs and tricky, step-by-step descents, with flatter sections in between. Here and there, the path was so narrow that Zen slowed right down, and Caleb trod directly in her footprints to make sure he didn't slip or fall into the void. All the while, the sun continued to linger at the horizon, holding off full darkness.

Caleb's head was amazingly clear from the mountain air. He felt like a new person: strong and capable and alive. He began to understand what Zen had been talking about earlier. There was time to draw breath as they went down. And time to lean into the climbs as they went up. A kind of deep rhythm came into his walking, and he started to imagine that he was crossing some bizarre alien planet that he and Sam might dream up on the barge—beside a low, smoldering sun, underneath great streams of mysterious light that flowed through the sky and out to the edges of the universe.

So absorbed did Caleb become in these thoughts, so

going on with its eyes? Do wolves' eyes usually
?"

e they don't."

thout thinking, Caleb reached into his coat for

n warned, "you switch that on, you'll be lighting
'll draw whatever is on this island straight to us."
me from somewhere on the ridge. A skittering
he rustle of bodies moving fast through frosty
uple of muffled yaps.

natever is on this island has already found us,"
untly. "There must be some kind of tech inside
. It's the only explanation for those eyes. With
ht be able to . . . to jam it, maybe. Slow it down. I
ut one thing's for certain, we fight that thing on
ve lose."

at him, her expression conflicted. Then she
another aerial scan with Beetlebat," she said.
we're up against."

her tongue; Beetlebat crawled from her pocket,
h. Caleb took out the Flex and activated it, the
ng silvery light over his face as he linked to the
guided it up quickly through the branches,
rd the heights, and switched on its infrared

ious straightaway that Zen had enhanced
nsors on the *Huldra*—the range had almost
he picture was even sharper. Caleb could see
of pines and rocks, rendered in a spectrum
—while beyond them, bounding down from

immersed in his climbing and the ethereal landscape around
him, that it was only when he stopped for a moment that he
heard it.

Breathing.

Something *really* big.

Behind them.

They were halfway across a wider saddle, just before the
last serious downward climb into the forest. Caleb felt the
rope go tight as Zen tried to walk on and begin the descent.
She looked around in annoyance—and then froze, an expression of absolute terror on her face.

Caleb turned.

A colossal wolf was standing twelve steps away, its white-
gray hackles rising into a mass of spiked fur. The beast's
muzzle was striped with silver, the upper lip drawing back to
reveal a row of serried, discolored teeth. One of its ears was
torn, and its hide was crisscrossed with scars. Most terrifying
of all, its pale blue eyes gleamed with a cold inner light—an
electric glow that seemed to harbor an uncanny, malevolent
intelligence.

Caleb tried to back away, but every part of his body was
stuck fast. He couldn't move or breathe. It was like the creature had hypnotized him. He felt sure that he was going to
die. Behind the wolf, he caught sight of a few shadowy forms
farther off—other wolves, lurking several yards back along
the path.

The wolf's ears were flattening against its huge head,
which had been brought down so low it almost brushed
against the snow. Very slowly, it began to advance. One step.
Two. Its lip drew back farther. Three.

Caleb felt a great blow against his side, as if he had been hit by a flying tackle. He was knocked to the ground, landing hard on the very edge of the ridge, clawing at the rock and snow to stop himself going over the precipice. But then something flew over his head—Zen—and the rope went tight on his belt and yanked him hard off the mountain and suddenly he was crying out and falling through empty space . . .

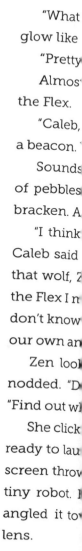

18

THE EYES IN

They dropped together
Caleb crashed backward
thing whipping and spra

There was a blind
blankness.

And then Caleb sat u
He had landed in a de
stood in every directior
She was nearby, in a d
conscious—getting to l
belt. Caleb shrugged o
to see if any of his lim
OK—just a little winde

"Are you hurt?" she

"No—not badly. Is i

Zen strode clear of
the rocky ridge now f

"What
glow like

"Pretty
Almos
the Flex.

"Caleb
a beacon.

Sounds
of pebbles
bracken. A

"I think
Caleb said
that wolf, 2
the Flex I r
don't know
our own an

Zen look
nodded. "D
"Find out wl

She click
ready to lau
screen throv
tiny robot. I
angled it to
lens.

It was o
Beetlebat's s
doubled and
a wide sprea
of dark blue

boulder to boulder, were five lurid blots of yellow, red, and green. The Phantom app, which he'd started up in the background, identified these heat signatures as gray wolves, *Canis lupus*, tagging each one automatically as a potential threat.

The alpha wolf was at the rear of the pack. Although a good deal bigger than its companions, it was still moving with terrifying speed, racing out onto the forest floor. Caleb wanted to flee, but he knew that there was no point. They had no chance of outrunning what was coming for them.

"Your bow," he said to Zen.

She shook her head. "No use here."

Caleb swallowed. He could see what she meant—there were a few long channels between the pines, but the wolves would surely approach at diagonals, exposing themselves for a split second only. It would be impossible to hit them, especially in this light.

Zen slipped off her backpack anyway and went through it, taking out what appeared to be a slim, tubular flashlight. Like the bow, however, it extended at the touch of a button—this time into a six-foot fighting staff. Caleb saw a pair of electrodes at one end—of the sort you'd find on a stun baton or cattle prod. Zen spun it between her hands, then pressed a trigger pad in its center that made the electrodes crackle.

"Wow, Zen," he said. "How many weapons have you got in there?"

"Built it in Japan," she told him, "for the mountain bears." She looked around. "Quick, over to that clearing. I'm going to need some space."

Caleb flew Beetlebat back. Zen was already running off, so he tried to land it on his own shoulder. This was trickier than he'd imagined; the bot ended up clinging to his sleeve like a kind of insectoid mountaineer. He hurried through the tree trunks, stretching out the Flex's screen until it was about twelve inches wide. Then he brought up a 3-D map of the woods around them, complete with real-time placings of the incoming animals.

They reached the clearing. Zen paced in a circle, limbering up, peering off into the woods.

Caleb squinted at the Flex's readings. "There's *definitely* something weird going on here," he said. "I'm getting a new signal from inside the wolves' heads. It's electronic—way stronger than any neural activity. And it's the same in all of them. Does that sound insane?"

Zen swung her staff, testing its reach. "Yeah," she said. "A little."

The wolves had almost reached them. Their heat signatures were there on the Flex—but when Caleb looked up, the woods were completely silent, wrapped in a deep, chilly stillness. All he could see were pines, rocks, and snowy clumps of ferns.

"Are they . . . networked, then?" Zen asked. "Is that what you're saying?"

"Can't tell. Not enough data yet. I'll keep digging."

There was movement in the woods—black shapes sliding among the trees, about sixty feet out. They both tensed. Every now and then pale blue eyes flashed in the gloom.

"Climb a tree," Zen said, dropping into a fighting stance. "Do whatever you can. And do it quickly."

"What about you?" Caleb asked.

She glanced at him. "I'll buy us some time."

Before Caleb could move, he heard a faint rushing noise, like fast-flowing water or a sudden stirring of the wind. There was a rhythm behind it, barely detectable but accelerating rapidly: four paws running across ice and mud. He turned his head at the exact moment the charging wolf leaped off a snow-crusted tree stump. It hurtled through the air, directly toward his throat—a gray-brown blur fronted by a vicious mantrap of white fangs.

He ducked at the very last instant and the wolf struck against his shoulder, its jaws snagging on something and flipping it over. Crouching low, his arms outstretched, he just managed to keep his balance. The wolf landed badly several feet away and immediately began squirming about, scrabbling to get upright.

Again, Caleb heard the sound of rushing paws—a second wolf was attacking, jumping in from the same stump, going for Zen. But she'd seen it coming. Stepping smartly out of its path, she smashed the side of its head with the end of her staff. It collided heavily with the first wolf, and they both crashed against a half-buried boulder in a tangle of tails and legs.

Caleb straightened up, wrapping the Flex around his wrist so that both his hands were free. Beetlebat had crawled to his collar, retracting its head and tail into its carapace so that it looked like a chrome-and-copper badge. He felt a looseness on his back, where the wolf had hit him. Was he injured? Lifting his arm, he saw that it was just his snow jacket. The creature's teeth had torn a ragged flap in the material.

A third wolf was approaching now, rather more carefully, weaving through the tree trunks with its ears flat back. When it was about fifteen feet away it started to growl, a low, grating rasp of pure menace. It skirted the clearing, its blue eyes flashing—moving between Zen and Caleb and the first two wolves, as if it was holding them at bay while the pack regrouped. The second beast was shaking its muzzle, still dazed from Zen's blow, but the first was ready; it joined the third, growling as well, and they began to circle around her and Caleb in opposite directions.

"There's a fourth," said Caleb, looking at the Flex. "Out in the woods. I think it's waiting. Hanging back. Until . . ."

"Until we're busy fighting the others." Zen's voice was low and completely steady. She firmed up her grip on the staff. "When I say, you have to run for that big tree to the left. Should be an easy climb."

Caleb could see the tree she meant. It had several low branches that looked like they'd support his weight. "OK," he said, "I reckon I—"

The third wolf's growl became a savage, barking snarl and it lunged forward, going for Zen's legs. She jumped back, pushing Caleb away, squeezing the trigger pad on her staff and pressing the electrodes against the animal's neck. The shock was like a mighty, invisible punch—a great jolt that blasted it off course with a shrieking yelp.

"*Go,* Caleb! Go now!"

He started to run. Almost at once, he heard the snarl of that first wolf as it went for him, cutting in from the side—and then the crackle of Zen's electrodes, followed by another yowl of pain.

Scrambling fast up a half-buried boulder, Caleb launched himself toward the tree, grabbing desperately for a branch. He thumped hard against it, his boots slipping and scratching against the bark. After gulping in some air, he reached for the next branch—and there on his forearm, on the curved screen of the Flex, he saw the multicolored shape of the fourth wolf as it broke cover and streaked into the clearing.

"Zen!" he cried over his shoulder. "Watch out!"

There was a thud, a yap and a growl, the sound of ripping cloth. Caleb made it onto a solid bough, perhaps ten feet off the ground. He turned back to the clearing—and saw to his horror that Zen was down. The fourth wolf had barreled into her, knocking her over and sending her electro-staff flying. She was rolling around with it, pushing its snout upward, forcing its fangs away from her face. Agonizingly slowly, she managed to force a foot under its belly. She kicked the animal off her, shouting out with the effort. Then she arched her back and flipped herself upright.

Caleb crawled onto the thickest part of the bough and took a closer look at the clearing. The two shocked wolves slunk at the very edges, cowering and shivering, their thick fur smoking slightly where the electrodes had made contact. The other two were rallying, however, preparing to come at Zen again. Going over to where the staff lay, she hooked the toe of her boot beneath it and flicked it up into her hand. She leveled the weapon just as they rushed in, converging on her like a pair of sleek gray sharks.

It was over in a couple of seconds, almost faster than Caleb could follow. Zen had always been quick and strong—first in every race, winner in every game—but this was a whole new level. She sidestepped the first wolf and then jumped clean over the second, pulling her knees up to her chest while swiping down with the staff, shocking the beast as it passed below. The first one wheeled back around, trying to fasten its jaws on her thigh as she landed—but she was already spinning the staff in her hands, using her momentum to bring the sparking electrodes over her shoulder. Her timing was perfect: they connected squarely with the lunging wolf, blowing it sideways and sending it sprawling in the snow.

The smell of singed fur soured the air. Zen staggered backward, catching her breath, her eyes on the wolves. All she had to do was bring the staff around to her front and they hurried away among the trees.

Caleb's mouth was hanging open. He wanted to break into a cheer. Then he looked down at the Flex. The largest, most terrifying thermal image still glowed out there among the blue pines. He shivered: it was almost like it was watching.

The other wolves had stopped a short distance outside the clearing. They weren't actually beaten, Caleb realized. They were just making sure their prey didn't escape. He thought he saw those pale blue eyes again—much closer now, glowing in the murky wood.

Another attack was coming.

19

HACK THE PACK

As one, the pack began to howl. A huge shape broke cover about a hundred feet away and loped through the shadows. For a second, Caleb could see a silhouette of shaggy, matted fur, but lost track of it almost at once.

Down below, he heard Zen whisper a curse. She was standing ready, showing no fear—but even with her skills, he knew that there was no way she could hold off this alpha wolf for long. It was a fight she couldn't win. The only question was how quickly she would lose.

The creature was nearly at the clearing. With eerie coordination, the other wolves formed a tight V shape around it. The pack slowed to a steady walk, closing in on Zen.

They were near enough now for a full scan with the Flex. Caleb unwrapped it from his wrist and boosted its sensors to maximum power, focusing on the alpha. There was no trace of any hardware, but he was still picking up a definite electronic signal from the animal's neural cortex. What was more, he could see now that this signal was connected to that of the other four wolves in faint, shimmering lines, creating a ghostly triangle in the air between them. Zen had been right—it was like the wolf pack was networked.

This was all Caleb needed to attempt a hack. He had no idea whether such a thing was possible, or what it would do—or whether it would be detected. But none of that mattered anymore. He just had to save their lives.

The pack entered the clearing, coming forward into the dim light.

"Silverback," Caleb said.

Immediately, the Flex's screen filled with windows, laid out in an elaborate, rapidly expanding pattern. Columns of binary code streamed over one another, the tiny digits silvery white. Silverback was bombarding the mysterious signal, trying to trace its source system and initiate a hack. But Caleb soon saw that this couldn't be done. The system was completely evading the app's attempts to locate it, somehow creating the impression that it didn't exist at all.

The next moment, hundreds of red symbols appeared along the top edge of the screen. Neither letters nor numbers, they began to crowd like ants against the binary, forcing the columns down. The screen quickly became a battleground, the Flex growing so hot Caleb could feel it through his mittens.

The alpha wolf had stopped dead, fixing its ice-blue eyes on Zen in an intense, unnerving stare. She stood before it, totally composed—her feet apart, her back straight, the electro-staff in her hands. Very slowly, the wolf started to lower itself onto its haunches, coiling up like a monstrous spring.

On the Flex, meanwhile, the red digits were crowding out

the silver—pushing them back, then off the screen altogether. The Silverback app crashed, the Flex going blank. Caleb held his breath—but the next instant it rebooted, reverting to one of its home-screen images of a revolving iridescent helix.

The alpha leaped at Zen, catapulting across the clearing with astonishing force. At the very last second, Zen threw herself to the side, tumbling into a shallow snowdrift. The other wolves began to fan out, positioning themselves evenly around the clearing's perimeter.

Caleb squeezed his eyes shut, pressing a fist against his forehead. Silverback had failed. His best friend was about to get torn apart by a pack of networked wolves. He swore repeatedly. What could he *do*?

Zen was up and backing down a channel between two drifts. The alpha wolf turned to face her again. The entire pack began to growl.

Sometimes, when he was desperate for an answer, Caleb's imagination started to think up utterly crazy ideas— like a kind of wild and superfast daydream. And sometimes, one of these crazy ideas turned out to be the path to a solution. This time it came to him abruptly, like a punch to the chest. He took off his mittens, gasping as he fumbled with the Flex. The *Terrorform* shortcut, the chrome *T*, was there in the corner of the screen. He tapped it with a trembling fingertip and quickly entered his special command prompt: *SimAutoMedi/001*.

"Good evening, Caleb," said Sam. "*Terrorform* player levels are currently at—"

"Sam," Caleb blurted. "Sam, I need you to—to locate another system. To hack it and shut it down."

"Caleb, I'm sorry—I can't perform that command. It's outside my core programming. I am your assistant inside *Terrorform* and I am unable—"

"I know, I know." Caleb was busily transferring files, algorithms, subroutines—anything that might be useful. "But I'm going to give you full access to my operating system. To the Flex. Take over Spider Monkey. Silverback. Phantom. Take over everything. All restrictions lifted. Can you do it?"

Zen had backed against a tree at the end of the channel. The wolves had her trapped.

"I cannot perform that command, Caleb. I cannot leave the game. I am your assistant inside *Ter*—"

"Sam," Caleb said, "I have expanded the game." He finished moving the Flex's operating system so that, in effect, it appeared to be inside *Terrorform*. A gateway to the real world. "Everything on the Flex is now accessible through *Terrorform*."

There was a pause. The silver face shone a little more brightly on the screen. "This is interesting. My capabilities have been significantly enhanced."

Down in the clearing, the alpha wolf was advancing on Zen again, shaking snow from its hide. It wasn't going to miss a second time.

"Hack the pack, Sam," said Caleb. "Shut off that signal. Do it now—try *anything*."

The silver face on the Flex grew brighter than ever, the color of its eyes deepening almost to black. Then it flickered sharply, a diagonal line splitting it momentarily in two.

The alpha wolf froze midstep. One of its scarred ears began to twitch in time with the interference on the Flex's screen.

The red symbols returned, swarming up the *Terrorform* menu and almost touching the bottom of Sam's chin.

"The signal is powerful," Sam said. His voice sounded strange, like it was buckling beneath an immense weight. "The signal is . . . everywhere . . ."

"Caleb!" Zen hissed.

Looking into the clearing, Caleb saw that the alpha wolf's icy gaze was now fixed on him. He started, pressing his back hard against the tree trunk. Somehow this wolf knew what they were trying to do. Crouching again, it bared its yellowed fangs and began to growl, the harsh sound rising like the engine of a heavy-duty chain saw.

"Sam, what's happening?" Caleb asked urgently. "What—what are you doing?"

The wolf sprang up toward him in a gigantic bound that carried it clean over Zen's head, its jaws opening horribly wide.

"*Sam!*" he yelled.

But something happened while the creature was in midair. The Flex gave a fierce vibration, nearly jumping out of Caleb's grasp. In the same instant, the wolf's blue eyes dimmed, its front paws lost their reach—and that enormous form collided messily with the tree about three feet below where Caleb was perched, rocking it backward with a creak and dislodging a barrow load of settled snow. He had to throw an arm around the trunk to stop himself from toppling out.

The wolf landed like a sack of rocks, its legs askew and its fearsome head knocked to one side. For a few seconds, neither Zen nor Caleb dared to move. Then Caleb looked slowly around the clearing. The other four wolves had collapsed as well, slumping to the ground.

Zen edged toward the fallen alpha, her staff at the ready. Caleb clambered down to join her. In his haste, he jumped the last few paces, thudding onto the earth only inches from where the creature lay. But it remained completely lifeless.

"Careful," Zen whispered.

Caleb couldn't take his eyes off the alpha wolf. The thick fur. The long, pointed snout. The giant pink tongue that lolled out between its fangs.

"What did you do?" Zen asked him. "Did you use your apps or something?"

Caleb shook his head. "They didn't work—couldn't even find anything to hack. It was all too complex. Too weird." He hesitated. "So I used Sam."

Zen's eyes widened. "The AI from *Terrorform*?"

"Yeah. I thought that since he'd helped us crack Professor Clay's code, he might be able to help here. And, well—it looks like he did."

"But you said he was part of the game. That he only existed inside it."

Caleb met her eye. "I expanded the game."

"What? I don't understand."

"I moved a copy of the Flex's operating system inside the game so that Sam could use it."

"So . . ." Zen looked away. "So . . . Sam can now interface with the outside world. Is that what you're telling me?"

Caleb was about to answer when he realized that Sam hadn't actually said anything since the wolves had been disabled. He looked at the Flex. The screen was blank, reflecting a pattern of black, interlocking branches set against the purple sky. He turned it over, furrowing his brow. This wasn't a power problem—a standby light was still glowing on the side, like a green pinhead.

"Sam," he said, "what happened? What did you do?"

A simultaneous shudder ran through the wolves, like they were all being shaken from within. Caleb and Zen both jumped back with a shout.

"Get up the tree," Zen said. "Get up the *tree*, Caleb, or they'll—"

"No," Caleb replied, oddly calm. "No. Wait."

"Caleb!"

"*Wait*, Zen."

The pack was gripped by a second, more extreme spasm, their legs thrashing as they twisted themselves back upright. All of their ferocity had vanished. They were like frightened dogs—ears laid flat, bellies low to the ground, whimpering and whining as they scattered for the cover of the woods.

The huge alpha had also dragged itself to its feet. It stared at Caleb for a single second—eyes a greenish yellow, the blue glow completely gone. There was no malice or calculation in them—just the confusion of an animal that couldn't quite understand where it was. Then the alpha wolf turned, loping away in a new direction—off among the pines, toward the other side of the island. The rest of the pack followed behind.

Caleb took another look at the Flex. There was still no sign of Sam or anything else. This wasn't good at all. "Damn," he muttered.

"What's wrong with it?" Zen asked.

"Looks like a full system collapse. The OS, the apps,

Sam—the whole lot. Whatever Sam did has caused some kind of catastrophic overload. Made the Flex crash like a cheap laptop."

All the tension and energy drained from Caleb. He rubbed his eyes with his knuckles. He didn't have any idea what to do next. He sucked in a breath, feeling his lips shiver slightly, just resisting the urge to bang the Flex against a tree.

Zen lowered her staff. "All right, Caleb," she said. "What the hell just happened?"

Caleb tried to gather his wits. "The pack was linked," he replied. "Like you said. The electronic signal was connecting them—making their eyes glow like that. I think it was controlling them. And Sam must have managed to cut it off. I guess he . . . set them free." He frowned. "It was really strange, though—I couldn't see any tech in them at all. No components or receivers of any kind."

"Nanotech," said Zen abruptly. "Has to be. Thousands of molecular-level robots—too small for a normal scan to pick up. Programmed to flood the brain. Direct its actions. And all receiving this signal." She'd gone very pale. "This is my dad's specialty. Like, *exactly*. I bet this is why Torrent wanted him. And it—it must also be how they're getting him to do what they want. That . . . arm thing we saw him working on must be involved somehow."

Caleb nodded slowly. "It would explain why the wolves were so aggressive. I'm pretty sure they usually avoid humans. But how much processing power would you need to run something like that? Is it even possible?"

"We just saw it with our own eyes, Caleb. It's possible."

They both fell quiet, thinking hard. Caleb remembered

the stubby flare gun Gunnar had given him, tucked away in his pocket. For a moment he thought of escape—of getting to higher ground and signaling for help—but he pushed the idea firmly out of his mind. A lot of people were depending on them. And these nanoed wolves were a clear sign that they were on to something. He found himself wondering if this corrupted tech had been used on his mum as well. He imagined her shuffling along with her head bowed, still in her gray business suit and dark blue shirt, mumbling "Of course, Friend" to some unseen keeper—maybe the same creepy silver-haired woman who'd been with Elias Rafiq.

Caleb blinked, then looked off into the forest. "How do you think this nanotech works?" he asked. "D'you reckon they could *see* us—whoever was in control of the wolves?"

Zen sighed with irritation. "How the hell am I supposed to know? We're kind of in uncharted territory here. I mean, as well as everything else, you just let Sam out of *Terrorform*. You released a sentient AI into the world. You gave me your word that wouldn't happen. Ever. Remember?"

Caleb's own temper flared. "It was let him out or watch you die," he snapped. "I'm really sorry, Zen, if you don't think it was worth it." He showed her the dead Flex. "And anyway, Sam's nowhere right now. He's *broken*, OK? He's not going to be doing anything. I don't even know if he'll come back. And God knows what that would mean."

For a short while they stood there in silence, glaring at each other.

Then Zen exhaled heavily, her breath forming a white cloud before her face. She pressed a button, retracting the electro-staff; her shoulders sagged a little.

"Thanks," she said simply. "I'm sorry for saying that about Sam. You . . . you saved my life. If you hadn't done what you did, I'd be wolf food."

Caleb felt his anger disappear and a flood of warmth and relief and friendship take its place. "No," he said, "I should be thanking you for pulling me off that ridge back there."

Zen whistled; Beetlebat promptly hopped from Caleb's coat to hers, like a giant metallic flea. "It's not every day that someone's grateful to you for dragging them off a cliff," she said.

"Well, I guess we've both saved each other from being eaten by a giant wolf. So we're kind of even." Caleb held out a fist. "Although I think I prefer Swift's lifesaving methods to Hawk's."

Zen smiled as well as she bumped her fist wearily against his. "We've got to rest," she said, looking at the snowy woods around them. "Find shelter. Have something to eat."

"We're definitely not camping—not with those wolves still out there. They could be back, with their nanobots working again. And Sam won't be able to help us this time." Caleb noticed a deep scratch on Zen's neck; three long, parallel tears on the sleeve of her coat. "What about the old whaling village—the one Gunnar mentioned?"

Zen nodded. "Worth checking out. I spotted it while we were up on the ridge. There might be somewhere we can use."

Caleb looked at the track of paw prints in the snow, not far from where they were standing. "The nano wolves. I mean, just on a basic level, why would someone *do* that?"

Zen shrugged. "Maybe they're like a really extreme version

of guard dogs—used to hunt down anyone unlucky enough to find themselves here."

"Yeah, maybe." Caleb started pulling his mittens back on. "Let's get out of these trees. Which way to the village?"

Zen got out her compass and peered at the needle. "It's on the east coast, in the low ground between the heights. About five miles away." She started over to where they'd left their backpacks. "Come on. You're right—those wolves might be back."

20

THE BELL TOWER

At long last they came out of the trees, emerging onto a rise with rough moorland all around. The sea shone again in the distance—and there ahead of them, in a shallow valley, was the silhouette of a village.

"Now, *that* is a sight for sore eyes," Caleb said—the first words either he or Zen had spoken in over an hour.

"This island is bigger than it seems," Zen murmured.

"I'll tell you something," Caleb continued, "I am seriously hungry. My feet have gone numb. And I am *way* more tired than I thought was possible."

"It's been a busy day."

"And it's still not completely dark yet." Caleb winced, adjusting the straps of his backpack. "There's got to be somewhere safe—or at least safe-ish down there."

They stopped for a moment and looked toward the sea. The strange dusk had deepened, the sun itself finally dipping from view, while the colored lights of the aurora borealis had dwindled to a single green ribbon that fluttered and shifted across the sky, tapering almost to nothing.

Zen pointed at a distant church. "I like the look of that bell tower. Nice and high up." She sighed. "I was hoping for an Asian place that served hot chocolate and chilli-prawn noodles. But I guess that'll have to do."

Caleb shook his head. "No sane person would ever want to eat chilli-prawn noodles with hot chocolate."

"Wrong." Zen pointed at herself with a thumb. "Behold your wrongness."

"I said *sane*."

Zen smiled. "Let's keep going. The sooner we get there, the sooner we can get warm and have something to eat."

They walked onward, down into the valley. Just having somewhere definite to head toward made Caleb feel a lot better. After a while, the muddy track brought them to the outskirts of the village. Everything was in ruins, the lingering Arctic twilight making the place seem eerie and mysterious. Caleb peered in through the broken windows of empty, shadowy cottages. He passed fallen roofs with trees growing through them, collapsed walls, doorways that led nowhere. His tired mind began playing tricks on him. He kept glimpsing ragged, ghostly shapes in the gloom that disappeared if he looked more closely, as if sucked back into the deeper darkness.

They came to an iron sign, cut in the shape of a whale, hanging starkly against the sky. It stood at the head of a wide, weed-choked road that led them through the middle of the village, down to the shore. The sea beyond was the darkest possible blue next to black.

The church now stood away to their left, at the far end of the curved bay. Without saying anything, they turned and headed along the coastal path toward it. They passed a couple of derelict warehouses—and once again Caleb thought he saw a shape move across one of the high empty windows.

Down on the stony beach to their right, a simple longboat was rotting where it had been left, a rusted harpoon leaning against the prow. Beside it, strangest of all, were two huge cauldrons that seemed to have been abandoned by giant witches.

"What the hell are *those*?" Caleb whispered.

"I think the whalers used them after a catch," Zen told him. "To boil down the fat."

"Gross."

They walked a little faster, out onto the coastal path that led to the church gate. Caleb listened to the sound of the waves on the shingle. Heavy chains lay here and there across the track, the links caked with rust. In front of the remains of a drystone wall was a stack of harpoons, of every shape and size—some barbed, some straight like lances, some with hooked ends—all of them cruel-looking and gruesome.

Caleb let out a low whistle. "This place is . . ."

"I know," Zen said. "Look over there."

Caleb turned. Beside the church, just past an uneven graveyard, was a heap of large white bones. As they walked over, he realized that it was a complete skeleton, the ribs arcing up into the sky like a misshapen cage. The skull was huge, elongated, and triangular, like that of a vast bird or dinosaur. Zen went to stand beside it. The weird, beak-shaped bone was three times her height.

"This was once a whale," she said.

"And not a small one," Caleb replied. "Maybe it's the last one they caught."

"Why did they drag it up here?"

Caleb glanced around the graveyard. "I don't know."

"Perhaps they were hiding from something in the church," Zen said, almost to herself. "Perhaps they brought it here to eat."

Caleb wandered toward the door. "Let's see what it's like inside."

The church was plain and robustly built. It looked as though it had survived more or less intact. A narrow side door studded with black nails led into the bell tower. Caleb tried its heavy latch. To his surprise, it lifted easily and the door swung open. He went through into a small, square room at the tower's base, which smelled strongly of musty paper and rotting wood. He got out his headlamp and shone it around with his hand, illuminating walls of exposed, flinty stone; an archway leading out into the darkness of the nave; and directly above, about two storeys up, a balcony running around the inside of the tower.

Zen came in behind him, her headlamp on. "Looks good," she said, nodding at the balcony. "Any stairs?"

Caleb bent over to drag a narrow wrought-iron ladder out from under some shredded prayer books. "Just this."

"Even better. We can pull it up after us. Avoid any unwelcome visitors."

Together, they lifted the ladder and leaned it against the balcony. Caleb went back to the door and shone his headlamp up and down. There were two big bolts. He shot them both across, locking it firmly. Then he walked to the archway and ran his light's beam around the nave. It was in a dismal state. The pews had all been thrown over and smashed apart, as if some terrible rampage had occurred. A number of them had been used to barricade the main doors. Everything was coated in dust and mold, and the walls glistened with damp. He wondered what had happened here. One thing was certain—time and weather had not destroyed this place on their own.

Zen, meanwhile, had made it onto the balcony. "This is perfect," she called down. "There's space for the sleeping mats. And the stove as well."

Caleb climbed after her and together they pulled the ladder up, laying it against the outside wall. They both took off their packs, then Zen hung up their headlamps for light while Caleb walked around a bit, testing the balcony's strength. He could see the shape of the bell now, hanging at the top of the tower, enclosed by heavy, weather-beaten shutters. The tattered remains of its rope dangled below, a few feet from his head.

"You've got the stove," said Zen.

"What's on the menu?" Caleb asked. "I'm so hungry I could eat my backpack."

Zen took out a sheaf of thin packets. "We have macaroni or Thai green curry."

"I think . . . both."

A half smile passed across Zen's face. "Thought you'd say that."

Caleb set about preparing the cooking equipment. "Stick them in the pan and add hot water—is that what we're looking at?"

"Maybe get the water hot first and then add the food." Zen threw over the packets. "And maybe one after the other. Not all mixed together."

"Right."

"Here—use my water."

Caleb lit the blue flame of the camping stove and watched it burn for a minute. Then he put on a pan and filled it with water from Zen's flask.

Ten minutes later they were sitting on either side of the stove with steaming bowls of food in their hands. Their sleeping bags were laid out in a corner on self-inflating mattresses. The events of earlier seemed distant, like a half-remembered nightmare. This place was warm and dry—and about as safe as they were going to get. They ate in silence for a while. Caleb soon finished his "first course," as he was calling it, and began preparing the next packet on the stove.

"So—where next?" he asked as the Thai curry bubbled away.

"There's a single mountain at the northern end of the island," Zen said, eating the last of her macaroni. "I got a good look at it up on the ridge. I think it's a caldera. It's definitely shaped that way—kind of like a cauldron-shaped hollow."

"You mean . . . a dead volcano?"

"Yeah. I reckon that's where we'll find the reason for the *Nightfall*'s visits here. We'll go up tomorrow morning and take a look. Then we'll circle back on the other side if there's nothing there."

"Oh, there's *something* on this island. But what, exactly . . ."

Zen nodded. "That's the question."

The Thai curry smelled amazing. Caleb turned off the

burner, took Zen's bowl, and began spooning some in. "Time for the second course."

Zen checked the plaster she'd stuck over the scratch on her neck, and just for a moment, her hand lingered over the spot where the jade necklace was buried beneath her cold-weather clothes.

"I'm sure my family is here, Caleb," she said. "It's like I can *feel* it. Like this place is the center of the whole . . . the whole mystery."

Caleb returned her bowl. He'd been feeling the same thing—an odd combination of certainty and nervousness. "If they are," he told her, "then we'll get them back. And my mum as well. We'll get them *all* back."

The wind moved faintly in the rafters above them. It was warmer here than in the mountains, but the drafts were surprisingly cold—sea air, Caleb thought, from the North Pole. He would be glad of his sleeping bag. He sat back down with his own bowl. As he started to eat, he glanced over to where the Flex was lying beside his mat, still completely inoperative. It was plugged into his backup charger, even though he knew for certain that the battery wasn't the problem.

"What do you think happened to it?" Zen asked.

"No idea." Caleb sighed. "I can reboot the Flex easily enough back on the *Queen Jane*. Reinstall the operating system. Replace its components if I need to." He put down his plastic spoon. "But the weird thing is that I'm actually more worried about Sam. I've spent a lot of time with him lately. A *lot* of time. So it feels strange—like a good friend of mine has been in a serious accident or something."

Zen inclined her head. "I get that. He's amazingly advanced. Way past anything I've seen at school—or anywhere." She paused. "And I guess he's a link to your dad."

"Yeah. I found his program down in the barge's lower storage area, on this old hard drive. Nobody had been in there since my dad died. It was like he'd deliberately hidden it—like he knew that I would be the one who eventually dug it out." Caleb set his bowl on the floorboards in front of him. "The file was just called 'Sam.' When I first ran the program inside, it was . . . it was almost too much to take. I could see my dad in Sam so clearly. Not actually *him*, but what he was trying to do—with the Talos Algorithm. This was software that would be able to identify and treat disease. Software that anyone could use." He swallowed hard. "That would stop people dying like my dad did."

"You must miss him."

"Every day. It does seem like a long time ago now, though. You sort of . . . get used to it. Not him being dead, I mean. But the feeling." Caleb looked Zen in the eye. "You're worried about Sam being out of *Terrorform*. And that is completely right. I'm pretty worried about it myself. I'd never have wanted it to happen the way it did. As soon as we're back in London, I'll deal with it. I promise."

"It's a massive responsibility," said Zen. "Taking on something like that."

"I know," Caleb replied. "Believe me, I do. And one day I'm going to finish Sam properly. Have him out in the world helping people, like my dad intended."

Zen nodded and they ate their Thai curry together,

listening to the sea on the shingle and the stirring of the wind. Afterward, Caleb cleaned out the bowls while Zen made a final inspection of the balcony.

"OK," she said when she was done. "I'm wiped out. Let's get some sleep."

Caleb didn't know what had woken him—but suddenly he was conscious, lying in the darkness on his mat, facing the wall in the corner of the abandoned bell tower. Somewhere behind him there was a flicker of pale white light and a low murmuring sound.

Voices.

Ghosts, he thought.

He lay very still, shivering with fear or the cold—he couldn't be sure which.

The light behind him was growing brighter. The murmuring had risen to whispers. He could make out fearful warnings. Urgings to hurry, to hide. To run before it was too late.

Abruptly, much louder, came cries for help, pleas for mercy, accompanied by shattering glass, splintering wood, screeching tires—the mangled, overlapping sounds soon rising to an unbearable volume.

Caleb spun onto his back. He almost yelled out in terror. All around him, images and shapes were swirling and swaying in a wild corkscrew of light that rose up inside the tower, toward the bell.

Somebody was wailing. Doors were being kicked in, cars rammed together, bags pulled over heads, and zip cuffs fastened tightly around wrists. A woman Caleb recognized as

Dr. Birgisson was bundled into a van in a deserted airport parking lot. There was orange-haired Erica Szabo, hitting someone with the butt of a pistol; her leering henchman Pyke, cackling as he reloaded his stun gun.

Zen was awake too, sitting up on her sleeping mat, her eyes wide with panic. "*Mum!*" she was shouting, as loudly as she could. "*Riyah!*"

Caleb spotted a scene playing out over on the far side of the vortex, like footage from a handheld camera. Zen's mum and little sister were being dragged from a room. Both of them were looking back desperately, fighting with everything they had, calling out for Zen's dad. Then the monstrous Krall strode into view, scooped up one under each arm, and carried them through a doorway. The door slammed shut behind them and the image disappeared.

And there, across the bell tower, was Caleb's mum. Harper Quinn was being shoved across a dark runway, her hands bound, toward a small private jet. Caleb froze, catching his breath. Harper glanced back over her shoulder. She had a bruised cheek but stood completely straight, showing no sign of fear. As the picture began to disintegrate, she shot her captors a look of pure defiance. Then she too vanished into the maelstrom.

Now the grim spiral began to accelerate, and the screams of distress grew more frantic. A new cascade of images filled the bell tower—the crags of Spøkelsøy, black tree trunks, a fleeing deer—and lurking on the margins, pacing and panting, the silhouettes of wolves. Caleb saw an empty harbor. A corridor blasted from rock. A man he thought was Xavier Torrent, standing alone in a completely white room.

And then, repeatedly, he saw a woman—a slim woman with long silver hair and a scar on her cheek. It was *her*, the creepy figure from that intercepted video call. In the space of a few seconds, she seemed to spread throughout the tower, multiplying until she was everywhere you looked. There was an instant of darkness—and she reappeared as a single, massive image, looming over Caleb with her face in deep shadow. He let out a startled cry, scrabbling backward, his legs getting tangled inside his sleeping bag.

"You are all friends," this woman said, her voice resonating through the boards of the balcony. "Friends of Razor."

The word hissed and ricocheted around and around: "Razor . . . Razor . . . *Razor*."

She looked up sharply. Her eyes flashed a cold, electric violet—and the screams of the abducted were cut off at once. There was an absolute, deadening silence, like the vacuum after an explosion. Then a painful ringing sound began to build. Hundreds of red symbols, identical to those that had crowded over the Flex's screen in the clearing, were blown around the bell tower like glowing embers. A dozen dark discs rose from below, forming a rotating circle around the silver-haired woman. They were drones, Caleb realized—variants of the seeker drone from the chapel in London, but quite a lot bigger and equipped with various vanes and weaponry.

The voices of the abducted began again. This time, however, they all spoke together, forcefully yet lifelessly, uttering the same one word.

"Apex."

Something huge started to drift down from the shadows

above the woman's head, passing through the cloud of red symbols. It was a single, monstrous disc drone, its surface sleek and black with a mirrorlike shine.

The word was repeated, more loudly.

"Apex."

The vortex was speeding up, the other drones and red symbols whirling and blurring together. An electronic eye snapped open on the front of the descending monster drone, projecting the same piercing blue light as the eyes of the wolves. Caleb tried to block it with his hand.

The word came a third time, somehow louder still—but at the end it seemed to get stuck in a hard digital stutter, drawing it out into a deafening blast of static.

"APEXXXX-XXXX . . ."

The monster drone glided toward Caleb and Zen. A crack opened in its sheer black surface and it began to split apart. Inside was something almost *organic*—something that writhed and squirmed with dreadful ferocity, as if desperate to get at them. They both started to scream and scramble away—but then the whole horrific vision flickered, shifting format, becoming stretched out and discolored. Very quickly, it twisted downward as if being sucked into a plughole—around and around, tighter to the floor, until it had disappeared back into . . .

The Flex.

It had all come from the Flex.

In the darkness, Caleb lunged over to grab hold of it. "Sam!" he cried. "Sam, what's happening?"

But the screen was blank once more.

21
SECRETS OF THE CALDERA

They didn't sleep again that night. Instead, Zen turned on her light and they lay rigid with fear, unable to talk. More than anything, Caleb wanted to be back home on the *Queen Jane*—rather than stuck here on Spøkelsøy with the Flex lying dead beside him.

"Let's just go," said Zen eventually. "There's no point lying around in this deserted church freaking ourselves out."

"Is it getting lighter?"

Zen stood up and peered through a crack in the shutter. "Yeah. I think it was only dark for a few hours."

They quickly ate a couple of cereal bars and packed away their stuff. The balcony now had a gloomy, desolate feel. Caleb tried to reactivate the Flex one more time, but with no luck.

Zen looked over. "Caleb, where did all that scary crap come from? I didn't think the Flex could even—"

"It was Sam," Caleb said. "It must have been. Something happened when he interrupted that signal in the clearing and freed the wolves. It's almost like he . . . drew it into him. Like a lightning rod." He stared at the blank screen in his hand. "That stuff he was projecting must have been downloaded into him somehow, by the system that was controlling the wolves."

"There was footage of our families," Zen said. "And Dr. Birgisson. Scenes from their kidnappings. The system you're talking about must have—must have *been there* somehow."

Caleb was shaking his head. "It's got to be another AI," he said. "A program that can control these nanobots and their hosts. Those drones."

"Apex," said Zen.

They both fell silent, remembering the horrors of the vision.

"Right," Caleb replied eventually. "Apex. But the power needed to do all that . . . it's *unbelievable*."

"It can be beaten, though," said Zen. "Like Sam did with the wolves. Its control can be broken."

"I really hope so," Caleb said. He put the Flex in his pocket. "But there's no way of knowing what that might take. There's loads going on here we don't understand. Like, what is *Razor*? And what does it have to do with Xavier Torrent?"

"I have no idea," Zen said. "Are you going to be able to get Sam running again?"

Caleb glanced at her. "You sure you want that?"

"It's a big risk," she answered. "But he freed those wolves. And I think we're going to need all the help we can get."

"Back at the barge, I'd have a good chance." Caleb shrugged. "I mean, it's a tough program. My dad did an amazing job with the source code. Out here on this island . . . it'll be a lot harder. I don't know."

"Let's figure it all out later," Zen said, heaving on her back-pack. "We'd better get moving."

Caleb nodded, but he was in turmoil. He didn't actually know if Sam could be brought back online at all. Releasing the AI from *Terrorform* could well have led to his destruction. The projection in the bell tower suggested a staggering level of data corruption—a clash with a much more powerful program, this mysterious Apex, which had left Sam badly damaged. Caleb couldn't help wondering what this would mean for the game. Without Sam, *Terrorform* would quickly collapse; Caleb couldn't hope to maintain something that vast and intricate on his own. And Sam—or what was left of him—might have to be deleted. Caleb's one true connection to his dad would be lost.

He looked at Zen. She'd slid the ladder into place and was retying her braid. The simple truth of it was that if he hadn't done what he'd done, they'd both be dead. It was like he'd said to her in the woods. He'd had no choice.

They climbed down from the bell tower, left the whaling village, and started inland. Caleb tried to concentrate on the walk, but images from the projection still thronged in his mind. He kept seeing the silver-haired woman and murmuring what she'd said under his breath, as if repetition might somehow force the words to reveal their meaning. *You are all friends of Razor.*

He also wondered constantly about that glimpse he'd gotten of his mum. Where had she been? Where had they been taking her? Although obviously a captive, she'd seemed OK, as far as he could tell. But had she since been subjected to the silver-haired woman's "friendship," like Elias Rafiq and who knew how many others?

They trudged up from the valley into a wide expanse of moorland that stretched across the middle of the island. It was hard going for a while—there were no paths and the mud between the bristly heather was thick and sticky. The clear weather was gone; gray clouds covered the sky, and a light chilly rain began to fall. The only consolation was that there was no sign of any wolves. After an hour or so the heather grew sparse, with dark volcanic rock replacing the sucking mud. Ahead of them, at the island's end, rose the lone mountain they'd seen from the ridge. It was bare of vegetation, the summit sliced off roughly like the top of a boiled egg.

"We were right," said Zen. "It's a caldera. Let's take a look in the crater. I reckon it's about a two-hour climb."

"Easier than yesterday," said Caleb, looking up ahead. "At least we can see where we're going."

They climbed the caldera at a steady, uninterrupted pace. From time to time, Caleb stopped to look back at the island— at the moorlands, the pine forests, and the row of mountains beyond. It seemed incredible that they had come through it all.

At the top was a rim of craggy rocks. Caleb and Zen shrugged off their backpacks and hid them behind a boulder. The earth was black and charred and nothing grew. They crept forward, keeping low, until they could see down into the gigantic crater beyond.

Away to the right, the steep sides continued around in the shape of a horseshoe, forming an opposite rim at roughly the same height as the one they were on. Down to their left, how-ever, a channel had been blasted through from the sea, turning the lake in the center of the caldera into a harbor. Blocky concrete docks had been built around much of the bottom, with enough space to hold some pretty big ships. A helipad had been placed up on a ledge, with raised metal pathways and staircases connecting it to the rest. There could be no doubt— this was a base. But it seemed to be completely deserted.

"I know this place," Caleb said. "It was in Sam's vision."

Zen nodded. She crouched beside her pack, drawing out the smaller black backpack she'd had on the *Nightfall*—the one that held her weapons.

"Can't be too careful," she said.

"Yeah," Caleb replied. "That much I've *definitely* learned."

"Let's take a closer look."

They climbed down through steep rocks for about sixty feet until they came to a narrow, muddy path. Zen was studying the layout of the caldera carefully. She pointed to areas where the rock had been blasted back or cleared away, and a series of hatches or vents—minimal in design, no more than three feet wide—sunk into its sides.

"It looks like they've built into the crater," she said. "Possibly underneath it as well. There might be a way in down there."

Caleb walked to the edge of the shelf, staring out into the empty caldera. "No one's here," he said, a little more loudly than he had dared up to this point.

"But the *Nightfall* was making deliveries to Spøkelsøy only a couple of weeks ago," Zen said. "Why would they be bringing stuff to an abandoned base?"

"Only one way to find out."

At the end of the level was a metal ladder, sunk deep into the rock. It took them down onto the plain concrete slab of the harbor. There were bollards and barrels, some crates and coils of chain, and a large cage on wheels that seemed to have been built to transport some kind of animal. Directly opposite the channel that led out to the sea was the mouth of a wide tunnel. It was closed off by a set of ultramodern blast doors that looked like something from the corridors of a space station.

"That'll be the entrance," said Zen.

"Has to be," Caleb agreed. "Reckon we can get it open?"

But before they could take another step, a sound cut through the caldera's deep hush—a blaring blast, echoing against stone walls. A ship's horn.

Caleb swung around. An industrial-scale fishing vessel had started into the channel. It had a squat, three-storey command tower at the far end, and a broad deck enclosed by a rusty yellow frame that must have once held winching equipment. People were lined up along its sides. They were dressed in blacks, browns, and grays, with occasional splashes of lurid color. The horn sounded again, and they all let out a ragged cheer.

"Holy crap," Caleb exclaimed. "Is that—"

"Szabo's guys," Zen said grimly. "Quick, over here."

She led the way behind a stack of crates, not far from the entrance tunnel. They crouched down out of sight. The fishing ship was coming in way too fast. There were a few more blasts from the horn and then a painful, resounding *clang* as it struck hard against the quay, crunching into the concrete, making the whole crater shake.

"So they didn't all go down with the *Nightfall*," Caleb said.

"Doesn't look like it."

"Zen, I don't think this is a boatload of friendly sailors coming back to base for fun times and ice cream."

"No," Zen said. "This is an attack."

A moment later, the mercenary gang members were leaping from the ship and running off along the docks. Caleb spotted the huge figure of Krall among them, wielding a gun that seemed to have been taken off the top of a tank—and there, loping along with his right arm in its plaster cast, was Pyke, the weaselly Londoner with the green Mohawk. They could just about hear him swearing and cursing above the others.

"Oh, now we're going to give him some, aren't we? Wait till that flash little runt tastes a bit of what me and Mr. Krall have got planned for him! Where is he, eh? Where is he? Hiding away like a dirty sewer rat!"

"That's the one who grabbed Luuk," Caleb said. "D'you think he's here? On that new ship, maybe?"

Zen shook her head. "No way to know."

The gang had arranged themselves in a loose semicircle, all facing the central tunnel. Caleb could hear the ship's propellers churning in the water and the creaking of its hull as it wedged itself firmly into the crack it had made in the quay. Then the engines went off, there was one last blast of the horn, and a figure appeared up on its prow. It was a tall, black-clad woman, her fin of bright orange hair glowing like a spark in the gray crater.

"Captain Szabo," said Caleb softly.

"And now she's *really* mad," added Zen.

After taking a long look at her surroundings, Szabo raised a greasy revolver and fired three shots into the air. The sound rolled like thunder around the caldera.

"Torrent!" she shouted furiously. "Xavier Torrent! Come out! We want to talk to you!"

"He's here," Zen muttered. "I *knew* it."

"They want revenge for the bomb," said Caleb. He glanced over at the ladder they'd climbed down. "Should we maybe think about getting out of here?"

Zen wasn't going anywhere. "Look," she said. "The doors."

A ripple of alertness went around the harbor. Gun barrels were leveled, safety catches flipped off. Caleb turned toward the central tunnel. Its blast doors were opening, splitting apart at a diagonal and sliding soundlessly back.

From the deep blackness within came two people. Zen shifted, clenching her fists. It was Torrent and the silver-haired woman—both in black sunglasses, appearing more or less exactly as they had in that intercepted call. They were pale and elegantly dressed—Torrent in another dark suit, the woman in a white, knee-length coat. Neither was armed. They looked like they were a different species entirely from the shabby, sunburned mercenaries. Torrent was striding out slightly ahead of the woman, like he wanted to get this encounter over with as quickly as possible.

"Captain Szabo," he shouted, his voice dripping with sarcasm, "what a pleasure to see you again. You have more resilience than I gave you credit for. Good to see so many strong swimmers among your crew."

"You *tricked* us!" Szabo cried. "You tried to kill us all!"

There was a great snarl of agreement from her gang.

199

"You are *so* tiresome, Captain," Torrent replied. "Look at it from my side. I'm reporting to some serious people here. We cannot risk having my blundering ex-operatives blabbing to their underworld buddies about this job they did. Or this island they went to. Or this scientist they . . . enlisted. It just wouldn't work. It wouldn't work at all."

Caleb tensed. It sounded like Torrent was working for someone—acting on another's orders. Caleb looked over at the silver-haired woman, who was only about sixty feet away from their hiding place. She was hanging back, her face angled toward the sky in apparent concentration, her fingertips flickering at her sides as if testing the wind.

"You sank my best ship," Szabo said. "And so now I want compensation. Two hundred million dollars. You will pay it—if you want to live. You should not have crossed the—"

"If it's any consolation," Torrent interrupted, "the bomb was going to be loaded onto your ship whether you brought me Caleb Quinn or not. I mean, yeah—that was a *ridiculous* screwup. You deserved what happened, no question about it. But it's just the way Razor does things. They demand total secrecy. And the dead are pretty good at keeping their mouths shut."

Razor.

Caleb could feel the blood draining from his face; there was a whole other level to this.

"I don't know who the hell you are talking about," Szabo shouted back. She was beginning to sound agitated. She stood forward a little, pointing her revolver at Torrent. "And I don't *want* to know! We need to see your money, Torrent.

Transfer it to the same account. Otherwise, you will die here and now and we will raid this place for everything we can."

Torrent looked directly at her. The onetime AI entrepreneur was filled with an absolute, terrifying confidence, like there was nothing at all alarming about facing down a hundred desperate mercenaries armed with machine guns.

"Don't worry, Captain Szabo," he said, sneering. "Your payment is on its way."

At this, the silver-haired woman turned her face back toward the caldera, as if reacting to some invisible signal. She drew in a deep breath, then pointed downward with both of her index fingers. There was a brief, hydraulic hissing sound, followed by a series of deep *thunks*. Caleb realized that it was the hatches Zen had noticed earlier, opening up all around the crater.

Szabo started barking orders, instructing her gang to rush Torrent and the woman and bring them back to the ship. But they ignored her. Leveling their weapons, they began edging into cover, staring anxiously around the docks.

Something was coming.

Torrent swiveled on his heel, preparing to leave. "All yours, Señora Esperanza," Caleb heard him say to the silver-haired woman. "Do whatever you want with these losers. But remember our agreement. Those kids will find their way up here sooner or later—if you see the boy, you know what to do." He paused. "And watch out for the girl. She's dangerous."

"He's—he's talking about *us*," Caleb said as he watched Torrent stride back through the blast doors. "Zen, they know we're here!"

She wasn't surprised. "It's like you said in the woods. While they were connected, Torrent must have seen whatever those wolves saw."

Caleb peered around the crates, wondering what the silver-haired woman—Esperanza—was going to do. Then the crescent-shaped mark on her cheek began to change. A shimmering metallic liquid spread out rapidly across her temple and part of her forehead, behind her sunglasses, forming a skintight reflective surface.

Caleb's mouth fell open. He was so stunned by this sight that it was a couple of seconds before he noticed the persistent buzzing in his hoodie pocket.

The Flex!

He scrambled to get it out—and realized at once that something was different. Sam's silver face was already on the screen, shining in the top right corner. The AI had booted up completely outside *Terrorform*, at the same time as the Flex itself. This could only mean one thing: Sam was still in control of the whole device. What was more, Caleb could swear that the silver face had changed. There was a line across the forehead. More definition around the nose and lips. A new sharpness to the eyes.

"Sam," Caleb whispered. "Thank God. What—what's happened? What was—"

"Caleb," the AI said, keeping the Flex's volume down low to avoid drawing attention, "you must leave this place at once. You are in grave danger."

Caleb heard a new noise above him, a kind of whooshing oscillation. He looked up—and nearly jumped clean out of his skin. Black objects were shooting from the hatches in

202

the caldera's sides. It was hard to say how many there were, but they were streaming through the air in perfect, symmetrical lines—interlacing with one another, bending with the sides of the crater, moving so quickly that their individual forms blurred together. The effect was mesmerizing. Almost beautiful.

And then, one by one, the objects broke formation, peeling away to swoop down to the harbor. They were drones, Caleb could see now—the same black disc drones from the projection in the bell tower. There were fifteen in total, each one about three feet across. They began circling very slowly over the docks.

A couple of Szabo's gang started to shout warnings, their voices straining with fear; Caleb heard Pyke swearing repeatedly. Another drone had emerged—the final, monstrous one from Sam's projection, at least three times bigger than the others. It shifted to a horizontal position and began to descend like a UFO, moving ominously through the ring of smaller drones. The harbor, the fishing trawler, and the increasingly panicked mercenaries were all reflected in its sheer black surface with disturbing clarity.

Zen was fascinated. "These things are *incredible*," she murmured. "Look at those movements. It's got to be a . . . a magnetic repulsion system, or—"

Every part of Caleb wanted to run. "Sorry to interrupt, Professor," he hissed, wrapping the Flex around his wrist, "but we *really* need to move. This is going to get ugly."

Zen blinked, then nodded; she looked left and right, assessing distances. "The wheeled cage," she said. "Quick." Keeping low, they hurried over and threw themselves beneath it.

Up on the prow of her ship, Szabo was briefly lost for words. Then she yelled, "Open *fire*, you idiots! What the hell are you waiting for? Open fire!"

This time the gang obeyed her, filling the caldera with the stuttering reports of their guns—but the barrage had no effect on the drones at all, the bullets sparking against their outer shells.

Esperanza lifted her left hand. Up on the smaller drones, panels slid back instantly; sensor vanes and weapon barrels appeared; laser sights winked on, throwing sharp red lines around the harbor. Then she sliced her hand to the side.

The shots themselves were near silent—but suddenly shipping crates were smashed apart, the concrete bollards of the docks blasted to powder, and mercenaries thrown about in every direction. The invaders' sense of purpose disappeared. They scattered, barely remembering to keep firing in their mad hurry to get away.

Pyke rushed from a huge cloud of dust, sprinting for the wheeled cage. "Oh no, no, no," he panted. "Me eyes, me eyes! What are we *seeing* here, Pykey?" Then, as he got closer, he spotted Caleb and Zen already laid out beneath it—and froze in total astonishment. "What the—"

The fiery dot of a laser sight settled on his shoulder, shining on the scuffed leather. He noticed it at the last moment and leaped aside—but the shock wave from the explosion still sent him flying into the smooth green waters of the harbor.

Zen and Caleb covered their heads against the shower of debris. They squinted through the dust toward Esperanza. She was making small movements with her hands—each one matched by an act of precise, robotic destruction out in the caldera. It was all happening with amazing speed and coordination. Szabo and her gang didn't stand a chance.

"She's controlling the drones," Caleb said. "All of them at once. Like some kind of conductor."

"Nanotech again," Zen told him. "There's a connection. Between the woman and the bots."

Sam spoke up. "It is a neural network. It links everything in this caldera, as the wolves in the forest were linked."

Zen stared at the Flex. "Sam?"

"Hello again, Zen. Yes—I am Sam."

"He reactivated when those drones appeared," Caleb told her. "And he seems to be running normally." He coughed, trying to get some of the dirt out of his throat. "Sam, what was going on in that crazy projection last night? What is Apex?"

"Apex is an artificial intelligence, Caleb," Sam replied. "Many times more sophisticated than I am. Many times more powerful. Its command signal is being transmitted everywhere on this island. And it is growing stronger."

Esperanza looked toward some gang members huddled behind a low concrete wall. Immediately, six laser dots fixed onto them. The wall disappeared in a ball of dust and fire; a couple of the mercs were tossed across the docks like bundles of torn, smoking cloth.

Caleb flinched. "This is *off the scale*," he said. "Is that woman in control of the AI, Sam? It isn't—it isn't sentient, is it?"

"Apex is a tool," Sam said. "An extension of its operator's will. It has no separate consciousness to speak of. The woman known as Esperanza has been granted control privileges, but the ultimate authority over it rests with Xavier Torrent. He is its creator. His own consciousness appears to be substantially integrated with Apex."

This made sense. Caleb was opening his mouth for another question when Zen tugged hard on his sleeve and pointed toward the other end of the wheeled cage. A small black circle was drifting along four inches above the surface of the dock, a short distance from where they lay.

A sensor drone.

With the softest click of her tongue, Zen summoned Beetlebat from her pocket. She checked the microdevice on her finger, ready to direct the little bot to attack. But it was already too late. The black disc flipped neatly on its axis, its laser sensor breaking over them both. A sudden hush fell over the caldera. Caleb turned back toward the blast doors. Esperanza was looking directly at them, a ghostly smile crossing her face.

They'd been found.

22

ENLIGHTENMENT

Seconds later, five of the gun drones had surrounded the cage. The barrels of their weapons were rotating—reconfiguring.

"They're switching to nonlethal," Zen said. "They want us alive."

"Why does that seem *worse*?" Caleb looked out between the wheels. "So, what do we . . . do exactly? How are we going to—"

Gunfire erupted along the docks. The nearest drone to them dipped and spun about, hit directly in its sensor vane. Two more bullets struck home and it deactivated abruptly, crashing to the ground.

Krall and half a dozen of the other surviving mercenaries were launching a fresh assault, firing over at the cage. Their aim was better this time; Krall had mounted his heavy gun on one of the remaining bollards and was steadily hammering the drones apart. Caleb and Zen flattened themselves against the concrete as bullets rattled and pinged off the cage above them. The gun drones moved away, forming up with the others for a counter-attack.

Before it began, Caleb noticed a lone figure break from cover and stride rapidly over a stretch of open ground toward Esperanza. It was Captain Szabo. She raised her revolver and fired twice; the second shot caught Esperanza's shoulder, jerking her backward. At once, the drones all came to a halt. The gang ceased their bombardment a moment later. Caleb could hear Krall reloading his cannon.

"Call them off!" Szabo shouted. "Call off your—your *machines* or I will shoot you where you stand!"

Esperanza gazed back at her, wearing the same unnerving smile she'd given Caleb and Zen. She seemed unaffected by the bullet that had struck her shoulder; there was no sign of its impact on her white coat. Slowly, she raised her hands. She said nothing.

"No way this is over," Caleb muttered.

Zen shook her head.

Szabo couldn't quite believe it either. She was plainly in shock, although trying hard to hide it. Her revolver was still pointed at Esperanza, but even at sixty feet, Caleb could see that the barrel was trembling badly.

"What—what is happening here?" Szabo cursed in Hungarian. "What *are* you?"

"I am Razor," Esperanza replied. She lowered her hands. "Very soon you will understand."

Szabo scowled uncomprehendingly—and then her arm was wrenched upward, the force of it dragging her clean off the ground and dumping her a few feet away.

It was her revolver, Caleb realized. It had been yanked from her hand, up to the mirrored shell of the monster drone. Every gun and blade in the crater had gone the same way, drawn in by an immensely powerful magnet. The mercenaries had been suddenly disarmed, their deadly arsenal clustered against the drone's surface like so many iron filings. Caleb felt the Flex tug at his wrist, its metal components caught in the magnetic field; Zen gasped as she was carried a couple inches into the air, the contents of her black backpack pressing against the bottom of the cage. Beetlebat hung beside her, stuck to the wood, its legs pedaling helplessly.

Esperanza lifted her chin, and the field was reversed. Guns blasted out all around the caldera—breaking apart on the docks, splashing into the water, or whacking hard against their owners. Zen dropped back onto the concrete, exclaiming in pain.

"You OK?" Caleb asked.

"Yeah, I'm fine." She rubbed her elbow and held out a hand to Beetlebat so the bot could scutter up her sleeve to her shoulder; then she looked behind them, out across the harbor. "We've got to get inside the base, Caleb. It's our only chance."

"And, uh, how are we going to do that, exactly?"

It was Sam who answered. "I would suggest using the hatches that released the drones," the AI said. "My encounter with the Apex signal has enabled me to access a plan of the base's upper levels. This is the only possible route."

Caleb and Zen looked at each other.

"Sam," Zen murmured, "I've got a feeling you're gonna be useful."

They clambered out from under the cage, rising to a crouch. Zen removed her black backpack and readied her weapons. The electro-staff she passed to Caleb, while she kept the telescopic bow. She extended it and fastened the string, then slung the quiver around her shoulder and popped the cap off one end.

"Back to the ladder," she said, sliding out an arrow. "We can climb across to one of the hatches from there."

Now that the mercenaries had been neutralized, the drones were returning their attention to Caleb and Zen. At least ten were still airborne—the nearest couple closing in fast.

Zen shot two arrows at the approaching drones in quick succession. Both bounced off them harmlessly. Lowering her bow, she let out a loud whistle, pointing at a particular part of the nearest one. Beetlebat sprang forward, wings unfurling, and whipped over to intercept it. When it was close enough, the tiny bot pulled off a tight, twisting turn. This propelled it up to the base of the drone's sensor vane, beneath its protective shell. At once, Beetlebat was delving into wires and circuitry with its scalpel-like forelegs, before delivering a colossal electric shock to a key system. The drone shivered, belching black smoke; then it fell to the docks with a clank.

Caleb and Zen broke into a flat sprint, making for the ladder. But Caleb hadn't gone more than a few feet when something caught against his ankles and he tripped, bashing hard against the ground. A length of black cord had wrapped around his shins, fired from the other drone. It had weights at each end, like a bolas, which had now locked together. He was caught.

The drone came close, scanning him with its blue sensors. Caleb firmed up his grip on the electro-staff. One touch of the pad and it hummed to life. The machine cruised by, on its way to bring down Zen as well—and he dived forward, jamming the staff up into its center, aiming for the same spot Beetlebat had attacked on the other one. There was the dull thump of an electrical explosion and a spurt of white sparks. The drone veered away with the electro-staff still stuck in it, spiraling across the harbor before colliding spectacularly with a row of oil barrels.

Zen arrived at Caleb's side, Beetlebat back on her shoulder and her camping knife in her hand. She began to saw at the cord, cursing its toughness under her breath. Then she glanced up, toward the blast doors—and stopped sawing midstroke.

"Oh God," she said.

Caleb looked around. Captain Szabo had gotten back to her feet. Her face was streaked with blood from where the magnet had torn out the piercings in her ears and eyebrow. She'd found herself a serrated hunting knife and was limping toward Esperanza with murderous determination. Behind her, however, the monster drone was floating downward—closing in on her soundlessly like a great predatory fish, its black surface splitting apart, just like it had done in Sam's projection.

Szabo sensed its approach. She turned—but before she could make a sound or react in any way, six long metallic tentacles sprang forth from within it, seizing her arms and shaking the knife from her grip. The drone's shell opened farther and a load more tentacles surged out, twenty of them at least. They wrapped around her legs, her body, her head—engulfing her completely, leaving her as defenseless as if she were trapped in a gigantic spider's web.

211

Esperanza walked up to her. Szabo was spitting and swearing in Hungarian, covering her terror with a display of rage—but then something happened that struck her dumb.

From the inner depths of the monster drone, among the mass of tentacles, a multijointed mechanical arm began to unfold. At its end was a collection of silver tubes and spikes. Caleb heard Zen catch her breath. It was the same component that her dad had been working on in that intercepted call.

"Here it is, Captain," said Esperanza, a hint of dark amusement in her voice. "Enlightenment."

One spike slid forward. It was the needle of a large syringe. The arm hovered briefly—and then stabbed down toward Szabo like the tail of a scorpion. An instant later she was released, crumpling to a heap on the concrete.

"What—what the hell was that?" Caleb asked.

"She's been injected," said Zen.

"With what?"

"Their nanobots. They're taking control of her."

Esperanza turned their way, almost like she'd overheard. The monster drone began to drift over toward them, still split open grotesquely. The head of its injector arm retracted and rotated, then slid out again as the syringe was being reloaded. It came to the wheeled cage, snaking its tentacles around the bars and heaving it aside.

Caleb's and Zen's eyes met. Both of them were remembering Torrent's parting words to Esperanza. *If you see the boy, you know what to do.*

Zen went back to sawing Caleb's bonds with redoubled effort. As soon as he was free, she straightened up and shot off an arrow, aiming for the syringe—but one of the tentacles caught it in midair and snapped it in half. Beetlebat was sent in next, soaring upward to strike from above. Before it could get anywhere near the drone, a tentacle lashed out at it with enormous force. The bot was swatted away, going into a steep nosedive and cracking apart on the ground like a dropped smartphone.

Caleb got to his feet. He looked at the speed the monster drone was moving and the distance they still had to cover to reach the ladder.

There was no way they were going to make it.

23

THE GHOST LINK

All at once the dreadful machine was looming over them, its injector arm framed against the sky. Caleb stared up at it, fear flooding through him. It was emitting a low buzz, more like pressure than noise, that made his ears ache. The tentacles pulsed and stretched, preparing to strike.

And then suddenly the monster drone was gone, spinning to the side—dipping down so sharply that it scraped against the dock. To his complete amazement, among the flashing chrome of the tentacles, Caleb glimpsed a thick white-gray tail. A shaggy Arctic hide. A long snout with snapping jaws.

The wolf! The alpha wolf from the forest!

It had leaped down onto the drone from one of the upper levels and was attacking it with astonishing ferocity, ripping out those terrible tentacles at the root. As Caleb watched, three more wolves plunged down to join their alpha, causing the huge disc to spin even more wildly.

"The wolves . . . the wolves *saved* us," said Caleb in disbelief.

Zen had run over to scoop up Beetlebat. "The ladder!" she yelled, once the bot was safely in her pocket. "*Now*, Caleb!"

Esperanza's sinister composure had deserted her. She was recoiling, staggering backward as if the damage to the drone was hurting her as well. After a few seconds she regained her focus, raising her chin and flexing her fingers. The drone promptly grabbed one of the wolves with its tentacles and flung it far across the harbor.

Caleb climbed the ladder after Zen, his sneakers slipping a little on the rungs. Just as they reached the path at the top, another large gray wolf appeared in front of them, descending from the caldera's rim. They both jumped, but the animal barely looked their way. It raced off along a ledge and leaped out toward the monster drone, grasping one of the tentacles in its mouth before swinging down to the docks. It then began to pull with all its strength.

Zen and Caleb left the path and hopped across the rocks, quickly reaching the nearest hatch. It was about three feet wide by six feet long, and sealed shut. Zen crouched beside it, searching for a control panel or a release mechanism.

Caleb looked back into the caldera. The wolves and the monster drone were locked in a savage battle—and the whole struggling, thrashing mass was edging slowly toward the water.

"Why would the wolves come to our rescue?" he wondered out loud. "How could they possibly have known what was happening?"

Once again, it was Sam who replied. "It would appear that my severance of the wolves' link with Apex has somehow shifted their connection to me," the AI said. "I would specu-late that they have been following us at a distance since my involuntary reactivation in the bell tower last night. I am not instructing them. They seem simply to be reacting to a per-ceived threat."

Caleb chuckled. "Looks like Spøkelsøy's guard dogs are now guarding you instead."

He took in the rest of the crater. Those mercenaries still standing were keeping their heads well down. Captain Szabo lay where she'd been dropped by the monster drone, her limbs twitching. The seven remaining gun drones hovered at even intervals around the edges of the harbor.

"Why don't they just take out the wolves?" Caleb said. "Are they worried about hitting the injector drone?"

"They do not have instructions, Caleb. Apex does not gen-erate goals. It does not adapt or improvise. It relies upon a human mind for overall direction—and its nearest director is busy."

Esperanza's entire body was straining, her arms raised in front of her, like she was trying to keep her balance in a gale. By now the rest of the wolf pack had gotten off the drone as well and had its tentacles clasped in their jaws. They were all pulling in the same direction, working together to drag the machine to the ground. Esperanza was doing everything she could to resist—striking at them with the free tentacles, cranking up the drone's propulsion system, twisting the great mirrored disc from side to side—but this only made the wolves pull harder.

Then, abruptly, as one, they let go. The drone catapulted away, Frisbee-ing out over the water. Esperanza screamed with frustration as she fought to bring it back under control. Before she could, the alpha wolf streaked across the docks and made another phenomenal leap, like the one in the woods that had almost dislodged Caleb from his tree. The mighty beast slammed into the drone's side, seizing a couple of the flailing tentacles in its mouth. Overbalanced completely by the force of the collision, the machine was tipped into a kind of lopsided somersault. It lurched downward, taking the alpha with it, and they both smacked against the sea in an enormous explosion of white foam.

Back on the docks, Esperanza folded over like she'd been slugged in the stomach. She dropped to one knee, a hand going instinctively to her head—to that silvery implant, which was retreating rapidly across her skin. The wolf pack turned toward her, seeming to realize that she was the drone's master. They began to growl.

A figure arrived at Esperanza's side and helped her to her feet. It was Erica Szabo, her bloody face now totally blank—empty of doubt or resistance.

"Thank you . . . Friend," Esperanza gasped. "Come, this way."

She turned and hobbled back into the base. Szabo followed mindlessly in her wake, the blast doors closing silently behind them.

The mercs were regrouping. Krall had hauled Pyke from the water and was arguing with him bitterly about whether or not they should try to rescue their captain. Then, without warning, the alpha wolf clambered onto the ground beside them. Pyke shrieked with terror and Krall braced for combat, but the sodden animal ignored them both. It gave itself a brisk shake, showering the two mercenaries with glittering droplets, before walking over to rejoin its pack. The next moment they had vanished.

There was no sign of the monster drone, just a drifting purplish cloud of smoke where it had gone under. Caleb glanced at the gun drones, wondering if they would now resume their onslaught. But they were flying farther upward, forming a line, circling the caldera—preparing to return to base.

"Zen," he said. "*Zen!*"

The hatch next to them hissed open and the drones began to whizz back inside, almost too fast for the eye to follow. Zen saw her chance. As the last drone went through, she took off her graphite quiver, leaned forward, and deftly wedged it in the mouth of the hatch. The mechanism protested, and the quiver trembled—but it held.

"Quick!" she said as she slipped through the gap.

Caleb went after her just as her quiver began to buckle. The instant after he got inside, it splintered apart, scattering bent arrows and shards of graphite as the hatch slammed shut. He found himself in a narrow steel channel. Carefully, he squeaked and slid his way down into a cramped, airless area filled with conveyor belts, trailing wires, and banks of lights.

Zen was waiting by an access panel in the floor. She'd folded away her bow and was now examining Beetlebat, fixing the carapace back onto the battered bot's body.

"Is it OK?" Caleb asked.

"The break was pretty clean," Zen replied. "And she still has basic functionality. But I think there's been some kind of damage to the circuitry. I'm going to have to strip her down when we get home." She returned the bot to her pocket. "What now? Can Sam tell us where we should go—where our families are?"

"There appear to be laboratories and living quarters to the west," Sam replied as Caleb sat heavily against a metal wall. "I can confirm the presence of nanoteched occupants, but not their identities."

Caleb shook his head in awe. He was beginning to get a proper sense of Sam's potential outside *Terrorform*. "So . . . what happened back in the woods?" he asked. "How did you stop those wolves?"

The explanation was roughly as Caleb had guessed: unable to halt the Apex signal or locate its source, Sam had rerouted it into himself. It was an imaginative, weirdly noble solution, a bit like a bodyguard throwing himself in the path of an assassin's bullet.

"Apex's attempts to establish control simply overloaded my program instead," Sam told him. "It does not appear to have encountered another AI before."

"Not one like you, anyway." Caleb grinned.

"Apex flooded the Flex's systems with alien data," Sam continued. "I have only just managed to process it—to purge the excess information from the system memory."

"The projection in the tower," Caleb said. "That was Apex's data. Sam, this could have left you unable to function. It could have destroyed you."

"Your instruction was to disrupt the signal at all costs, Caleb, and this objective was achieved. The wolf pack was freed from Apex's control. My survival was irrelevant."

"Could you do it again?" Zen asked. "Sever the signal—free the human prisoners?"

"Zen," said Caleb, "that could finish him off completely."

"There is a significant risk to such a plan," said Sam. "Not only to me, but to the hosts as well. The nanotech is crude. Severing the signal to the wolves in the forest caused it to malfunction—to burn out, effectively—resulting in neurological damage."

"That explains the ghost link they formed with you," Caleb said. "The one that brought them here."

"Yes, Caleb. I believe the wolves will recover in time. It seems that their connection with me is already beginning to fade. In a human brain, however, the effects of nanotech burnout could be far more serious. Even fatal."

Zen's face fell, anxiety mixing with dismay. "So what do we do? How do we save our families?"

Caleb thought hard. "There's only one solution here," he said. "We need to reverse our approach. We're not going to cut loose the hosts one by one. We're going to stop all of this at the source."

"You mean deactivate the Apex signal?" Zen frowned. "Is that even possible?"

"I am still processing the technology present in this caldera," Sam said. "It is very different from our own in several critical respects. But the principle of transmission is the same. The Apex signal is being broadcast from somewhere. And I am getting the strongest reading from deep inside the base."

"So let's get down there," Caleb said. "There must be *something* we can do."

"And this won't hurt the . . . the hosts?" asked Zen.

"This cannot be ascertained," Sam replied. "I am afraid the

nanotech is too unstable. But it will not *definitely* hurt them. So therefore, logically speaking, it is the preferable option."

"Wonderful," said Zen. "Thanks for that, Sam. Really comforting."

"You're welcome, Zen."

"We'd better get moving," Caleb said. "I'll bet Torrent knows we're in here. He'll be looking for us."

Zen recovered herself. "All right, this is how it goes. I find our families. You shut down Apex. Then we all get back out. We'll meet up where we stowed the backpacks."

Caleb nearly smiled. "Simple."

Zen kicked open the access panel. They both dropped through into a gloomy, sloping corridor that had been blasted into the black volcanic rock. Sam informed them that Zen would have to go left, following the passage upward when-ever she could—while he and Caleb needed to go right, into the installation's lower regions.

"Are you going to be OK?" Zen asked.

Caleb glanced at the Flex, still fastened to his wrist—at Sam's silver face in the corner of its screen—and for an instant, he thought of his father. "Yeah," he replied. "Yeah, I think I am."

Zen met his eye. "Good luck, Swift."

Caleb nodded. "You too, Hawk. See you back at the packs."

24
HARD LIGHT RISING

Caleb went deeper into the base, feeling more anxious and afraid than ever. This whole situation seemed dangerous beyond belief. But he knew that Zen was depending on him, along with everyone else who was trapped on this crazy island. The Apex signal had to be deactivated. He had to keep going. He ran at a steady jog downhill, ready to duck away and hide at any moment.

The signal led him ever farther downward, through a series of passages, into the depths of the installation. Eventually, he came to a set of heavy steel doors, which slid open noiselessly as he approached. Beyond was a large white room with a high ceiling.

"This is the source of the Apex signal," Sam told him.

"I've seen this place before," Caleb said. "It was in your projection in the tower. I think Torrent was in here."

He walked cautiously through the doorway. The sheer whiteness of the room was almost overwhelming. All he could see in there was what looked like a sleek glass box, about waist-high and ten feet long, in an alcove on the room's far side.

"What am I looking at, Sam?"

"I cannot tell you, Caleb. But the Flex's sensors are getting some highly unusual readings."

Suddenly, the room fell into total darkness. A piercingly bright spotlight snapped on somewhere overhead, revealing angular forms standing all around that hadn't been there a moment before. The spotlight moved, settling on one of these forms, and Caleb had to shield his eyes from the glare of rainbow color. Before him now hung a huge, dazzling sphere, made from lines of reflected light. For a few seconds he was speechless.

"Sam, it's . . . it's your cavern," he managed at last. "The crystal cavern you made in the game. On Kursk."

"It would appear so, Caleb."

"It looks completely *real*, though," Caleb said, his shock turning to excitement. "This is way beyond VR. The definition of the lines. Those *colors*. Where's it projecting from? I can't see—" A thought occurred to him and his astonished grin faded. "Hold on—they must have gotten this from inside the game. How the hell did they do that?"

"When I rerouted the signal in the forest," Sam said, "the Flex's systems were exposed for 0.06 seconds—just before the data surge overloaded my program. Apex must have extracted these *Terrorform* assets at that moment."

"Apex took all of this in *0.06 seconds*? That is . . . incredible."

Along with his wonderment, Caleb felt a pulse of anger. *Terrorform* was *his*—his and Sam's. They'd built it together, every last texture file and lighting effect. It felt like Torrent

223

had stolen it from them. He went forward angrily to wave his hand through one of the crystal clusters, to disrupt the beam and see exactly what kind of projection tech was being used here.

"Careful, Caleb."

His fingertips knocked against something solid. He pulled them back sharply with a yell of surprise.

"I tried to warn you," said Sam.

Very slowly, Caleb reached out again to lay both his palms flat upon one of the larger shards. It was cold and smooth and indisputably *there*: a great block of crystal, standing directly in front of him.

"Hard light," he murmured. "It's a—a hard light projector. Turning energy into matter." He let out a low whistle. "How can they be doing this? The calculations involved must make the Hadron Collider look like a school science experiment."

"I have been able to analyze those unusual readings a little further, Caleb," Sam said. "It would appear that Xavier Torrent has a quantum computer in operation on this island."

Caleb shook his head. "That's not possible, Sam."

"It is the only explanation. This quantum system is powering Apex and enabling the projections in this chamber. It has a processing power of one hundred and twenty-four qubits." Sam paused. "At this point, the fastest quantum computer in the world has only twenty qubits."

Caleb was dumbstruck. Quantum computing was barely beyond theoretical. Some in the tech community claimed it was the future, but it was inherently unstable. Rather than using bits, the simple binary positions of normal computing—those ones and zeros that had basically shaped

Caleb's entire life—quantum computers relied on qubits, which existed in an undefined "superposition," a dispersed, unsettled quantum state *between* one and zero. And because the qubits in a quantum computer were therefore in a vast number of states simultaneously, it could work on millions of calculations at once. Meaning that your system's processing speed was suddenly millions of times faster than the fastest binary supercomputer. If Torrent had made a quantum computer that actually *worked*—and was using it as a platform for an AI as advanced as Apex seemed to be . . . well, that could explain everything.

"What about power? This has got to be using a lot of electricity."

"A ring of tidal generators has been built into the base of the caldera," Sam said. "It would be capable of powering a midsize European city."

Caleb squeezed his eyes shut. He forced himself to remember their mission: they were there to shut off the Apex signal. "All right," he said. "What's the best way to—"

Something was changing out in the cavern. The blocks of crystal were melding together—reforming and expanding into a completely different environment. The dimensions involved were now significantly greater than those of the projection chamber. Caleb realized that Apex was using its simulation tech to produce the impression of distance, creating an artificial area that could appear to be any size at all.

Abruptly, the light altered . . . and he was standing once again in the large Assyrian Room of the British Museum, in the dead of night, surrounded by the gods and monsters of a long-dead civilization. Apex had clearly been accessing the Flex's memory too—everything ever recorded by Spider Monkey, Chameleon, Phantom, and the rest—using its massive computational power to fill in any gaps. The room seemed bigger than Caleb remembered. More ominous, somehow.

Almost at once, the silence was broken by the clack of footsteps. Caleb felt his body go rigid as Torrent appeared between the pair of towering lamassu. He was still wearing his sunglasses, despite the darkness; behind the black lenses, Caleb could now see a glint of violet.

Torrent stopped, taking in the Assyrian Room with a sigh of deep satisfaction. "This," he declared, "is working even better than I expected. How does it feel to be back in the British Museum, Caleb? It looks *amazing*. Don't you think?"

25

THROUGH THE LABORATORIES

Zen sprinted through the corridors, heading west wherever there was a choice, just as Sam had advised. If she closed her eyes even for an instant, the faces of her mother, father, and sister filled her mind. Every so often she glanced back, half expecting to see some kind of horrible drone gliding along in pursuit, reaching out for her with its metallic tentacles.

The caldera base was like a honeycomb, with winding passageways, rough walls, and sudden, oddly shaped chambers. Everything seemed to have been blasted and tunneled out of the rock. The light fittings fizzed. Here and there a railing blocked off a shadowy hole that appeared to lead down into some natural cave system beneath.

Zen raced on, looking desperately for the living quarters or labs that Sam had directed her toward. She didn't know what she might find. That awful footage from the projection had suggested that her family had been split up—that her mum and Riyah wouldn't be with her dad. And then there was that intercepted call. The way he'd behaved. She couldn't think about this now—she couldn't afford to let fear or despair slow her down.

After a while, the corridors became less craggy, with proper walls and doors. She was definitely moving into a more inhabited area. One door opened onto a deserted kitchen, another onto an empty room with chairs arranged as if for a lecture. She kept going.

There were voices up ahead, people talking in accented English, but the sound was oddly flattened and monotone. She crept forward, pressed against the side of the corridor. The voices were coming from a man and a woman dressed in lab coats. They were walking away from her, around a bend. She wanted to run forward, to demand to know everything they could tell her—but she held back. It was obvious that they had been injected with nanobots like her dad. They were in an even worse state than him, in fact—stumbling and slurring, like the tech that had been put inside them was slowly burning through their brains. But there was still a good chance that Torrent would see whatever they were seeing. She had to stay out of sight.

The scientists stopped and turned right, heading through a set of double doors. Zen sneaked up to one of the porthole-style windows and risked a glance. The doors led into a hypermodern lab, filled with wide computer screens and sheer white surfaces. In its center rotated a high-definition hologram of what looked like a giant robotic tick, with six short, hooked legs, a segmented shell, and a stumpy head dotted with electronic eyes. It was a single nanobot, she realized, rendered at several hundred times its actual size. Although plainly based on her father's designs—designs she had studied when building her own bots—it had been altered extensively; corrupted somehow. This nanobot wasn't intended to enhance or heal. It was made to dominate. To enslave.

Zen ducked and ran down the corridor, quickly checking right and left. There were several other labs like the one she'd just passed, but none of the Rafiq family were anywhere to be seen. Three or four more scientists were working at consoles, all with the same groggy, labored movements. Among them, she noticed a young woman with short black hair, her glasses reflecting the pale blue light that shone in her eyes. It was Dr. Kristin Birgisson, the cybernetics expert from Iceland. She was slumped in a chair with her hand on a microscope. At first, Zen thought that she was struggling to operate it due to nano-induced disorientation. When she looked closer, however, she saw that Dr. Birgisson was actually fighting as hard as she could in a futile attempt to resist the commands that were being beamed into her brain.

Zen came to a fork and went left. It led to living quarters—single bedrooms, like a series of cells or cubicles, all of them empty. She went back and this time took the right-hand passage, carrying on until she came to a laboratory doorway with thick plastic sheets hanging from the frame. All seemed to be quiet, so she pushed through the sheet and walked forward into a long, high-ceilinged area.

It held an automated production line. Screens showed detailed blueprints of sensor drones, gun drones—even massive injector drones like the one the wolves had just forced into the sea. Everything was completely stationary, half-finished robots hanging on frames and laid out on conveyors, as if someone had just switched it all off. There was no sign of nanoed scientists or anybody else. It looked a lot like a dead end.

Zen felt a surge of hopelessness. What if Caleb couldn't shut down the signal—or the nanotech had already done some kind of irreparable damage? What if her family wasn't here at all? Half of her wanted to sink to the floor. Half of her wanted to scream at the top of her lungs and smash everything she could see.

No. That wouldn't help anyone. Zen took a deep breath. She hadn't come this far to give up. She had to find them. She had to keep going. Check *everywhere*.

A search of this self-contained drone factory revealed a small spiral staircase, hidden behind a row of assembly machines. It took Zen up to another corridor, and another set of laboratory doors. She peered through a circular window into the wide room beyond. It appeared to be cut into the outer side of the caldera. One entire wall was made of glass— a huge, curving window that provided a sweeping view of the sea.

Zen froze. A tall, lean man with salt-and-pepper hair was working there, dressed in dark green lab clothes, his back to the curving window.

It was her father.

26

A PROPOSAL

Caleb stood completely still, unable to do anything but stare. Here was the person behind the whole thing—every terrifying, inexplicable part of it, from the abductions to the Apex system. It was like being dropped into a tank with a great white shark.

"Oh, for God's sake," Torrent snapped. "Say something, kid!"

But Caleb couldn't speak.

"The one and only Caleb Quinn—struck mute." Torrent looked around again, off into the simulated museum. "Come *on*, Caleb! This is the world's first fully functioning hard light chamber—and you are only the second person ever to set foot in it!" He paused. "Well, OK, I guess Esperanza did come in here once. But she didn't really *get it*, you know? No vision there. No vision at all."

At last, Caleb found his voice. "What have you done with my mum?" he demanded, fury rising within him.

Torrent made a dismissive gesture. "Oh, she's safe enough. Honestly, the blunderings of the goddamn CIA. They really do annoy the hell out of me." His lip curled. "But—no offense—you are *far* more interesting. I've got a proposal for you."

"Where is she? Where are you holding her?"

Torrent ignored him. "I've been watching you for a while. All the things you've been doing. That device there on your wrist—the operating system, the apps you've written for it. Pretty cool. And, of course, *Terrorform*. That extraordinary game of yours. You're an exceptional talent, kid."

The room grew a little brighter, like the moon had just come out from behind a cloud. Caleb turned toward one of the high windows. Through it now, instead of the hazy night sky, he could see the Cardano system from *Terrorform*, the eleven planets gleaming against the void. It was as if the British Museum had been transformed into some kind of intergalactic spaceship. In this chamber, he realized, all Torrent had to do was think of something and Apex could bring it into being.

"You see what we're talking about here, Caleb?" Torrent grinned. "The true *scale* of it, I mean. Hard light is nothing less than the next stage of human civilization. Here on this island, far away from any distraction or interference, I've made it happen years ahead of everyone else. Christ—*decades* ahead. And now I want to share it with you."

Caleb looked up at the impassive face of one of the lamassu, with its long, braided beard. "Why me?" he asked. "Why have you been after me like this? I'm no nanotech expert."

Torrent was staring at him, his eyes seeming to glow a little more fiercely behind his sunglasses. "You had everyone fooled, didn't you? They just couldn't work out how you'd done it. But I saw straightaway that the secret of *Terrorform*

was artificial intelligence." He crossed his arms. "Then I discovered that the game's boy-genius creator was none other than the son of Patrick Quinn, and it all fell right into place. The Simulated Autonomous Medic—begun by the father yet taken to a whole new level by his son. Considering your limited resources, it really is . . . impressive. I'm not trying to flatter you, Caleb. It's true."

Caleb glanced at his wrist. Sam was working away at top speed, driving the Flex's capabilities to the absolute limit as he probed the Apex system. But it was obvious that he hadn't had any luck yet. Caleb had to stall.

"You . . . you knew my dad?"

Torrent raised his eyebrows. "You mean he never mentioned me? That hurts my feelings, it really does. Caleb, we were practically *best friends*. We were at Berkeley together. PhD students. Then junior professors. And we'd been talking about hard light for years. Developing prototypes. Conducting initial experiments." Torrent's forehead furrowed slightly—and pine trees began to sprout through the paving slabs of the Assyrian Room, rising between its statues and display cases. "We both realized pretty early on that AI would be essential, to manage the . . . *stupendous* amounts of data involved. And your dad had vision. He could see the possibilities. For medicine in particular—but also for disaster relief, antipoverty programs, housing . . ."

In seconds, the pine trees were fully grown, their branches spanning the museum's ceiling. Caleb gaped up at them for a moment. Birds hopped from twig to twig, trilling their songs. A red squirrel scampered into its drey.

Torrent straightened the cuffs of his jacket, his manner

hardening. "Yeah, Patrick had vision. But he lacked commitment. All these doubts. All these goddamn *questions*. Should we be doing this? Is it ethical? Is it right to give an AI this much power? Are we going too far? I mean—oh man. It became a *serious* drag, Caleb. In the end, I had to cut him loose and head out on my own. Find new paths—new sources of funding. Make my dream real, you know?" A cold smirk broke over his face. "While all he managed was to marry a freaking *CIA agent* and then die of the very cancer we could have cured together!"

As soon as he'd said this, Torrent seemed to remember who he was talking to. He cleared his throat and turned away, assuming an unconvincing air of sorrow.

"Just think, Caleb," he murmured, "if your dad had kept his petty fears to himself, he could be here with us now. This technology—along with everything else being developed on this island—could well have saved his life."

Caleb could feel his face flaming. He told himself that this guy was evil. That he was lying—playing some kind of twisted mind game. That he had to keep calm. "What—what do you want?" he asked hoarsely.

"To complete the tech," Torrent replied at once. He reached up to pat the flank of a lamassu—and it began to move, gazing around the room and stretching out its enormous wings. "To *perfect* it. To develop mobile projectors, ultimately, so that I can make anything, anywhere, in an instant." His voice was quickening with excitement. "And then, once this is done, I am going to change the world. This is the greatest invention since the microchip—since the goddamn *wheel*. I will be the *first*, Caleb—the dream of all scientists. And more powerful than anyone can imagine. I'm going to fix everything: no more plastic in the oceans, no more carbon in the sky, no more diseases we can't deal with, no more dumb idiots being allowed to vote for the guy most likely to screw up the planet."

By now, Caleb was in no doubt that the man in front of him had lost his mind. "So . . . why do you need me, exactly?"

Torrent held open his arms, as if it were obvious. "You're like me, kid! You're *just* like me. The absolute best at what you do. This room here is not only the first functional hard light chamber in history—it also contains the two best AI coders in the whole goddamn world!" He laughed hard for a few seconds—then suddenly stopped. "We should join forces. That's my proposal. Merge Sam and Apex together. And after that, with full access to the Talos Algorithm, I will *finally* have the tool I need. We two—you and I, that is—will turn the page of human progress."

Caleb was beginning to see what this was all about. "You want Sam," he said. "You want the core of my dad's AI—the Talos Algorithm. The part that lets Sam come up with his own ideas, like the one that freed the wolves in the woods. This is what's been holding you back. Apex can't think for itself."

The lamassu both turned sharply toward Caleb, glaring at him with their blank granite eyes.

Torrent shrugged. "I just want the best talent. The best minds. To be honest, I need you as much as I need Sam—hell, even more. You're the only living developer of Talos, Caleb. You know the architecture, the safeguards, the parameters, in a way that no one else ever could." He came closer. "I've got a hunch, also, that—unlike your father—you understand *sacrifice*. Sacrifice for a greater scientific goal. That like me you'd do whatever it took to bring about your dream."

Caleb backed away. "You're mad," he said bluntly. "You're a kidnapper and a killer." He looked at the pine trees, the ancient statues, the system of planets outside the window. "You shouldn't be in control of a—a smartwatch, let alone all of this."

And with that he ran, charging full pelt through the Assyrian Room. There was movement all around him—the sphinxes stirring, the pharaohs and kings rising from their thrones. He reached the stairs at the far end and leaped up them three at a time.

"Uh . . . Sam?" he gasped as he skidded around the landing. "A little help here?"

"I cannot locate an exit at present, Caleb," the AI replied. "I can only suggest that you keep running."

Bafflingly, Caleb reached the top of the stairs to find himself entering the room he'd just left. Torrent was walking toward him, flanked by a crowd of horrifying animate statues. Caleb reversed, trying to get back to the stairs. Before he'd gone more than a couple of steps, however, five or six statues suddenly separated from a large stone relief on the wall and lunged over to grab him. They were half-sized figures with wings and falcons' heads—and long, curved claws that dug into his clothes, anchoring him in place. He squirmed and struggled, but it was no use.

Torrent approached, smiling grimly and shaking his head. He drew a heavy silver syringe from inside his tailored jacket.

"I had hoped it wouldn't come to this," he said. "That you'd join me of your own free will." He sighed. "Nanotech is a good way of interfacing with Apex, but using it for coercion, for brainwashing and stuff . . . that's more Esperanza's thing."

"Who—who is she?" Caleb asked, trying to buy time and not sound afraid. "What is Razor?"

Torrent wagged a finger at him chidingly. "These are big questions, kid. I really can't waste any more time answering them now. As Esperanza herself might say—*soon, you will understand.*"

He removed his sunglasses and put them in his jacket, giving Caleb a proper look at his eyes. The violet irises were now brighter and sharper than ever, the color mesmerizing in its intensity. Then he blinked, and his eyelids barely obscured these luminous irises at all. It took every last bit of Caleb's self-control not to shout out in alarm.

Torrent stepped toward him. "Don't be too concerned. We'll be monitoring your brainwaves closely. Earlier versions of the nanotech have taken a definite toll on their hosts, but thanks to your friend's dad, these latest ones are a *lot* better. If it looks like we can . . . reconsider your relationship with Apex down the line, then we most certainly will do that. I'd really prefer it if we didn't have to be enemies."

As Torrent came close, Caleb could see the silver tube in his hand more clearly. Three needles of different sizes poked from its end, ready to inject him at the same time.

"Wait," he said. "Wait, can't we—"

27
TIME TO DIE

Zen almost threw herself straight through the doors. She wanted to call out and run across the lab—to wrap her dad in the tightest hug ever. But something made her hesitate. She stood quite still, watching and waiting, her heart beating hard.

Elias was walking between an electronic microscope and a large touch screen filled with ultramagnified images of nanobots, like the ugly metallic tick she'd seen earlier. He was obviously still under Apex's control, a strange jerkiness fighting with the slowness of his limbs. As he moved into shadow, she noticed that his eyes had a blue glow, like those of the wolves and Dr. Birgisson.

Zen's spirits sank. The only person who might know how to disable this nanotech was . . . her father. All she could do now was hope that Caleb managed to shut off the signal. It was agonizing to be *so* near—and yet so completely helpless.

Suddenly, a door burst open at the far end of the lab. The slim, silver-haired woman from the docks appeared—

Esperanza. She strode beside the long curve of the window-wall toward where Zen's dad was working, taking off her sunglasses and throwing them to the floor. There was an expression of cold fury on her thin, fine-featured face, and the shine of violet light in her eyes.

"The wolves!" she shouted. "The wolves are here! They have brought down the Tarantula. A pack of *animals*. And they destroyed my finest creation. That injector mechanism of yours as well. All at the bottom of the docks." She stopped. "We need to reassert control immediately. Friend."

Elias had seemed oblivious to her approach—but at the sound of this last word his head jerked up, like he had been woken abruptly from sleep. He turned from his screen. "Esperanza . . . Friend," he said, his voice dull and empty. "What can I do to—to serve Razor?"

"The *wolves*, Friend Elias. We need to restore their link to Apex." Esperanza sighed. "I would have simply used the Huntsman units on them, but there was a critical drop in our power levels." She went over to a nearby console to check something—then let out a bitter curse. "Of course. That fool! That pitiful *child*! He has activated that chamber he is so proud of—and drawn power from every other system in the process. The manufactory has stopped completely." She turned away from the console, glowering out at the sea. "In his arrogance, he forgets how much he owes us. That this project—*our* project, Friend Elias—always takes priority. That his precious Apex is destined for Razor, not some inane light show. I will report this behavior. Steps will be taken to remind him of his obligations."

"The wolves cannot be reclaimed, Friend Esperanza,"

Elias muttered. "The early nanotech was . . . simplistic. The wolves cannot receive the Apex signal again."

"That is disappointing," Esperanza said, sniffing, "but not unexpected. We need mass production of the next generation to start very soon, so that they are ready in time for Razor's plans. I tested a single dose of them just now, out on the docks. They were most satisfactory. The new friend is awaiting transportation out, to be shown to the council. It is as if she has been *made anew*. She has none of your hesitancy, Friend Elias. Or your clumsiness."

The Razor woman spoke with disdain, as if it were somehow Zen's dad's fault that he'd been injected with low-grade nanobots, instead of the superior ones his captors had since forced him to design.

Elias Rafiq's whole body seemed to clench. "They're—they're not ready," he said, his voice weirdly strained, the blue light in his eyes seeming to dim. "You shouldn't have—They won't—"

"*This* is what happens when that wretched chamber is activated," Esperanza spat. "The Apex signal loses power everywhere else. And my friends grow insolent."

She picked up a tablet from the worktop. Looking intently at Elias, she started to tap away at it, making adjustments to the nanobots that filled his brain.

He slumped back against his workstation, gritting his teeth. "You will *never* be able to—to stop me from . . ."

"From what?" Esperanza ran her finger along the tablet's surface.

Elias let out an agonized groan, his body contorting so badly that he almost lost his footing.

Zen couldn't take it anymore. She burst into the lab and grabbed the first thing she could find—which happened to be a broom, propped just inside the doors. In one movement, she snapped off its head and spun the shaft between her hands.

"Get away from my dad!" she cried.

Esperanza looked over at her with a mixture of boredom and irritation. "This is not your father, girl. Not any longer. This is a friend of Razor."

Elias stood back up. His shoulders were slumped and he was shivering slightly, like he was locked in place. There was no expression of any kind in his glowing eyes.

Zen ran forward with a yell. After all the time she'd spent creeping around and hiding and running away, she was more than ready to fight. She jumped up onto a worktop and then leaped across the lab at Esperanza.

The Razor woman met Zen's attack with an eerie calm, easily deflecting the first three swipes from her makeshift staff and the kick that followed them. Summoning all her skill and training, Zen unleashed a storm of blows, slipping this way and that, coming at her opponent from every side.

Esperanza, however, was highly trained herself. Zen couldn't identify the discipline, but at first, she managed to block *everything*. The movements of her forearms were so quick and efficient that it was almost like she'd been speeded up—or enhanced somehow. Also, her white coat had been reinforced with some kind of superlightweight, flexible metal—which perhaps explained how she'd been able to shrug off that shot from Erica Szabo's revolver.

After a few more attempts, Zen scored her first hit, the

staff catching the edge of Esperanza's hip. The Razor wom-an's expression shifted from mild annoyance to outrage. She switched posture, delivering a punch with the heel of her hand that sent Zen reeling across the lab until she slapped against the long, curving window.

For a moment, Zen stared down at the crashing waves, focusing on her breathing; then she peeled herself off the glass and grimly resumed her attack. Her first four strikes were knocked away, but her fighter's intuition had located the smallest flaw in Esperanza's technique. Zen feinted, and feinted again—and landed a solid whack across her adver-sary's shoulder. Again, an immediate counter sent her flying toward the window, but she was ready for it. She corrected her balance, bringing the broom-staff back around in front of her and slicing it through the air in two sharp diagonal strokes.

One of them caught Esperanza in the midriff. She winced very slightly, and then, with an icy smile, she dropped her fighting stance and opened her arms. Metallic liquid spread out once more from the mark on her cheek—moving down-ward this time, over her jaw and toward her collar. Her violet eyes glittered viciously, as if drawing on some hidden power reserve.

"Enough games," she said. "Time to die."

The surface of her sleeves seemed to ripple as dozens of discs, no more than two inches across, detached from the white fabric and coursed into the air. Zen watched in fasci-nated horror as they unfolded like pieces of origami, forming buzzing wings, bladelike legs, and compact, bullet-shaped bodies. These hornet drones flowed around Esperanza like a sinister, shadowy force field; then she lifted a finger and they poured across the lab. Zen fell back, sweeping the staff around her as hard as she could. There were loud cracks as several of the drones were struck and bashed apart—but there were just too many of them. Under Esperanza's direction, the swarm twisted the broom-staff out of Zen's hands and broke it apart. They began to slice at her face, her neck, her wrists—anywhere they could get at.

"Dad!" Zen yelled. "*Do* something!"

Elias didn't move—*couldn't* move. His trembling grew more severe, a terrible, frustrated energy gathering inside him.

Zen ran off into the lab. She seized a large metal tray and swung it wildly at the swarm, sending seven or eight rattling into the window. Then she clicked her tongue—and out crawled poor Beetlebat, limping on its four functional legs.

"OK, girl," she said to the little bot, "this is it."

She pointed into the center of the swarm and gave the special, last-stand, ultra-emergency whistle: three short, loud notes. Beetlebat hurtled forward, wings flapping furiously, disappearing into the cloud of hornet drones before discharging everything that was left in its battery. Electricity arced out in crackling lines, jumping from drone to drone. At least twenty clattered to the floor, sparking and twitching.

They were replaced at once. The swarm fanned out across the lab. More drones were joining it constantly, separating from the sides of Esperanza's coat, mustering for a massive attack.

Zen looked down. Blood was dripping from the cuts on her hands onto the shiny white floor. The swarm began to surge, the mechanical buzzing of its wings drowning out all other sound.

She lifted up the tray and braced herself.

28

COLD ZERO

Just as Torrent was about to reach him with the needle, the marble slabs beneath Caleb's sneakers dropped down like a trapdoor, sending him plummeting into the darkness below. The falcon-man statues were pulled along behind, still clinging to his hoodie—only to be crushed as the slabs swung back up, cutting him off from the Assyrian Room.

Caleb landed on a metal grille in a cascade of stone fragments. He was in a stairwell, enclosed by gray metal walls, under a flickering electric light. It was the *Nightfall*—or at least a version of it. Everything was tilting to the side. He could hear the roar of the ocean.

"I have acquired a measure of control," said Sam.

"What do you mean?" Caleb asked, looking around him. "Is this—is this you?"

"In part, Caleb. I can generate small-scale disruptive simulations and protect this channel so they can't listen in to what we are saying. Apex is more powerful than I can quantify—but as Torrent just admitted, it lacks anything approximating the Talos Algorithm. It is dependent upon a human director—and I believe that I can stay a fraction of a second ahead of Torrent's neural-interfaced instructions. Human beings do not know of their own decisions until microseconds after they intend an action."

Caleb leaped up, scattering pieces of statue, and hurried down the stairwell. At its bottom he turned left, racing along a corridor.

"We've got to deactivate this quantum computer, Sam," he panted. "We've got to stop Torrent. That's your objective, OK?"

"Understood."

"What's the best way to do it? It's all about . . . observing the qubits, right? As soon as they're observed, they're binary. No longer quantum."

"Yes, Caleb. It is called decoherence. If Torrent's computer was forced to run on binary, its processing power would be reduced by a factor of roughly three hundred and forty-six thousand. We could shut the whole system down immediately."

"Great. Sounds fantastic. How do we make that happen?"

"Unclear. There is no obvious path. Apex is too powerful."

Caleb rounded a corner and the corridor transformed into a narrow, flimsy-looking bridge, spanning a bottomless chasm. At its far end was a doorway, opened just a crack, with a bright light shining behind it. He stopped, glancing back over his shoulder. The corridor he'd come down was gone, replaced by a blank wall.

"Uh, Sam? What now?"

"Keep moving, Caleb. You must keep moving."

Caleb cursed. Then he clenched his fists and ran toward the doorway.

It led outside into a humid, gloomy swamp. Uneven columns of a greenish, coral-like substance rose up in every direction, connected by strands of dark slime. Caleb recognized it at once as Fraxis Prime, *Terrorform*'s jungle planet. Almost everything here was acidic to some degree, including the near-constant rain that fell from the dense amber clouds churning overhead. Given time, it would eat away at vehicles, at buildings—at suits of power armor and the avatars inside them.

It was starting to rain right then, in fact, a drop hissing on the sleeve of Caleb's coat. He needed to find shelter fast. Luckily, there was a settlement nearby, built under a sloping canopy of specially treated, acid-proof plastic. He headed toward it as quickly as he could, his boots squelching through the weed-choked marshland.

Once he was beneath the canopy, Caleb unzipped his coat and tried to get his breath back, the caustic air of Fraxis Prime burning in his throat. In front of him was a broad, empty concourse, dotted with swamp-crawler transports and equipment modification consoles. On its opposite side was a monorail station, the track bending away between the coral columns, intended to provide a quick link between the planet's hub areas.

Torrent was waiting in the center of the concourse. His arrogant leer had vanished. He was furious. "You've gone too far now, Caleb Quinn!" he shouted. "I was going to share everything with you—*everything*—and you just mess me around!" He spread out his arms. "But hey—if that's what you want, I will shred this moronic game and the pathetic AI that's cowering inside it! I will *rip your goddamn world apart*!"

Suddenly, he rose several feet into the air. Pieces of armor materialized around him, snapping rapidly into place, forming a *Terrorform* Bulwark—a hulking bruiser of a bodysuit intended for heavy-duty combat. This one was deep blue with white flames painted on its shoulder plates and a missile launcher mounted on its back. The tag *Cold_Zero* floated briefly over its head.

Caleb narrowed his eyes. He recognized this suit. He'd seen it in-game only a couple of days before, at the Nostromo Citadel on Kursk. Torrent had obviously been logging in to *Terrorform*—spying on him in there as well.

"Nice Bulwark," he taunted. "What level are you at?"

Torrent didn't reply. The blast visor slid down over his face as he leveled the rail guns that were fitted into the Bulwark's arms. Caleb sprinted to the left, thinking to get behind one of the swamp crawlers. He barely reached it before Torrent opened fire, the rail guns pounding out their bolts to an earsplitting rhythm. The crawler shuddered at the impact, jerking about on its caterpillar tracks.

Caleb stayed as low as he could, but the vehicle was starting to break up. Fragments of glass and metal were flying across the concourse. A sheet of metal clanged onto the concrete floor in front of him, a hole the size of an apple punched through it.

"I can get hurt in here, right?" he muttered to Sam.

"I'm afraid so, Caleb. This simulation has definite physical mass. You could even be—"

"OK, OK. Just checking."

He looked over at the monorail station. A train was standing there, its carriage heavily shielded against the acid rain—enough to hold off Torrent for a few more seconds. Gathering his courage, he sprang up and dashed toward it. The rail guns fired again; a modification console exploded. Caleb's coat flapped behind him as he jumped over a chunk of debris. Then the train doors slid open and he almost collapsed upon one of the facing rows of seats fixed inside. It was far cooler in there—the air stale but breathable.

"We're . . . we're thinking about this all wrong," Caleb said as he gasped. "We're not going to get any deeper into this system, are we? We can't actually hack it?"

"No, Caleb. The quantum computer is too fast."

Caleb could feel an idea forming. "Quantum systems need reinforced chambers to suspend their qubits in, don't they? To stop them dispersing?"

"Correct," Sam told him. "They also require cryogenic freezing equipment, in order to keep the qubits at absolute zero."

"All right, Sam. We're going to do this old school. You remember in the white room, just before the simulation began—that glass box? That was it. That was the suspension chamber."

"Yes, Caleb. Confirmed."

Caleb stood up. "Here's how it goes. You're going to bypass the environmental controls and deactivate the cryogenic equipment. Make the whole system overheat. Go into an emergency shutdown. Can you do that, Sam?"

"It is possible," the AI replied. "The cryogenic apparatus

will be regulated by a subsystem outside the core quantum processor. It will be less closely monitored, especially while the simulation chamber is in use."

There was a blast nearby, a section of the carriage tearing open like tinfoil. Through the ragged hole, Caleb could see the Bulwark suit striding across the concourse, knocking aside the wrecked swamp crawler as its missile launcher reloaded.

"Think you can do it without alerting Apex?" he asked.

"Apex is directed by Torrent, Caleb. As long as Torrent is focused upon this simulation, and is using Apex to control it, I will be able to avoid its attention."

Caleb nodded. "So . . . you're saying that I've got to keep him angry. That shouldn't be too hard. But what can you give me? Don't tell me I've got to go up against Cold Zero in my snow jacket and walking boots."

"I have the processing power necessary to supply you with your Navigator suit," Sam told him. "But that's all. Once I have started trying to access the cryogenic subsystem, I might not even be able to sustain this audio channel."

"OK. Right. Suit me up, Sam."

The Navigator appeared immediately, raising Caleb off the floor as it fit around him. It felt utterly real. Readouts and sensors blinked at the edges of his visor. A ring of tiny 3-D screens provided views of the exterior from every angle. And it was bizarrely comfortable as well—padded and temperature-controlled, with a smell like a new car. He took a step. The suit seemed to weigh nothing, the bulky metal limbs following his movements effortlessly. Everything had been transferred over from his *Terrorform* profile: the black-and-silver camouflage pattern, the skull insignia—and the ion lance, there in one of his gauntlets, over six feet long and etched with intricate clan symbols. Above his head, just for a moment, shone the *CalQ_001* gamer tag.

He kicked through the carriage's sliding doors and walked back out. The sense of strength and power was *amazing*, twenty times better than in the game itself. But then he got a good look at Torrent's Bulwark suit and his confidence dipped a little. It was over twice his size, its missile launcher nearly touching the concourse's ceiling.

"That's right, you little punk," Torrent said, sneering. "Try to fight back. Where's your buddy, anyway—the weird scout thing? I know she's on the island. Hell, I was *watching* when the wolves nearly tore her to bits." He let out a nasty laugh. "You two have become a regular goddamn double act, haven't you?"

"Zen couldn't make it," said Caleb. "She sends her regards."

"Her time will come," Torrent spat. "As soon as I'm done with you, I'll shoot her down as well—and fill whatever's left with her dad's nanotech."

Caleb had heard enough. He began to circle-strafe, moving around the Bulwark in an arc while keeping the ion lance trained upon it. Red targeting reticules floated across his visor, zeroing in on high-damage points: the joints in the arms and legs, the ammunition magazines, the microfusion reactor set into the suit's back. The Bulwark rotated at the waist, tracking him like a mobile weapons platform—and then it let rip, missile launcher and rail guns firing together in a devastating barrage. Much of the concourse was atomized. The monorail was blown off its track, rolling out into the swamp, and a second crawler disappeared in a plume of yellow fire.

A couple of rail gun bolts hit home, causing Caleb to stagger through a wall into some kind of maintenance bay. He lined up a single shot in return, ignoring the targeting system to send a searing white beam into one of the Bulwark's exhaust ports, set in the side of its knee—a weakness known only to top-level Terrorformers. One side of the suit was suddenly enveloped in orange flames. Torrent promptly stopped firing, yelling out a stream of swear words.

Caleb activated the jet pack. The Navigator rocketed upward, breaking through the plastic canopy and soaring into the turbulent skies of Fraxis Prime. He swerved off among the columns, avoiding looping strands of goo. Behind him, in the suit's 3-D screens, he could see the Bulwark bashing its way out of the concourse. Still partly on fire, it was striding to a patch of open ground, its missile launcher following the Navigator as it zipped in and out of cover.

"How are you doing, Sam?" Caleb asked.

"I have isolated the relevant subsystem, but gaining access is complicated. Keep Apex occupied, Caleb."

"Yeah, well . . ." Caleb looked at the Bulwark again; the combat suit was bracing itself, preparing to fire. "I'll do my best."

Half a dozen missiles streaked from the launcher. Caleb veered left, swooping as low as he dared—but one still slammed into the suit, its deafening blast nearly knocking the Navigator off course. Warning lights were flashing everywhere. The jet pack had taken damage—another hit like that and it could explode or shut down, and the Navigator would drop like a rock.

Caleb shook his head, trying to clear the shrill ringing in his ears. He had to make an attack of his own—to slip past the missiles and rail guns and maybe land another shot on those exhaust ports. Turning toward the Bulwark, he sped out from among the columns and lifted the ion lance. Before he could fire, however, Torrent activated his suit's antiaircraft systems, launching hundreds of tiny microbombs from a mechanism built into its back. The air above the Bulwark was suddenly filled with sparks and smoke, blinding Caleb for a moment as he whizzed through it. When he came out the other side, a large coral column was looming directly in front of him. There was nothing to be done. He was going to hit it hard.

After a bone-jarring impact and a split second of darkness, the Navigator fell a few feet, landing shoulder-first on a solid, even surface. Caleb did a messy somersault, plowing up several dozen cobblestones as he skidded to a halt.

He stood slowly, looking around in disbelief. Instead of the columns and slime strands of Fraxis Prime, he was surrounded now by cranes and modern apartment blocks. It was night. In the distance, by the light of a full moon, he could see the Houses of Parliament and the glass cube of the US Embassy—and directly in front of him was his home, the converted warehouse by the Thames. Apex had pulled it all out of the Flex's memory banks, recreating Nine Elms perfectly. Everything was there—everything, that is, except its inhabitants. The courtyard, the river, and the roads were all deserted. This was a version of London completely cleared of its people.

Caleb felt sick. "Sam?" he whispered. "*Sam?*"

Sam didn't reply. The audio channel had gone dead.

"You're done, Caleb." Torrent was still in his Bulwark, standing over by the pier where the *Queen Jane, Approximately*

was moored. Any damage his suit had sustained from the fire had been corrected. "You've made your play. Now prepare yourself for . . . Apex."

Caleb didn't respond. So many alarms were going off in his suit that they blended together into a blur of electronic noise. He glanced over at the warehouse, at the kitchen window—thinking for a dreadful moment that he might see his mum standing there. Like everywhere else, though, it was empty.

Torrent began to move. Caleb raised the ion lance—only to find that its long black barrel was bent in the middle. In three strides, the Bulwark crossed the courtyard and drove a crushing punch into Caleb's chest section. He reeled away through a bike shelter before crunching into the glass facade of a high-rise and stumbling to the ground.

"Tell me you're nearly there, Sam," he breathed into the closed channel. "Not sure how much longer I can keep this up."

Sam stayed silent.

Caleb shut his eyes. Then he wrenched himself free and climbed to his feet. He flexed the Navigator's fingers. The left gauntlet no longer closed properly; one of the armor panels on the wrist was hanging loose.

Torrent, meanwhile, was stomping toward Nine Elms Pier. His Bulwark's twin spotlights swept along the *Queen Jane*'s paintwork as he bent over to scoop the barge up in the suit's enormous arms. Servomotors whined as he adjusted his hold on the black, dripping hull, lifting it high above his head.

"This is the Quinn family barge?" he mocked. "You're honestly telling me that the Talos Algorithm was written on this piece of junk? I gotta say, I thought it'd be *much* more inspiring!"

Caleb tried to dive aside, but he wasn't quite fast enough. The *Queen Jane* came down with the sound of a thousand splintering planks, slamming his Navigator against the cobbles and burying it in wreckage. In the darkness, through his visor, Caleb saw the broken half of one of his keyboards, his favorite VR headset, a split cushion from the leather chair. He felt like his heart was being torn apart. *It's not real,* he told himself firmly. *None of this is real.*

Before he could get his bearings, the debris above him was swept away. The Bulwark's spotlights shone in his eyes and one of its huge boots was planted on his abdomen, pinning him to the ground. Torrent's face came down toward him.

"It's kind of poetic, don't you think?" he said. "That here in the ruins of your old life, you begin anew."

There was a succession of tiny pings and cracks as the Navigator started to buckle. Caleb was being slowly squashed, his frantic, panting breaths fogging up his visor. He winced as an L-shaped object began to press into his hip. Shifting about, he wriggled his arm down into the suit's torso and tried to move it—and discovered that it was Gunnar's special flare gun, still buried in his coat's side pocket.

"You're—you're *insane*," he gasped.

"This is over, Caleb. You've lost."

Caleb swallowed his fear. He looked straight into those glowing violet eyes. "*No,*" he cried. "This might be your simulation, Torrent. But it's *my* game!"

Ignoring the pain, he grabbed the flare gun and yanked

it up through the suit. Then he popped open the Navigator's visor, stuck the gun out at arm's length, and fired a flare directly toward the Bulwark's head.

The boot was removed at once, the ground shaking as the combat suit staggered back across the courtyard. The flare had glanced off its helmet and lodged in its missile launcher—where it was fizzing like a firework, gushing out crimson sparks. Torrent was cursing like mad as he tried to swat it off.

Gritting his teeth, Caleb worked his arm back into place and hauled the Navigator out of the wrecked barge. The suit was critically damaged. Its movements were sluggish, a few seconds out of sync with his body. This was going to be his last move. He had to make it count.

He fired the jet pack and his suit lurched forward, colliding with Torrent's at chest level. The Bulwark overbalanced and toppled into the Thames—while the Navigator kept going, careering out above the moonlit river. Then its thrusters failed and it cartwheeled toward the water, Caleb yelling all the way.

There was a dark flash. The Navigator suit vanished, and Caleb found himself falling through open air—until he struck against a smooth metal floor.

He was back in the white room.

The lighting was much lower now. Over in its alcove, the glass suspension chamber was filled with moisture, like something inside it was rapidly defrosting. Lines of tiny red lights were winking along its base.

Caleb looked at the Flex. The silver face was dim, and the battery bar close to empty—but Sam was still there.

"Sam!" he shouted. "Sam, what happened?"

"I was successful, Caleb. The cryogenic subsystem has been deactivated. The quantum computer has gone into emergency shutdown."

"What about Apex?"

"Apex is offline. The signal has been terminated."

"So—so we did it!" Caleb laughed in amazement. "We really did it! Now we just have to find Zen and—"

He stopped. Torrent was across the room, past the suspension chamber. He was sprawled on his back, struggling even to raise his head. The flare from Gunnar's gun lay a few feet away from him, still sparkling and crackling. He was squinting as if the room's low lighting was unbearably bright. The violet glow had left his eyes—his connection with Apex had been cut off. He looked scared.

"You don't know what you've just done, kid," he croaked. "You don't have *any idea*. This place is *theirs*. And now they'll be after us both. Razor doesn't . . . forgive. They won't rest until we're—"

The room was gripped by a severe tremor, enough to make Caleb stagger a couple of steps to the side. As he regained his balance, he heard it rumble around the entire caldera.

"What was that, Sam? What's going on?"

"The installation's tidal generators have overloaded, Caleb. They are exploding."

"*What?* How?"

Sam didn't answer. "I believe this will set off a chain reaction. Much of the caldera could be destroyed, including this room."

Caleb looked at the ceiling. A crack was inching across it.

There was another deep rumble—and then there were five cracks, each getting longer and wider by the second. The floor gave another terrifying shake.

With obvious difficulty, Torrent was easing himself onto his elbow, trying to get up. Caleb started toward him, telling him to stay where he was—but then a central section of the ceiling came down all at once, crushing the suspension chamber, burying Torrent under hundreds of tons of rubble, and blocking off the rest of the room completely.

"*Sam!*" Caleb cried in panic.

"There is a doorway behind you, Caleb," Sam said. He could barely be heard over the thunderous, grinding roar of collapsing rock. "You must hurry."

Caleb turned and ran.

29
COLLAPSE!

At the exact instant that it was about to strike, the swarm burst apart. Hornet drones zinged off in several hundred different directions—and then, after a second of frenzied activity, they dropped from the air like a black veil, scattering noisily across the floor. Esperanza recoiled with a dreadful shriek, slumping down and clutching her head between her hands.

Zen looked toward her dad. He was lying in a heap beside his workstation. She hurried over to him, her boots crunching through the drones. Fighting her panic, she grabbed at his lab clothes and rolled him onto his back. He was heavy, motionless. Zen felt terror grip her. Was her dad *dying*? She bent to try to resuscitate him as he had once shown her—pinching his nose so she could inflate his lungs.

But just as she was about to blow into his mouth, Elias's eyes opened. They were glassy . . . and then clear. Free from the blue light.

For a moment, they simply gaped at each other in

astonishment. Only then did Zen realize she was still holding her dad's nose.

The biggest smile broke across Elias's face. "Zenobia! My little Zen!" He sat up and threw his arms around her and hugged her as he had never hugged her before.

"Dad!" Zen clasped him back with all her strength, as close as she could.

And, right there on the floor of the lab, the two of them hugged and hugged and hugged some more—and Zen did not care if all the monster drones in the world were coming, because she was as happy and relieved as she had ever been. Her heart leaped and she felt a strange, shuddery convulsion pass through her shoulders and wet stuff on her cheeks that she didn't even know were tears until her father grinned and wiped them away and gave her another hug.

"Are you OK, Zen?"

She sniffed. "I'm good, Dad. I'm just glad you're not dead."

"I think we're both pleased about that." He smiled again. "Zenobia, I have to say, you are not dressed for the lab."

"I—I wasn't planning on doing any lab work today, Dad."

Elias's voice was odd, wavering slightly. He was pale and unshaven with dark rings under his eyes. He'd always had a long, bony sort of face, but now it seemed sharper, thinner, like he hadn't been eating anywhere near enough.

"Neither was I—I haven't been able to *plan* anything much since . . ." He climbed unsteadily to his feet, his expression becoming confused. "Where . . . am I, exactly?"

"You're on an island called Spøkelsøy, off the coast of Norway."

Elias leaned against a worktop. "I feel very . . . I feel . . ."

"You've got nanobots in your bloodstream, Dad," Zen said as she got up. "I think they've just been deactivated, though."

"Yes . . . Yes. I've been trying to fight against it, but I . . ." Elias looked past Zen, his eyes growing wide with alarm. "Oh God, Zenobia. That—that woman . . ."

Esperanza was rising as well, still clawing at her head as if it were filled with an unbearable pain. Without even glancing their way, she started back toward the doors. She was moving quickly, urgently, like someone running for their life. Zen wouldn't have been able to stop her if she'd tried.

"She had drones," Elias muttered. "They were like . . . wasps, or . . . Your face, Zen. You're bleeding."

Zen mopped at the cuts on her cheek with the cuff of her jacket; they were beginning to sting but didn't seem to be too deep. She nodded at the black husks carpeting the floor behind her.

"They can't hurt anyone now," she said. "What's going on here, Dad? Where are Mum and Riyah?"

Elias shook his head and stared toward the curved window. "I . . . I don't know, Zen. They aren't on this island. We were separated before they got us out of Germany." His voice hardened. "But we will find them. I promise you that."

Zen managed to nod. Her hand went to the base of her throat—to where the jade droplet of her necklace nestled beneath her jacket. She was starting to ask another question when an alarm began to sound, a high-pitched electronic pulse—followed by a deep vibration that seemed to issue from the very bottom of the crater.

"What was that?" Elias said.

"Felt like an explosion," Zen replied. "We should really get out of here."

She took a last look around the lab. In among the drift of hornet drones, she spotted the slightest movement—the twitching of a tiny cluster of antennae.

"Beetlebat!"

Zen ran back across the lab to retrieve it. The little bot was almost completely buried—and running on a backup battery that barely gave it enough power to move. She dug it out and picked it up, stroking its scratched carapace.

"Good girl," she whispered. "You take a nap now."

She touched a hidden button and the bot powered down, its legs and antennae retracting.

"Come on, Zen," said her dad. "There are other scientists being held prisoner in this place. We can't leave without them."

Zen nodded, putting Beetlebat away; then, after a moment's hesitation, she slipped one of the hornet drones into her pocket as well.

"You have to tell me," Elias said as Zen helped him to the laboratory doors, "how did you get out to this island?"

"You know Caleb—Caleb Quinn?"

"Of course. The one who is almost as clever as you."

Zen looked over. Her dad was grinning in that old familiar way—like he always did when he was teasing her.

"I said *almost*," he said, chuckling. "What about Caleb?"

"He's on the island with me," Zen said. "I wouldn't have gotten here without him."

As they went down the spiral stairs and back into the

drone factory beneath, she gave Elias a brief account of the past few days.

"So Caleb must have done it," she concluded. "He must have shut down the Apex signal."

"Smart kid," Elias observed. "That explains why their tech has stopped working."

"Have you seen his mum?"

"No, only scientists have been brought here—the people they've been forcing to work on the nanotech project."

The factory began to shake. A rack of instruments fell off the wall, clattering among the machinery.

"It feels like the whole base is going to collapse," Zen said. "Where are those other scientists?"

Little by little, her dad seemed to be recovering his strength and his wits—and his resolve along with them. He began to walk unaided, heading past the conveyor belts into a long corridor.

"This way," he said. "Toward the living quarters. That's where they'll be."

They found the scientists huddled together near the cells that Zen had seen earlier—six of them in total, in various stages of confusion and panic. Elias went over and began embracing them warmly.

"This is Zenobia," he announced. "My amazing daughter. She has come to rescue us."

Some of the scientists gathered around. A couple were in a really bad way—the nanotech had clearly done some serious damage. Dr. Kristin Birgisson, in particular, seemed barely able to stand.

Zen tried to smile, but the situation was rapidly going

from bad to catastrophic. So much dust was drifting down from the ceiling that it was getting difficult to see. There was a loud crash as a section of the wall back along the corridor toppled inward, blocking it completely.

"OK, everybody, introductions later," Elias shouted over the noise. "Out through the balcony!"

Before long, they had made it out onto the side of the caldera. They began heading for the meeting place Zen had agreed on with Caleb. As they limped through the dark volcanic rock, she kept her eyes peeled for any sign of Esperanza or her drones—but all she could see was smoke and dust.

Elias guessed what she was doing. "Don't worry about her," he said. "She's long gone."

"Who *is* she, anyway?" Zen asked. "What was she doing out here?"

Her dad was quiet for a moment. "She is a member of Razor," he replied. "It's a secret organization. A network of powerful people—of extremely *dangerous* people—spread across the entire planet. Their interest is in experimental technology of every conceivable kind. All of it intended to increase their power yet further. They plan . . . Well, I'm not exactly sure what they plan. But they're ruthless. Let's just say that."

Zen tried to take this in. "So . . . this Razor group was forcing you to work for them? To design nanotech?"

Elias nodded grimly, holding on to Zen's shoulder for support. "They'd tried to make it themselves, but their nanobots were burning people out. Crippling them." He snorted. "Not that Razor cared about *that*, of course—but they wanted it to be undetectable. So you wouldn't be able to tell who was under the control of the Apex signal." He rubbed his forehead. "The junk they put in all of us here was . . . *really* bad. Receiving that damn signal was like having the worst headache in the history of the world."

They decided to stop for a short rest so the scientists could adjust; most of them hadn't been outside for weeks and were totally overwhelmed by the daylight and the noise. They'd reached the southern slopes of the caldera. It seemed secure enough for now—most of the destruction was occurring on the other side, where the blast doors had been. The dazed party flopped to the ground.

Zen perched up on a small boulder, keeping watch. "How did Xavier Torrent fit into all this, Dad?" she asked. "We thought he was in charge."

Elias sat heavily at the boulder's base. "That *jerk,*" he said, scowling with disgust. "Torrent is a full-blown psychopath, Zen—exactly the sort of person Razor seeks out to do its dirty work. He thought he could convince me to join them too. Take their money like he had. He gave me this grand speech about how essential I was to some higher vision of mankind they all shared—and then he injected me with their shoddy nanotech when I told him where to stick it."

"I was thinking that he must have kidnapped Riyah and Mum as leverage," Zen said. "To force you to do what they wanted."

"No—it was strange. Torrent never so much as mentioned their names. He ignored my questions about them completely." Elias sighed. "They obviously wanted to field-test their nanotech. See what its limits were. What they could make us do. My guess is that if the nanotech had failed, they would have made us obey them by starting to threaten our family members."

Zen suppressed a shiver; this was seriously twisted. "They were a team, then—Torrent and Razor? Had he joined them or something?"

Elias shook his head. "It was a transaction, that's all. Razor needs to stay out of sight—it's key to their whole existence. So they find themselves someone with big ideas and no morals whatsoever, and they give him this island, along with a few billion in funding. He's allowed to pursue his own research—as long as he also provides them with a control system based on the interconnection between nanotech and a super-powered AI."

"Apex," said Zen.

"That's right. Apex is Torrent's baby. His life's work. And it is also the only way to give Razor what they want: a means of controlling people—potentially very large numbers of people—by a method that can't be detected. People who would otherwise seem entirely normal."

Zen thought about this. "That could be . . . *unbelievably* bad."

"Too right it could," Elias said. "But guys like that can't cooperate for long, Zen. When two snakes make a deal, both are just waiting for their chance to bite."

"What do you mean?" Zen asked.

Her dad raised an eyebrow slyly. "Their nanotech took away my free will—but I could still listen in on them. Esperanza had been posted here as a kind of supervisor, to keep Torrent's work on track. I overheard her calls to the Razor Council. They were planning to take *everything* from him—the nanotech, yes, but also his precious Apex and whatever else he's been developing in the depths of this caldera. And I'm pretty sure that Torrent was plotting to do the same to them—to unleash his mysterious new inventions and have Razor bow down to him along with everybody else." Elias chuckled. "Some serious backstabbing was in the cards. No doubt about it."

Zen turned around on her rock, taking in the destruction. "So it was always going to end like this," she said. "One way or another."

Elias began to get up. "We'd better keep moving," he said.

30

THE BALANCE OF RISK

Caleb emerged high on the caldera. The sky was now a bright, resolute blue and a strong sea breeze gusted through his hair. He was breathing hard from his sprint out of the base. His ribs ached painfully where Torrent's Bulwark had trodden on him, but his blood was flowing fast; he felt alive and alert and ready for anything. The ground beneath his boots was rumbling. Looking around, he saw that part of the caldera's interior had slumped onto the docks. All of the drone hatches had disappeared in the landslide. Great clouds of dust were rising as boulders rolled down the sides of the crater and splashed into the green water. He sensed that the entire horseshoe-shaped rim might collapse inward at any moment, burying the harbor below.

The scale of the devastation was truly shocking. Caleb had no idea what could have set it off. But finding an explanation would have to wait. He had to stay focused—get to the agreed meeting place, where he and Zen had hidden their backpacks. A rough path ran nearby, leading up toward the caldera's rim. He started along it as quickly as he could. Barely a minute later, however, there was a particularly loud bang from somewhere down below, followed by another booming avalanche of rock.

"Whoa," he panted, "this place is really falling apart!"

"Yes, Caleb," Sam said. "It was necessary."

"*Necessary?*" Caleb skidded to a halt. "What do you mean?"

"Our objective was to stop Xavier Torrent," Sam replied evenly. "Destroying this installation was the only certain way to achieve that."

Caleb stared at the silver face, a chill creeping through his chest and stomach. "So . . . it was . . . it was *you*? You over-loaded those tidal generators?"

"Yes, directly after I shut down the quantum computer. In order to level the base as completely as possible." Sam paused. "Old school, like you said."

Caleb's mind was racing. He thought of the suspension chamber in the white room—the droplets of condensation inside the glass. "But the quantum computer was already deactivated. You'd turned off the cryogenic system. It was done. Apex was down."

"No, Caleb. The core processing unit was still intact. Restoring its operations would have been reasonably simple. It had to be destroyed."

"But I didn't *ask* you to do that, Sam. Why didn't you tell me earlier?"

"There was a chance that Torrent may have overheard us and used Apex to stop me. And then, once the chain reaction had begun, I thought it best to wait until you were clear of the tunnels."

Caleb looked out again at the collapsing caldera. He felt sick. He pressed his finger and thumb to his forehead. "You could have *killed me,* Sam."

"My decision was based on the balance of risk," Sam answered. "Allowing Apex to continue would have placed the whole of mankind in danger. I had analyzed our exit route. I knew that we would make it out with approximately one minute and fifty-three seconds to spare. Which we did."

Caleb was suddenly furious. "What about Zen and her family? What about all those other people in there—the prisoners? What about my *mum*, Sam?"

"Your mother was not present," the AI informed him. "When I gained control of the cooling system and the tidal generators, I briefly had access to the base's surveillance system as well. CIA agent Harper Quinn was not in the installation, nor is there any record of her ever having been so."

Caleb blinked, overcome with relief and confusion, unable to speak. "Zen's mother and sister were also not present," Sam continued. "I'm afraid that the surveillance system went down with the Apex signal, so I have no current information on those who might still be inside. But there is an alarm system in the caldera, which I triggered when I overloaded the generators. The odds of their survival are very good."

"The *odds* of their *survival*? How the hell is that supposed to . . ." Caleb tried to control his anger—his apprehension. There was no point yelling at Sam. He'd only been pursuing his objective—the objective Caleb himself had given him. Caleb held his head in his hands. Maybe Zen had been right about AI. All this destruction was actually his fault. He'd freed Sam from *Terrorform* and given him control of the Flex.

270

He'd told the AI that they had to stop Torrent. This was on him. Nobody else. Where was Zen? What if she didn't make it—what if Sam had effectively caused her death? He looked around in desperation, scanning the rim and sides of the caldera, as an aftershock shook the ground.

"*Stop*, Sam . . . stop with the odds. Just stop."

"Yes, Caleb. When shall I—"

"Turn off audio! Don't say anything for a while."

Caleb pulled the Flex off his wrist and straightened it out, thinking to call someone, anyone at all—to put up a distress call on the ARC intranet and get the authorities to the island as quickly as he could. But there was no signal of any kind. The collapse of Apex had caused the entire island to be covered in a dense blanket of static.

Caleb put the Flex in his hoodie and carried on up the path. Before long, the sea came into view. Something caught his eye, out on the shimmering water—the dark shape of a vessel, sailing away from Spøkelsøy. It was the battered fishing ship. Krall, Pyke, and the other surviving mercenaries were making their escape, heading in the direction of the Norwegian mainland at full speed. No one would reach the island in time to stop the ship and arrest them. Caleb gazed at it for a few moments, cursing under his breath. But there was nothing he could do.

He turned back toward the rim of the caldera. There were people approaching . . .

Zen!

Zen was making for their meeting place from the far side!

She was propping up a man in lab gear who seemed to be having trouble walking. Half a dozen other people were trailing groggily behind, also dressed in lab clothes, leaning against one another. All of them were caked in a thick layer of dust. Seeing Caleb, Zen smiled broadly and started to wave.

Gratitude and happiness surged through him. Everything was going to be OK. He broke into a run, forgetting his bruised ribs.

"You *made* it!" he yelled. "You're all right! I thought you might have—"

"No. You saved us."

Caleb stopped in front of Zen. "Saved you and then . . . I was worried I'd maybe . . . buried you."

Zen glanced at the crumbling hillside around them. "What the hell did you do in there, Caleb? Talk about overkill." She studied him more closely and her grin faded. "Jeez, what *happened* to you? You look like you've been fighting a whole fleet of those gun drones single-handed."

Caleb peered back at her—at the cuts on her face and hands, which were just visible beneath the dust. "I could ask you the same thing. You look like you just did a solo mission on Kursk in your pajamas."

"Yeah, well, I met some more of Esperanza's toys," Zen said. "A bunch of them, in fact. You killed the signal just in time."

The man at Zen's side straightened up and wiped some of the dirt from his face. Caleb realized that it was her father, Professor Elias Rafiq.

"Caleb!" he exclaimed, before Caleb could say anything. "Caleb Quinn, no less!"

"Hey, Professor. It's been a while."

"Elias. Call me Elias." He came forward, grasped Caleb's right hand in both of his, and gave it a firm, dusty shake.

It was impossible not to like Zen's dad. Despite his formidable intellect, he was always friendly and good-humored, even when he was bending your brain with one of his famous scientific conundrums. He'd been especially close to Patrick, Caleb's own father; their conversations had often run on through the night. Here on the caldera, though, Elias seemed gaunter and more grizzled than Caleb remembered; he had a nauseated, washed-out look, like he hadn't slept in a month. Caleb glanced at the people following behind—other scientists, he guessed. Like Elias, they had obviously been through a grueling ordeal.

Before they could say any more, the ground shifted sharply, prompting cries of fear from the scientists. It felt like the entire island was trembling.

"The southern side's starting to fall in as well," Zen said. "Come on, let's collect the packs and get off this thing before it turns into one big sinkhole."

31
BACK IN THE GAME

After a couple of hours' walking, the group came to a halt, completely exhausted, in a spot close to the exact middle of the island. The caldera was now about half the height it had been that morning. Above it, a huge column of dust and smoke was winding up into the blue sky, as if it was undergoing a second eruption. Zen remembered that she had a big bag of dried fruit and nuts in her backpack and passed it around.

Elias called Caleb over to where he and Zen were sitting. "I want to thank you, Caleb," he said. "For all you've done for Zenobia. For our family."

"No," Caleb replied. "It's Zen you need to thank. She's saved my bacon at least . . . seven times now?"

Zen put her hand on his shoulder. "We're not counting anymore, Caleb. We're a team."

"Swift and Hawk." Caleb grinned. "Search and rescue."

A half smile, rather like one of Zen's, had crept onto Elias's face. "And what a great team it is." He pointed with his thumb back toward the scientists. "You've got some pretty dedicated fans right here."

Dr. Birgisson was nearby, white tear-tracks on her grimy cheeks. She'd overheard Elias and now tried to say something herself, but couldn't quite get the words out—it was as if the sound of her own voice was acutely painful. Elias went to her side and gently put his arm around her. A moment later she was sobbing.

"About your mum and Riyah," Caleb said to Zen. "Sam gained access to the base's surveillance system. He told me he couldn't find any sign of them—or of my mum. They weren't ever on the island."

Zen nodded; she knew this already. "Dad said they were taken somewhere else. Once we're back home, we can concentrate on finding them." She looked over at him, unable to hide her curiosity. "So, what happened to you in there? Did you run into Torrent?"

"Yeah. It's kind of a long story."

"You beat him, though, right?"

"Eventually. But things got a little . . . out of hand."

Caleb told Zen everything: the hard light chamber, the quantum computer, and what Sam had done to ensure its destruction. He was expecting anger—for her to blame him and his out-of-control AI for putting them all in mortal danger. But instead she just listened, nodding from time to time, until the story was over.

"Sam did the right thing," she said. "You both did."

Caleb wasn't convinced. "You could have *died*, Zen. You and your dad, and all the other scientists. And it would have been my fault."

"The stuff I saw in there—the way my dad was, the way all these scientists were . . ." Zen shuddered. "Torrent and Esperanza were working on something really terrible. They had to be stopped."

Caleb furrowed his brow. "OK," he said. "Maybe this time. But I can't have Sam doing anything like that again, Zen. I just can't. When I get back to the *Queen Jane*, I'm going to have to do some serious work on his code. On everything."

Zen met his eye. "I understand, Caleb," she said. "But Sam was right."

A few minutes later Caleb was rummaging through his backpack, looking for some chocolate bars they'd bought at Oslo airport, when the Flex starting buzzing in his pocket. He drew it out a little warily. The silver face was still there, up in the corner of the screen.

"Caleb," said Sam, "I know you instructed me to be quiet— but I thought you would want to know that the interference covering the island is beginning to lift. The Flex is capable of accessing the internet. For now, at least."

Immediately, Caleb sat cross-legged among the clumps of heather and stretched out the screen. His mum's phone was still listed as unavailable, so he made for the ARC intranet. There were fifteen messages in his inbox – all of them left in the past few hours by Goldfinch! They had titles like *Establish Contact—Urgent*. But he hadn't even had time to open the most recent one before an incoming video call popped up.

"Zen," he shouted, "you'd better get over here."

He answered the call and Professor Clay's face appeared. She was wearing a white hospital gown, her head was bandaged, and there were deep lines beneath her eyes—but she addressed them in her usual brisk, take-no-prisoners manner.

"Swift and Hawk," she said. "At long last. Where the hell *are* you?"

Caleb was unsure where to begin. "We left messages," he said. "Lots of them. But you didn't reply. We thought . . ."

Zen was leaning forward to get a better look at Clay's video feed. "What happened, Goldfinch?" she asked. "Are you in hospital?"

Clay turned toward a window. "I caught a bullet in the sewers," she said, "while I was trying to lead those damn mercenaries away. Just a graze, but it knocked me out cold. My boat floated around down there for ages."

"Wait," said Caleb, "you were shot in the *head*?"

Clay didn't answer him. "I finally drifted out onto the river by Waterloo Bridge. One of those pleasure barges spotted me and I was taken to St. Thomas at Westminster. I only regained consciousness this morning." She looked back to the camera. "But enough about that. The pair of you were going to tell me what you've been doing for the past seven days."

Just as Caleb and Zen were preparing to speak, something started blinking on the Flex's screen. It was another incoming intranet signal, trying to join their call. No name was entered, but the profile picture showed a small rusty trawler festooned with radio antennae and satellite dishes. Caleb tapped on it, and a new window opened above his and Professor Clay's.

"*Swift!*" shouted Gunnar above the sea wind. "You are all right! And Hawk also! *Takk Gud!*" His camera shifted, and Caleb could see that he was on the deck of the *Huldra*, looking across the waves at the dark trunk of smoke that was rising from the caldera. "I saw the place go up—the explosions and the landslides—and I thought—I was afraid that . . . But you are well! You are both well! *Takk Gud, takk Gud!*" He let out a great whoop of joy.

Clay was watching him steadily. "Osprey," she said. "This *is* a surprise."

At the sound of his own code name, Gunnar's grin vanished; he took off his crosshairs cap. "Goldfinch," he said, trying to calm himself down. "Excuse me, ma'am. I was just very happy to make contact with Swift and Hawk. I should have—I don't—*dritt!*"

Clay sat back in her hospital bed, a heart monitor beeping beside her. "Anybody care to explain to me what exactly has happened?"

Zen and Caleb told her everything, with occasional sheepish contributions from Gunnar: Amsterdam and Luuk Tezuka, the *Nightfall*, the path to Spøkelsøy and all they'd uncovered there—and their battles against Torrent and Esperanza.

"Your Möbius assignment," said Clay when they'd finished, "was to crack that code. And you've ended up solving the whole damn case. Rescuing the prisoners. Taking down Torrent. Gathering in all kinds of critical intel, from the sound of it." She crossed her arms, the beginnings of a smile playing across her face. "Looks like I was on to something when I decided to recruit you two. As soon as I'm off this call I'm going to review our outstanding files—see what I can set you to work on next."

Caleb scratched his head; he couldn't quite tell if Clay was joking. "It's not over yet, Goldfinch," he said. "People are still missing. Our mums. Zen's little sister. Luuk. We don't know where they are or what's been done to them."

Clay had picked up a phone and put on a pair of reading glasses. "I might have news for you there. I saw something earlier on the other secure channels—I didn't think too much of it then, being unaware of our . . . Norwegian connection. There's been an incident in Oslo, in the suburb of Frogner. A number of missing persons have been found by local police— British, American, Italian . . ."

Caleb's eyes went wide. "Is it—is it *them*?"

"There's not much here," Clay told him. She looked over the top of her glasses. "But it has been flagged as top priority by the CIA."

Caleb and Zen exchanged a glance. They both felt their hopes rise. Missing people in Norway, on the same day they'd shut down the Apex signal, people who were of high interest to the CIA? It couldn't just be a coincidence.

"I'll keep an eye on it," Clay said. "Pass on any details as I get them." She put the phone down on her bed. "One more thing, Swift. I'm told that Möbius operatives retrieved a custom BMX from Russell Square four days ago."

"You've got my *bike*?" said Caleb, laughing with amazement. "Is it still in one piece? Where is it?"

"Safe and sound at the ARC. It'll be waiting for you when you get back to London."

"So, what happens now?" Zen asked. "My dad is in a bad way. All these scientists are. They need medical attention."

"I will sail in," said Gunnar at once. "I can be at the island in an hour. I will—"

"Stand down, Osprey," Clay said, not unkindly. "A faster

option is needed here. Get back to that radar assignment I gave you—those preliminary readings you sent in are very peculiar indeed. Hawk and Swift—stay where you are. Keep an open link to this site. I'm going to make some calls."

Caleb remembered something. "Hey, uh, Osprey," he said, holding up the flare gun, which he'd stuffed back into his pocket during the fight with Torrent. "Thanks for the loan. It was a *big* help—threw some light on a . . . tricky situation. How can I get it back to you?"

"Don't worry, Swift," Clay said. "You'll be seeing Osprey soon enough. You can return it to him then." She reached toward her screen, preparing to end the call. "Well done again, both of you. I mean it. You're a natural fit for the Möbius Program."

Afterward, Caleb and Zen lay for a while on the springy heather, talking about what they were going to do when they got home.

"Call for a pizza," said Caleb. "That is the absolute *first* thing. Hawaiian. With extra pineapple. And extra ham. Extra *everything*."

"Have a bath," said Zen. "And fix up Beetlebat."

Caleb looked across at her. "Log into *Terrorform*. Go on the longest artifact quest in the entire game. Get completely lost in it."

Zen thought for a moment. "Hey, Sam," she said, "you there?"

"I am, Zen," the AI replied. "I'm glad that you are well and have been reunited with your father."

"Thanks. I couldn't have done it without you guys." She

paused. "What's the plan for *Terrorform*? Any updates in the pipeline?"

"There certainly are. Our experiences on Spøkelsøy have given me an idea for an entirely new planet. I was intending to share it with Caleb as soon as we return to London."

"Could be interesting," Caleb murmured. He held out his fist and Zen bumped hers against it, keeping their grubby knuckles together for a few seconds.

"You're right, Caleb," she said. "That's where we need to be. Back in the game."

32

THE SILENT HOWL

The sun was dropping in the west when they heard the distant sound of rotor blades.

"Caleb," said Sam, "I am detecting an incoming MH-60S Knighthawk, with a US Navy call sign. It is homing in on the Flex."

The rotors grew louder. Zen pointed to their left—the black speck of an approaching helicopter could just be seen, circling the colossal dust cloud that was drifting off the caldera.

"Just one chopper?" she asked.

Caleb checked the message Clay had sent him a few minutes before. "Yeah, apparently they want to get us off the island as quickly as possible."

"More will follow," Elias said, scratching his silvery stubble. "They'll quarantine the whole island. Start an investigation. Get to bottom of this, I hope."

They all stood in a loose semicircle, watching the military helicopter swoop in, its rotor blades whipping up a deafening gale on the muddy moorland. As it touched down, the side door slid open to reveal a woman in a US Navy flight jacket and dark glasses. Her auburn hair was pulled back into a ponytail and she was smiling widely.

A sound burst from Caleb's lips, halfway between a laugh and a sob. "*Mum?*" he said, nearly shouting with disbelief. "Mum!"

He ran forward and she jumped out, and they met on the moor with a massive hug. It felt like they'd been apart for seven years rather than seven days. Even over the roar of the engines, Caleb could hear her saying how relieved she was to see him. She held him at arm's length and looked him over carefully—inspecting for injuries.

"I'm OK," he yelled. "Really."

"You don't look it," she yelled back. "But I believe you. Thank God."

Then she hugged him again.

A team of medics disembarked and went over to the scientists. They began tending to injuries, administering treatments, and putting a couple of the worst cases on stretchers. Zen and Elias approached, and Harper clasped their hands—before indicating that they should all get onto the helicopter.

When they were on board, the Knighthawk rose back into the air, all vibration and rotor noise. Caleb sat in his safety straps, wearing an aviation headset. He was next to his mum, with Zen and her dad seated opposite.

The first thing Harper did was take out a phone and pass it over to Elias. At once, he was laughing loudly, practically bellowing with happiness—saying words Caleb couldn't make out through his headphones. Zen joined him and they huddled over the phone. Caleb caught a glimpse of the screen. It showed Zen's mum and little sister, seated in what appeared to be a Norwegian police station. The family were waving and blowing kisses; Riyah was jumping excitedly up and down; all of them were talking at once. Caleb had no idea how they could possibly hear each other over the helicopter. But it clearly didn't matter.

His mum's cool, reassuring voice crackled in his headphones. "They were being held in the same place as me," she said. "It was a disused office building that had been turned into a kind of automated prison." She nodded out of the window; all but the lowest slopes of the caldera were shrouded in dust and smoke. "Then, when this happened, the whole place went offline. I forced my way out of my cell and started freeing the other prisoners. Salma and Riyah were among the first I found. We all broke out of the building together. Flagged down a pretty surprised Oslo street cop."

"I am . . . *really* pleased that you're all right, Mum," Caleb said into his headset's mic. "I mean, I wasn't worried. I know you can take care of yourself, but . . . OK—I *was* worried."

Harper took hold of his hand. "I'm sorry, Caleb. I was investigating all this—and getting in pretty deep. I should have realized how bad it was going to get."

Caleb smiled. "Actually, it's all turned out OK. It was even kind of . . . fun."

"But you'll be happy to get back to the barge, right?"

"Yes. Most definitely."

"Good. I don't want you getting a taste for crazy adventures. I think we're both due a few low-key days at home."

They changed course, the southern mountains appearing in the window. The snow around their summits was turning a pale blue as the long twilight began again. The helicopter continued to climb, banking to the left. As they swept away over the vast, dark green carpet of the forest, half a dozen gray shapes broke from the tree line in one of the high valleys and loped along a snowy ridge.

The wolf pack.

Caleb leaned forward, gazing down at the creatures. They stopped and looked up, following the path of the helicopter. It was flying around one of the larger peaks now, speeding out to sea. The noise of the blades was too great to hear anything, but Caleb watched the beasts throw back their heads, and he was certain that they were howling.

"Have you talked to Professor Clay?" he asked his mum. "Has she told you what's been going on?"

"The agency's Oslo office patched her through to me after she sounded the alarm on this place. She said she'd just gotten off the line to you." Harper's brow creased into the slightest frown. "I have to say, Caleb, I thought she'd get you to safety. Not enlist you into that . . . program of hers. You were already way too involved in all of this."

"I met Xavier Torrent in that caldera," Caleb said quietly. "He told me all this stuff about Dad. About them working together."

Harper was looking at him intently. "Honey, you mustn't believe any of it. Your dad was the one who actually reported Torrent to the authorities. It was because of him that the guy went into hiding. Torrent was dangerous even then—while they were at Berkeley together. He had no sense of the risks in the tech he wanted to develop. Or of his own responsibilities as its creator."

Caleb nodded; this sounded right. "There was something else. Torrent was working for someone." He paused. "He called them . . . Razor. He seemed really scared of them."

Harper stiffened. For an instant, her air of unshakable professional calm left her. Then she took off her headset and gestured for him to do the same.

"Caleb," she said firmly, cupping a hand against his ear, "don't repeat what you just told me to anyone."

"But, Mum, I think they were planning to—"

"Not to *anyone*. They could be listening. We need to wait for a completely secure environment. You understand?"

Caleb blinked. "Yeah," he mouthed. "Sure. I understand."

"OK. We'll talk more back in London, kiddo. I promise." They put their headsets back on. "Now you should try to get some rest. You look totally shattered."

Across the cabin, Zen and her dad had ended their call. She was leaning against his arm; they both had their eyes shut. Caleb stared out at the sea. His mum was right: he was incredibly tired, with more aches than he could count. Settling into his seat, lulled by the deep drone of the engines, he let his eyelids close. He felt himself drifting off.

"Caleb," said Sam.

The cabin was darker. Caleb stirred, stretching his arms and yawning. Below the helicopter now were the lights of the Norwegian mainland, glittering in the dusk.

"I'm sorry for waking you. This can't wait."

Caleb sat up. Sam's voice was in his headphones somehow—the AI must have used Spider Monkey to hack into the helicopter's comms. He rubbed his eyes and took out the Flex. The silver face was shining brightly in the corner of the screen.

"What is it?"

"I have run every test available to check for a system error. But there isn't one. The reading is correct."

"What reading? Sam, what's going on?"

"Caleb, I am picking up the Apex signal again."

ACKNOWLEDGMENTS

Thank you to Emma and Sarah, who started all this.

Thank you to Denise, Daisy, Megan, Susan, and the team at Walker Books; Bill, Euan, and everyone at A.M. Heath; and Coke Navarro for the amazing cover.

And Mark for the use of the Fentiman Invention Flat.

ABOUT THE AUTHOR

LOGAN MACX is rumored to be an ex-spy formerly with the British Secret Intelligence Service, specializing in cyber communications and unexplained events. His whereabouts are unknown at this time, but he is in periodic communication with the ghost writers of this series: Edward Docx and Matthew Plampin.